LEONTINE BLYTHEWOOD

The Duchess's Unclaimed Heir

First edition

This book was professionally typeset on Reedsy.
Find out more at reedsy.com

Contents

1

The Mourning's Duchess

I never thought I would wear this dress. The heavy black silk of mourning, layered in somber folds, pressed against my skin like the finality of a closed door. When the dress had been made—a year ago at my mother's urging, for occasions I'd hoped would remain distant—I had thought it an unnecessary extravagance. I hadn't foreseen standing in it at my husband's funeral, swallowing back tears as I dressed for a day I hadn't imagined would come this soon.

"Let me help, Your Grace," Mary murmured, her hands gentle yet efficient as she buttoned the row of tiny onyx buttons running down my back. Her fingers hesitated at my waist, and I knew why. Though I was only in the early stages, my growing belly was beginning to change my form, pressing gently against the fabric in a reminder of everything left uncertain.

"Thank you, Mary." I held myself still as she finished, avoiding the mirror. I could feel her eyes on me, filled with concern—a concern I was too weary to address.

"If I may, Your Grace," she said tentatively, "you could perhaps rest today. It's hardly fitting for a woman in your condition to endure such strain."

I closed my eyes, letting her words sink in before answering. "I must go, Mary. If not for him, then...for the child. For what's left of us both."

Mary gave a silent nod and reached for my black veil, lifting it with care before draping it over my head and shoulders. I caught a glimpse of myself in the mirror—a shadowed figure cloaked in grief, the faint outline of my unborn child beneath the mourning gown. The sight shook me, and I clutched the bedpost to steady myself, summoning a deep breath.

I forced my gaze from my reflection. "That will be all, Mary. I can manage from here."

With a reluctant curtsy, she left, casting one last worried glance over her shoulder before slipping from the room. The silence that followed pressed down on me, and I lingered, feeling the weight of the empty space where my husband's presence should have been. It was a strange ache, one I hadn't anticipated—a hollow feeling that spread from my chest to my very fingertips.

Finally, I made my way to the door and stepped into the hall, where the low hum of hushed voices echoed through the corridors. The house was full of people, each murmuring their sympathies, every head dipped with a sorrow that felt both genuine and hollow, as if rehearsed. Yet I felt like the only one truly mourning, the only one who had loved him in her own way, the only one who carried a piece of him within her.

The procession to the chapel seemed both endless and fleeting, and I barely registered the familiar surroundings as I passed by the portraits of ancestors long gone, men and women who had once inhabited these halls and now watched me with silent, painted eyes. I wondered what they would think of me, of this young, suddenly widowed Duchess who carried the Duke's child without his protection, without his guidance, without any clear path forward.

By the time I reached the chapel, my hands were cold, my heart fluttering in a strange, quiet panic beneath my ribs. The coffin stood at the front, draped in the family crest, a cold and impersonal symbol that felt painfully inadequate for the man I had known, for all the moments that had passed between us.

I made my way to the front pew and sat down, folding my hands in my lap, letting the silence of the room settle over me. Around me, the Duke's relatives filled the seats, their expressions a mix of solemnity and something else—a kind of hungry curiosity, as though they were already calculating their next move.

As the ceremony began, I felt the pressure of my growing child against my hand, a reminder that I was no longer grieving alone. My husband's absence was one thing—an ache, a hollow space—but the thought of my child facing that same absence for a lifetime, never knowing its father, never being known by him, was almost unbearable.

The priest's words washed over me, and I struggled to keep my mind focused, to hold back the surge of grief that threatened to unravel me. I barely heard the eulogies, the scripted condolences, all spoken by people who had known my husband only as the Duke. Not as the quiet, reserved man I had spent quiet mornings with, not as the man who had once held my hand in his as we spoke softly about the future we thought we'd have.

Then came the final blessing, and with it, a wave of finality that left me feeling both numb and painfully awake. The congregation began to rise, preparing to pay their final respects, and I felt my heart beat faster, my pulse quick and shallow. I knew I would have to join them, to approach the coffin and say my own goodbye. But my legs felt as if they were weighed down by the same stone that marked his resting place.

I felt a hand brush lightly against my shoulder and turned to see Lady Henrietta, one of the Duke's elderly aunts, her face wrinkled with age and yet devoid of softness. Her sharp eyes fell immediately to my belly, lingering there with a look I couldn't quite decipher.

"Take care, child," she whispered, her tone as dry and brittle as her hand on my shoulder. "Your condition must not be...compromised."

I nodded stiffly, understanding the message beneath her words. My value to them now was tied not to myself but to the child I carried—their potential heir, a means to their own ends. The realization made me want to retreat, to hide this life within me from their calculating eyes, but I had no choice. This child was all that I had left, all that I had left of him.

With the ceremony concluded, I made my way to the coffin, each step feeling as though it carried me through thick, heavy water. When I reached the polished wood, I laid my gloved hand upon it, feeling the coolness seep through the fabric.

"I'm here, Rupert," I whispered, the words catching in my throat. My hand rubbed my slightly enlarged belly. "Our baby is here, too, to say goodbye to you on your last journey. We're here, together."

I looked down and kissed the surface of my husband's coffin. "Rest in peace, my love. Sleep tight and have sweet dreams."

The room seemed to close in around me, and for a moment, I let myself imagine he could hear me, that he would somehow know that I would protect this child with everything in me, that I would ensure our legacy, his legacy, lived on.

With a final, shuddering breath, I straightened, allowing the curtain of my black veil to fall across my face. I turned to leave, feeling every pair of eyes upon me, every silent calculation, every whispered assumption. I was the Duchess in mourning, the widow with a growing belly, and they all waited to see what would become of me.

As I moved down the aisle, past faces both sympathetic and predatory, I held my head high, feeling the pressure of their gazes but determined not to let it break me. The Duke may have left me, but I was still here. And as long as I was, I would carry his memory and his child forward, despite the weight, despite the loss.

2

The Widow's Burden

T he house felt heavier after the funeral. Silence settled in the corners and along the empty halls, pressing down as though even the walls bore witness to my grief and isolation. Days seemed to stretch endlessly, one slipping into the next without distinction, until time itself felt as hollow as I did.

I remember when my husband found out I was pregnant. His joy was palpable, almost childlike, as though the news had breathed a second life into him. Despite his failing health, he would rest his hand gently on my growing belly, his eyes lighting up with every flutter I described. He would ask me repeatedly about my condition, urging me to rest as much as possible. He calculated the months, counting down to the day our child would enter the world.

But I knew. I knew his excitement held a silent desperation. Rupert wasn't just counting the time to my labor—he was measuring it against his own remaining days. Each time he mentioned the approaching birth, my heart grew heavier. Would he still be here to see the baby? To hold them in his arms? His frailty was a shadow over our happiness.

When he passed, before my belly had even fully rounded, the silence he left behind was unbearable. I sighed heavily, wishing with every fiber of my being that he could have stayed longer, stayed to witness the life we had created together. I could imagine it all so vividly—his smile as he kissed my forehead, his gentle touch as he cradled our child, his warmth radiating through the room. But all of it was gone.

Today, I sat alone in the drawing room, my black skirts spilling around me like spilled ink on fine paper. I had never known the weight of widowhood, but now, sitting in the stifling quiet, I understood it as a burden no one had prepared me to bear. Perhaps because, deep down, everyone had expected that I would be the one to live under the protection of my husband—not to become his legacy's protector. And now, I was left to face a future that felt both uncertain and ruthlessly unkind.

Maybe things would be different if my husband were still alive. I wouldn't have had to face all this alone. I wouldn't be afraid of facing an uncertain future either.

A letter from my family arrived, offering formal condolences and urging me to "take care" for the sake of my unborn child. The viscount and viscountess— my parents—meant well, I supposed, but their words were as thin as the country air I'd left behind. They hadn't fully understood my life here, nor the struggles I would face on my own. My family came from modest means, and our title, though noble, lacked the influence and wealth that were abundant among the Duke's relations. We were country folk—my mother had taught me embroidery, my father had drilled me on decorum, but we were far removed from the world I inhabited now, with its ruthless nobles and whispered intrigues.

In this place, I was a lamb among wolves, easy prey in a world that demanded fierceness and cunning. I'd come to London to marry, to fulfill my duty to my family, thinking myself fortunate when I secured an arrangement with a Duke. But now I understood that I was not one of them. In fact, I had never been less certain of my place.

A quiet tap at the door drew me from my thoughts. Mary entered, a worried look etched on her face.

"Your Grace, I thought you might want some tea," she said, setting a tray on the table. "You've hardly eaten today."

I offered a thin smile. "Thank you, Mary. You've been too good to me."

"Only what you deserve, Your Grace," she murmured, but her gaze lingered a moment too long. I could see the worry in her eyes—perhaps she feared, as I did, that there would be no end to these whispers, no mercy from those who seemed poised to tear me down.

I picked up the cup of tea, warming my hands on the delicate porcelain, and tried to find comfort in its familiar scent. I sipped slowly, letting the liquid settle in my stomach. The simple act soothed me, even if only for a moment, until the silence crept back in.

The whispers had started almost immediately after the funeral. I heard them in the hushed conversations of servants and saw them in the thin-lipped stares of distant relatives as they passed me in the halls. At first, I dismissed it as part of the usual idle chatter, but soon I could no longer ignore the underlying malice in their glances or the sly edge to their words. It was clear that the rumors were circulating—insidious, twisting rumors that hinted at the most unforgivable of sins: that my child was not my husband's.

And without my husband here to defend us, they circled closer each day, like vultures drawn to the scent of vulnerability.

The Duke's cousins were the worst offenders, men and women who had barely acknowledged my existence during my marriage, yet now seemed intimately invested in my life. Lord Frederick, the Duke's distant cousin, had taken to appearing in the drawing room unannounced, his gaze always fixed on me with a too-curious interest.

"Good morning, Your Grace," he greeted me, his smile stretched thin as he entered the room without invitation. I struggled to maintain a composed expression, though his presence seemed to drain the warmth from the room.

"Good morning, Lord Frederick," I replied, keeping my tone cool.

He settled into the chair opposite mine, uninvited, and his eyes fell almost immediately to my belly, barely beginning to swell beneath my mourning gown. The glint in his eye was unmistakable.

Without waiting for an invitation, he settled into the chair across from me. His eyes swept over me, lingering a beat too long on the faint swell beneath my mourning gown. Though the fire crackled warmly in the hearth, his presence seemed to chill the room.

"I felt it only proper to visit," he began, leaning back with an air of practiced casualness. "The Duke's passing has left a void in the family, and I wish to ensure that you are...managing."

"Your concern is noted," I replied, my tone polite but cool. "The estate has been busy, as you can imagine, but we are persevering."

He hummed thoughtfully, his gaze unwavering. "Of course. The Duke was more than my cousin; he was a pillar of this family. His loss is deeply felt."

I inclined my head, though the words felt hollow. Frederick had scarcely spoken to my husband during his lifetime, yet here he sat, cloaked in the pretense of familial devotion.

"And now, I must say, the family was quite...surprised," he said, voice oozing with false sympathy, "to learn of your condition. And so soon after the Duke's passing."

I met his gaze, though every nerve in me wanted to look away, to flinch from the implication beneath his words. "Indeed. My husband and I were blessed," I replied, refusing to let him see the impact of his words. "Though his health declined, we still held hope for a family, even to the end."

"Fortunate indeed," Frederick murmured, his lips curling faintly. He leaned forward, clasping his hands loosely. "Though such matters inevitably invite questions. A title as significant as this...naturally, it demands clarity."

Anger flickered in my chest, but I forced it down. "My child is my husband's," I said firmly, meeting his gaze without faltering. "There will be no uncertainty."

He gave a small, dismissive hum, as though indulging my explanation. "And yet," he murmured, almost to himself, "a title of this magnitude...one can hardly allow sentiment to cloud matters of inheritance."

I gripped the edge of my cup, anger flashing through me. "My child will inherit the title, Lord Frederick. Of that, you can be assured."

He tilted his head slightly, as if considering my words. The faintest trace of a smirk tugged at the corners of his mouth. "Of course, Your Grace. Provided the child...is his," he said, his tone laced with mock deference. "But, as you know, the family has its...responsibilities."

His gaze was unrelenting, and the weight of his insinuation pressed down on the room like a storm cloud. For a moment, silence stretched between us, taut and suffocating. Then I shifted slightly, placing a hand on my stomach in a gesture that felt both protective and dismissive.

"I thank you for your concern, Lord Frederick," I said, softening my voice to something almost apologetic. "But I find myself quite tired. The pregnancy, you see—it takes its toll."

His expression faltered just slightly, though he recovered quickly, rising to his feet with an exaggerated air of politeness. "Of course, Your Grace," he said, inclining his head. "Rest is paramount in your condition."

The words hung between us like a heavy curtain. I met his gaze, unblinking, though my knuckles whitened against the porcelain cup in my hand. He lingered for a moment longer, then rose and inclined his head.

"Good day, Your Grace," he said smoothly, before leaving the room as silently as he'd entered.

I inclined my head in return, watching as he lingered a moment longer, as though searching for something in my expression. Finding none, he gave a faint, almost mocking smile and made his way to the door.

As it clicked shut behind him, I exhaled slowly, the tension in my shoulders easing only slightly. His unspoken accusations still hung in the air, heavy and inescapable, a reminder that the whispers in the halls would not be silenced so easily.

Exhaustion and frustration weighed on me, pulling at the edges of my composure. I could almost hear the gleeful gossip that would spread through the house by evening. The Duke's relatives were vultures circling, biding their time until they could claim what they saw as rightfully theirs. And with every day that passed, I felt them encroach on my position, questioning not only my virtue but my very right to be here.

I rubbed my belly repeatedly. So, now they're after me by accusing me of doing indecent things and carrying another man's child.

"I wish you'd waited for the birth of our child, Rupert. I don't think I would be in this situation," I muttered as I looked down and rubbed my belly repeatedly.

I had nothing but this unborn child to protect me—a child I carried with pride and yet with an ache that grew each day, knowing they would never

9

know their father's kindness or quiet strength.

After Lord Frederick left, I sat alone by the fire, my gaze fixed on the dancing flames, my thoughts muddled by the conversation that had just taken place. The weight of the accusations lingered like a storm cloud, and I struggled to shake the uneasy feeling that had taken root deep within me. The quiet of the room felt oppressive, the silence only broken by the soft crackling of the fire. Just as I reached for my abandoned teacup, a footman entered, carrying a letter. He held it out with a quiet bow, his expression unreadable.

"Your Grace," he murmured before retreating.

The envelope was simple, sealed with an unfamiliar mark. For a moment, I hesitated, dreading what fresh attempt to control or undermine me it might contain. But when I broke the seal and unfolded the paper, my breath caught.

The handwriting was unmistakable. Bold and elegant, each curve of the letters seemed to call out to me, reaching across the abyss of his absence. It was my husband's.

Tears blurred my vision before I could even begin reading, and I pressed a trembling hand to my lips as the first line greeted me:

My dearest Evelina,

The fire's warmth pressed against my skin as I read on, his words pulling me into the depth of his love, his pain, and his foresight.

If you are reading this, I am no longer with you. It is a thought that shatters me even as I write. But I must think beyond my grief and prepare for what lies ahead—for you, for our child. My greatest regret is that I cannot be there to protect you both.

Tears sprang to my eyes, blurring the ink on the page. My hand shook as I brushed them away, willing myself to focus, to read each precious word he had left for me. His voice seemed to rise from the paper, gentle and filled with love, speaking to me as if he were still beside me. He spoke of his hopes for our child, of his dreams for the family we had so desperately wanted. He spoke of his trust in my strength, of his confidence that I would protect our unborn child with all that I had. His words were tender, filled with regret that he could not be here to shield us from the dangers he feared might come.

And then, at the end, his tone shifted.

There are those who will seek to harm you, my love, or to challenge the legitimacy of our child's claim. For this reason, I have made provisions to ensure your safety. There is a man you must contact, should the need arise. His name is Lord Jeremiah Langley, Viscount of Ravenscroft. He is an old friend, one I trust implicitly. Though his methods may seem... unconventional, his loyalty is beyond question.

My husband's trust in such a man confounded me. I could not reconcile the notorious rake with the ally he had chosen to protect me. Yet here was his name, written in my husband's own hand, etched with finality and purpose.

I clutched the letter to my chest, its folds crinkling against the pounding of my heart. His words were a lifeline, a beacon in the overwhelming darkness. But they were also a challenge. Could I truly place my faith in this man? Could I trust his guidance when my very instincts screamed for caution?

The firelight blurred again as fresh tears fell. My husband had thought of everything, even in his final days, even as death loomed over him. His love had reached beyond the grave to shield me and our child from the wolves at the door.

I read the last lines once more, my fingers brushing the ink as though I could feel the warmth of his hand.

Evelina, I know you will find the strength you need, for it is within you. Trust this man, if you must. But above all, trust yourself. You are more capable than you know. And remember, my love for you and our child will endure beyond this life.

The sob that escaped me was quiet, almost soundless, but it carried the weight of my grief and love. I folded the letter carefully and held it against my chest, letting the warmth of the fire seep into my chilled bones. My husband was gone, but his voice lingered, guiding me forward when I felt I had no direction.

Yet, here was my husband, in his final words to me, asking that I place my trust in this man.

The flickering light played over the paper, illuminating his instructions with a warmth that felt almost like his presence. A part of me resisted the idea, wanting to stand firm and prove myself capable alone. But as I thought of the encroaching family members and their thinly veiled threats, I knew I could not fight them without help.

There was too much at stake—my child's future, my own safety. And yet, the thought of inviting another unpredictable element into my already fragile life filled me with apprehension. Perhaps Lord Ravenscroft could help me, perhaps he was exactly what I needed to keep the wolves at bay, but I was not ready to place my trust in a man I barely knew, one whose reputation inspired more fear than comfort. Lord Ravenscroft might be the last person I would choose to turn to, but if he was the man my husband trusted, then he would have to be the man I trusted as well. But, I'm still not sure about that.

I took a deep breath, my gaze drifting to the darkened window. The night outside was as uncertain as the path before me, and I could only hope that, when the time came, I would make the right choice—whether that meant reaching out to Lord Ravenscroft or standing my ground alone. For now, all I could do was wait, and watch, and try to find the strength my husband believed I had, even if I wasn't yet sure I believed it myself.

And while I wasn't ready to place my trust fully in the enigmatic Lord Ravenscroft, I knew one thing with certainty: I would do whatever it took to protect my husband's legacy and the life growing within me.

But for tonight, I let myself mourn, let myself feel the ache of his absence and the weight of the path ahead. As I cradled the letter, I whispered softly into the flickering quiet, "I will not fail you."

3

Poison and Peril

T he tea tray arrived promptly at four o'clock, as it always did. The cups clinked softly as Mary arranged the table, her movements brisk yet careful, a comforting presence in a house that felt colder by the day. Across from me sat Lady Henrietta, the late Duke's aunt, her sharp eyes fixed on the embroidery she held, though it was clear her true focus was on me—watching, waiting, judging.

"I must say, my dear," she began, her tone laced with an edge of judgment, "it is remarkable that you manage to appear so... composed under the circumstances."

I folded my hands in my lap, resisting the urge to let her words sting. "Thank you, Lady Henrietta," I replied evenly. "It is my duty, after all, to ensure the Wakefield name is upheld."

Her lips curved into a faint smile, though it lacked warmth. "Quite so. And yet, I do wonder how long one can maintain such grace, particularly with so much at stake."

I forced a polite smile, unwilling to rise to her bait. It was always like this with Rupert's family—an endless parade of barbed compliments and veiled threats, each one designed to remind me of my tenuous position. They had made no secret of their doubts about my pregnancy or their belief that a male heir from another branch of the family would better serve the estate.

"Evelina, my dear," Lady Henrietta began, her tone seemingly polite but carrying an edge. "You know, given your condition, it would be prudent to have someone assist you with the estate matters. Early pregnancy can be quite delicate, and it's important you rest for the baby's sake."

I looked up, surprised but careful to keep my face neutral. "Thank you, Lady Henrietta, but I assure you, I am perfectly capable of handling the estate. Rupert entrusted it to me, and I wish to honor his confidence in my abilities."

Lady Henrietta's lips curved into a smile that didn't quite reach her eyes. She set down her embroidery, her gaze fixed on me. "You are strong-willed, my dear, and I admire that. However, managing an estate as grand as Wakefield can be daunting, especially for someone as... inexperienced as yourself." She paused, then added, "My son, Cedric, has offered to help. It's simply practical, given the circumstances."

"I appreciate the offer, truly," I said, trying to keep my tone even, "but I am confident in my ability to oversee the estate. I know it's what Rupert would have wanted."

Lady Henrietta sighed, her expression one of exaggerated patience. "You may think so, Evelina, but experience is what makes the difference. You are still so very young, and with a baby on the way, it would be wise not to overexert yourself. Cedric could relieve you of the burdens, at least until you are feeling stronger."

I clenched my hands in my lap, resisting the urge to let her words sting. "With all due respect, Lady Henrietta, I know my limits. This is my child, my husband's legacy, and I intend to fulfill my duties as he would have wished."

Lady Henrietta's eyes narrowed slightly, her smile fading. "Evelina, there is no shame in accepting help. You may think you know what is best, but without the proper experience, you risk making mistakes that could cost more than you realize. Rest, my dear. Leave the heavy decisions to those who understand them."

The tension in the room seemed to grow, the air heavy with unspoken words. Mary poured the tea, her brow furrowed slightly as she glanced at me, a silent question in her eyes. I gave her a small nod, signaling that I was fine, and she placed a delicate porcelain cup before me.

"Thank you, Mary," I said softly, taking the cup. I raised it to my lips, the scent of chamomile and mint wafting up to meet me. I focused on the warmth of the tea, letting it soothe the tension that knotted in my stomach.

At first, there was a faint bitterness, sharper than usual, but I dismissed it as an oversight in brewing. Then, the reaction came swiftly and mercilessly. A sharp, twisting pain in my abdomen, sudden and brutal, forced a gasp from my lips. It was like a knife, searing through my insides, a vicious agony that stole my breath. My heart raced uncontrollably, and cold sweat beaded on my forehead. Nausea surged, violent and unrelenting, and I clutched my belly in desperation. The pain radiated through my entire body, building to an unbearable crescendo as my vision blurred and darkened. My chest tightened, each breath more labored than the last, until I could no longer hold on.

The cup fell from my hand, shattering against the hardwood floor, the sound distant as I doubled over, clutching my belly. The pain was relentless, radiating in violent waves that seemed to tear through my very core.

What happened next was a blur of pain, fear, and chaos.

"Your Grace?" Mary's voice came from somewhere far away, panicked and high-pitched, but I couldn't answer her. My vision blurred, the edges of the room darkening as the pain intensified, spreading like fire through my veins. My breath came in ragged gasps, my heart pounding wildly in my chest, each beat a desperate plea: The baby.

The pain clawed at me, twisting my insides with a cruelty that left me breathless. I felt the muscles in my abdomen tighten and spasm, an awful pressure building as I collapsed to the floor, my knees hitting the ground with a jolt that sent another spike of agony through me. My hands gripped my belly, my fingers trembling as I tried to protect the life inside me.

"Evelina!" Lady Henrietta's voice broke through the haze, sharper now, tinged with real concern. She dropped her embroidery and rushed to my side, her hands gentle but firm as she tried to support me. "Mary, fetch the physician! Now!"

"Yes, my lady!" Mary's voice was frantic, the sound of her hurried footsteps fading as she left the room.

Lady Henrietta knelt beside me, her usually stern expression softened by worry. She placed a hand on my forehead, her touch surprisingly tender.

"Breathe, my dear," she urged, her voice low and calming. "Focus on your breath. You must stay calm, for the baby."

I tried to do as she said, but the pain was unbearable, each wave more brutal than the last. Tears welled in my eyes, and I clutched my belly, a desperate whimper escaping me. "The baby..." I gasped, my voice barely a whisper.

Lady Henrietta's eyes met mine, and for the first time, I saw genuine fear in them. "The baby will be alright, Evelina. You must stay strong. Hold on, my dear. The physician will be here soon."

She supported me as I writhed in pain, her arms steadying me as I was guided to lie down on the settee. Every movement felt like another knife, slicing through me, the pain radiating through my entire body. My head swam, the room spinning as nausea churned in my stomach, bile rising in my throat. I clenched my teeth, a desperate whimper escaping me as I fought to stay conscious, to stay present. My vision faded in and out, the faces around me blurring as the pain dragged me further into a haze.

"Hold on, Your Grace," Mary's voice pleaded, trembling and desperate. Her hand was on my forehead, cool and gentle, but it did nothing to quell the fire raging inside me. My body convulsed, my muscles locking up as I curled in on myself, a scream tearing from my throat as another wave of pain hit—sharp, excruciating, and unending.

Lady Henrietta's voice was a constant, soothing murmur, her hands holding mine as I struggled. "Stay with us, Evelina. You are stronger than this. You will get through it, for the baby."

And then, darkness claimed me.

* * *

When I awoke, the first thing I noticed was the faint scent of lavender, likely from the linens Mary had placed over me. The second was the ache that pulsed through my body, a deep, throbbing pain that seemed to echo with every beat of my heart. It was a reminder of how close I had come to losing everything.

"Your Grace," Mary whispered, her voice trembling. "You're awake."

I turned my head to see her sitting beside me, her eyes red and swollen, the worry etched into her face as plain as day. Her hand was resting lightly on mine, her fingers cool against my fevered skin.

"What...what happened?" I croaked, my throat dry and raw. My voice barely sounded like my own, hoarse and weak.

"You collapsed," she said, her voice breaking. "The physician was here—he said it was poison, Your Grace. In the tea."

The words hung in the air, heavy and suffocating. Poison. Someone had tried to harm me, and in doing so, had risked the life of my child. A cold chill spread through me, a fear unlike any I had ever known.

My heart raced as I instinctively moved a hand to my stomach, terror gripping me. "The baby?"

Mary's eyes filled with tears. "The physician said...you were lucky. The baby is still with us, but he warned you must rest. No stress, no overexertion."

Relief flooded through me, tempered by a wave of anger and fear. My hand tightened over my stomach, a fierce protectiveness surging within me. I had thought they wanted to strip me of my position, to remove me from the estate—but this? This was an act of violence, one I hadn't believed them capable of.

Relief and fury warred within me, each emotion vying for control. Someone had tried to kill me—and, worse, my child. "Who?" I asked, my voice sharper now. "Do they know who did it?"

Mary shook her head. "No, Your Grace. But the butler found something—traces of powdered veratrum in the tea leaves. It's a plant toxin, common enough in some medicinal preparations, but fatal to a pregnant woman even in small doses."

The name chilled me. Veratrum, a poison that often mistaken for harmless herbs if one weren't careful—or intentional. Its effects were insidious: violent nausea, sharp abdominal pain, and the potential to induce miscarriage or worse.

Mary's voice faltered as she added, "The tea canister was tampered with. The butler discovered the faint residue in Lady Henrietta's cup as well, but it seems she drank only a sip before switching to her usual Earl Grey. The physician believes the dose in hers was too small to cause harm."

I stared at her, the implications chilling. "So, the poison wasn't meant for her. It was meant for me."

She nodded, her face pale. "Yes, Your Grace. Whoever did this wasn't just after you—they were after the baby. They knew exactly what they were doing."

My stomach twisted—not from the lingering pain, but from the betrayal that threatened to suffocate me. Someone in this house wanted me gone, and they were willing to risk murder to achieve it.

"There's no way to know who...who did it. It could be anyone," I whispered as I began to get goosebumps down to my bones

"Yes, Your Grace. Anyone in the house."

Her words sent a chill through me, the realization dawning that I was surrounded by enemies, hidden in plain sight. I had been naive to think that they would only come for my title, that they would leave me and my child unharmed. I had underestimated their ruthlessness—and it had nearly cost me everything.

I sat up slowly, ignoring Mary's protests, and reached for the small desk beside the bed. My hand trembled as I pulled a piece of parchment toward me, dipping the pen into the ink with a resolve I hadn't felt in days.

"Your Grace," Mary said hesitantly, "what are you doing?"

"I am done waiting," I replied, my voice firm despite the exhaustion that lingered in my body. "They want me gone, Mary. They want this child gone. And I will not sit idly by while they try to take everything from me."

I began to write, the words flowing with a clarity born of desperation and determination:

Lord Jeremiah Langley, Viscount of Ravenscroft,

I write to you in great need, under circumstances I could never have foreseen. I require your assistance, as your late friend, my husband, instructed me. My position has become untenable, my safety and that of my unborn child gravely threatened. I implore you, as one whom Rupert trusted, to come to Wakefield and offer your aid.

I signed my name with a flourish, the ink drying quickly as I folded the letter and sealed it with wax.

My hand settled instinctively over my belly, feeling the soft curve of new life beneath. This child, his child, was my duty to protect, even if it meant accepting the help of a man I had never met.

"Mary," I said, handing the letter to her, "this must go out immediately. It cannot wait."

She hesitated, her brow furrowed with worry. "Do you trust him, Your Grace? This Lord Ravenscroft?"

I looked down at my hands, still shaking, and took a deep breath. "I don't know," I admitted. "But he is the only chance we have."

Mary nodded, taking the letter with a determined expression. "I'll see to it."

As she left the room, I leaned back against the pillows, my hand once again resting over my belly. The fear still lingered, but beneath it was a spark of something new—a resolve to fight, to protect the life growing within me.

They had tried to take everything from me, but they had underestimated my will. If they wanted to destroy me, they would have to face me head-on—and I would not let them win.

4

The Wolves at My Door

After yesterday's terrible incident, rest was supposed to be my priority. My body ached, my mind was heavy with the fear of what could have been, and yet I could not truly rest. The letter I had sent to Lord Jeremiah Langley was still on its way, and the house seemed quieter than ever, each shadow in the corners a reminder of the enemies hiding in plain sight.

I had expected the arrival of the physician for a follow-up or perhaps a sympathetic visit from a neighbor. What I did not expect was the sudden appearance of Lady Henrietta and her son, Cedric Harland.

The sitting room was far too warm when they entered, despite the coldness they carried with them. Lady Henrietta swept in with her usual air of authority, her gaze sharp as it roved over me reclining on the settee. Cedric followed, his demeanor as pleasant and smooth as ever, the practiced smile of a man who knew how to charm his way past suspicion.

"My dear Evelina," Lady Henrietta said, her tone sweetened with just enough syrup to make it cloying, "we simply had to come. After yesterday's dreadful ordeal, I could not leave you unattended in such a state. Cedric and I are here to ensure you have all the support you need during this... delicate time."

I sat up straighter, gripping the arm of the settee to steady myself. "I appreciate your concern, Lady Henrietta, Lord Harland," I said evenly, keeping my tone polite. "Mary has been more than capable of attending to my needs."

Lady Henrietta gave a small, dismissive wave of her hand. "Oh, I am sure Mary does her best," she said, her eyes lingering on the maid, "but managing an estate like Wakefield is no small task, and your health must come first. It would be a shame to risk the baby's wellbeing over matters that others could handle with ease." She glanced at Cedric, her meaning clear without needing to say more.

Cedric stepped forward, his smile widening as he sat down opposite me. "She's right, Your Grace," he said, his voice warm and persuasive. "You've already been through so much. Allow me to take some of the burden off your shoulders. I can oversee the estate for you, handle correspondence, manage the tenants—whatever you need. You should be focused on rest and the child."

I gave a small nod, keeping my expression neutral despite the unease twisting inside me. "That is generous of you, Lord Harland," I replied, my voice calm. "But I cannot make such a decision lightly. I will need time to consider."

Lady Henrietta's lips pressed into a thin line, though she quickly replaced the expression with another saccharine smile. "Of course, my dear. Take all the time you need, though I would urge you not to delay too long. Every day that passes without proper management risks undoing all that Rupert worked so hard to build. Cedric is here for the family, for the legacy. It's what Rupert would have wanted."

I forced a polite smile, even as my heart clenched at the mention of my late husband. "I will take that into consideration," I said evenly.

Lady Henrietta leaned forward slightly, her eyes narrowing. "You know, Evelina," she began, her voice softening, "I truly am worried about you. Yesterday was a frightful experience, and I cannot imagine the toll it took on you—not just physically, but emotionally as well. Rest is what you need, not the burden of running an estate. Please, my dear, for the sake of the baby, consider our help."

Cedric nodded in agreement, his eyes sympathetic. "It's understandable that you want to honor Rupert's wishes, but you must also think of your own health, Your Grace. We only want what's best for you."

I could see the calculation behind their words, the subtle push to make me give in, to relinquish control. My stomach tightened again—not from pain, but from the unease their proposal sent coursing through me. Their presence alone was enough to unsettle me, but the way Cedric spoke, as if he were already taking charge, made my pulse quicken with dread.

"I appreciate your kindness, Lord Cedric," I said, feigning gratitude. "And I will certainly consider it. For now, however, I think it best that I rest. The physician was quite clear about avoiding undue strain, and I find my stomach is still unsettled from yesterday's events."

Lady Henrietta's gaze narrowed slightly, the false smile faltering for a moment. "Of course, Evelina," she said after a pause. "You must take care of yourself. Cedric and I will leave you to rest, but do let us know if there is anything we can do to assist."

Cedric stood, giving a short bow. "Please don't hesitate, Your Grace. We are family, and family looks after each other. You can count on us."

As they rose to leave, I fought the urge to let my exhaustion show, keeping my expression composed until the door closed behind them. Only then did I release the breath I had been holding, sinking back into the settee as the tension drained from my body.

Mary entered moments later, her eyes wide with concern. "Your Grace, are you alright? They didn't upset you, did they?"

"No more than usual," I said, managing a small smile. "But their intentions are clear, Mary. They want Cedric here, close enough to finish what the poison could not. I cannot let that happen."

Mary nodded, her hands twisting nervously in her apron. "What will you do, Your Grace? Until Lord Ravenscroft arrives..."

I thought of the letter I had sent, the ink still fresh in my mind. "We hold them off, Mary," I said firmly. "For as long as it takes. This child is the Duke's heir, and I will not let them take that away—not from me, not from him."

Mary's expression hardened, her worry giving way to resolve. "I'll keep a close eye on them, Your Grace. They won't get away with anything under this roof."

Her loyalty was a balm to my frayed nerves, but it was not enough to ease the weight pressing down on me. The wolves were at the door, and I could not let them in.

5

A Visitor in the Night

The darkened silhouette of Wakefield Hall loomed before me, stately and vast against the night sky. I shifted uneasily in my saddle, gazing up at the imposing structure with a mixture of familiarity and dread. I'd known it once, years ago, though not well. But enough to feel its character, to sense the kind of household it must be under the rule of a man like *Rupert Harland, the Duke of Wakefield.*

Rupert and I had been unlikely friends—a curious bond forged through a shared tour in the Peninsula. He was a man who inspired trust through his steadiness, a rare quality, even among friends. I was never his equal; I lacked his sense of duty and restraint, he'd once told me so to my face, with a half-smile, a little too honest. Yet, when I received Evelina's letter, there was only one answer I could give.

Sliding from my horse, I felt the crunch of gravel beneath my boots as I approached the grand doors. Rupert had left me with a final request: to see to his wife's well-being if anything happened to him. The letter had come months ago, soon after he realized his health was beginning to decline. Yet it wasn't until Evelina's own letter arrived, desperate yet cautious, that I truly understood what he had meant. He had known this place would become hostile territory for her without him.

If only she had been more pregnant, I thought grimly, as I climbed the wide stone steps. Had she been showing the unmistakable signs of bearing a child, her protection might have been simpler. But the whispers I'd already begun to hear on my way into town were crueler than I had expected. Rupert's relatives were sharks, drawn to weakness, and she was barely past the early signs of her pregnancy.

"Lord Ravenscroft?" A footman stood at the door, his expression stiff with disapproval. I nearly laughed; his look implied a wealth of judgment for the "guest" who had come under a clouded reputation.

"Yes, I am expected," I replied curtly. There was no need to charm the household just yet; that would come later if it proved useful.

The servant led me inside, the familiar scent of aged wood and polished silver pulling memories I'd long left behind. The estate was the very heart of aristocratic tradition, a grand, sprawling place that demanded respect. My gaze took in the high ceilings, the portraits of long-dead Harlands glaring from their gilded frames as if to assess me. I had always been something of an interloper here, a man who straddled the worlds of respectability and scandal. Now, I felt it keenly.

"His Grace's widow will see you shortly," the footman informed me before bowing and disappearing into the hall.

And so, I waited, my mind restless as I considered the woman I was about to meet.

I hadn't known Evelina well, but I remembered Rupert speaking of her with a fondness rare for a man of his station, who'd had little choice in his marriage. She'd come from a country family—a viscount's daughter, raised in simpler ways, thrust into the merciless world of the ton. From what I'd gleaned, she'd spent most of her marriage doing her best to adapt, perhaps even thriving in her quiet way, until fate decided otherwise. Now, she was a young woman, a widow with a fragile claim to her position, left to fend for herself against Rupert's calculating relatives.

A young widow, a reluctant duchess—and a pregnant one, at that. I didn't even know if she had the stomach to survive this, though I knew Rupert had believed she did. For her sake, I hoped he'd been right.

When she entered the room, her presence seemed small against the grand, echoing walls of the drawing room. She wore black, the weight of her mourning gown cloaking her delicate figure, which was made even slighter by the visible curve of her early pregnancy. I noticed the way her fingers trembled as she clasped her hands together, and for a brief moment, the vulnerability there unsettled me.

"Lord Ravenscroft," she greeted me with a steady, if tentative, voice. Her eyes, soft but serious, searched mine. There was no evidence of the rumors in her face—no shadow of scandal or treachery. Only quiet strength tinged with sadness. I inclined my head.

"Your Grace," I replied, my voice low. "Thank you for receiving me."

She gestured for me to sit, though she remained standing. She seemed to be measuring me, and I didn't blame her. I could imagine how absurd I must seem to her—a rogue, a man with a reputation that likely invited whispers of impropriety even before I'd stepped foot in this house. And now, I'd been summoned to her side by her dying husband. The Duke had placed his trust in me, a choice that I knew must seem outlandish, if not reckless, to a woman who had so much to lose.

"I received your letter," I said gently, hoping to ease the stiffness in her posture.

"Yes." Her gaze softened, though she remained guarded. "You were...an unexpected answer, I must admit. I had not thought my husband would ask someone...like yourself, forgive me, to come to my aid."

A smile tugged at the corner of my mouth, but I resisted the urge to respond with my usual sarcasm. Instead, I simply nodded. "Rupert was never one to make decisions lightly, Your Grace. He knew what might happen here without his presence. He wanted you and his child to be protected."

She lowered her eyes, and I saw her shoulders sag slightly, as though the weight of everything finally had the freedom to rest upon her. It was there, in the curve of her body beneath the layers of mourning silk, in the way her hand drifted instinctively to her stomach.

The sight unsettled me. She was so young, carrying both the weight of a dukedom and a child, barely past her girlhood, her face framed by dark curls that spilled beneath her mourning veil. But she was not yet beaten; there was a fire there, even if it was still dimmed by grief. Rupert had seen it, and now I saw it too. And it was enough to convince me that I would stay.

"I'm sure you're aware of the rumors," she said quietly, her gaze lifting to meet mine, steady despite the tremor in her voice. "They think to remove me if they can."

I nodded, understanding immediately the threat that lay between her words. "Yes, I heard about that."

"I...I don't know how I am to fight them. I was not trained for battles of this kind. Not like you were."

A wave of protectiveness washed over me, surprising in its force. Rupert had been wise to summon me, even if I was the last person anyone would think of as a suitable protector for a duchess. And as I looked at Evelina, this delicate woman with a resolve that seemed half-formed, I realized the depth of Rupert's concern. He had understood that she would be a target, an easy prey, vulnerable to those who cared little for the child she carried.

"My loyalty was to Rupert," I said slowly, "and it remains so now. If he asked me to protect you, then that is what I intend to do."

For a moment, a flicker of relief passed over her features, and she gave a single, slight nod. "Thank you, Lord Ravenscroft."

"Please," I replied, offering her a wry smile. "Call me Jeremiah. If I'm to help you, formalities will only slow us down."

"Very well...Jeremiah," she said, her lips softening with the hint of a smile. There was something sincere, almost grateful, in her expression, and I felt a strange comfort in knowing she'd allowed me this small concession.

We sat in silence for a moment, the understanding between us fragile but enough to set the course ahead. I knew it would not be simple—she had been left to face not only her own grief but also the machinations of a family who saw her as an obstacle. But if Rupert's faith in her had been strong enough to call me here, then I would match that faith.

As I looked at her, I made a silent vow to uphold that trust, for Rupert's sake, and perhaps for hers as well.

6

Unlikely Allies

I sat across from Lord Ravenscroft—Jeremiah, I corrected myself, as he had insisted. The morning light filtered through the high windows, casting long beams across the drawing room, softening the otherwise severe decor of the Duke's home. We didn't continue our conversation last night because I felt that Jeremiah was tired after the long journey. So, I asked to come in the morning and try to engage him in conversation. I studied him, trying to piece together what it was Rupert had seen in him, something that would make a Duke place his family's future in the hands of a man known as both a rake and a soldier.

Jeremiah, for his part, seemed perfectly at ease under my scrutiny. He sat with a quiet confidence, his gaze patient, steady, as though he were used to being examined and found wanting by society's more refined circles. And yet, when he looked at me, I saw no judgment, no dismissiveness, only an unwavering respect that felt strange and, admittedly, disarming.

"I'm apologize if I disturbed your rest, I just wanted to continue last night's conversation," I said while trying to smile.

"It's alright, Your Grace. It's as it should be." Her voice remained as calm as before. "So, what shall we talk about first."

I looked up, curiosity piqued. "You knew Rupert well, didn't you?"

A small, fond smile touched Jeremiah's lips. "Yes, I did. We met years ago."

I held his gaze, searching his face for any trace of insincerity, but there was none. "Why did you come?" I found myself asking, the question slipping out before I could stop it.

Jeremiah's eyes softened, and he let out a breath, almost as if he, too, were testing the truth of his answer. "Because Rupert asked me to. And because..." He hesitated, his brow furrowing. "Because I believe it is the right thing to do."

"Why do you feel this is the right thing?"

Jeremiah smiled. "Your son is the rightful heir to the duchy of Wakefield, so it's only right that I do all this."

His overly diplomatic answer made me want to ask further questions, I wanted honesty from the person who would be my partner in the future. The person who might become my most dangerous enemy if I'm not careful. "Why do you want to help me? We are strangers."

"Think of it as returning the favor."

"A favor?" I asked, furrowing my brow.

"Yes, a favor. When I was in a particularly difficult situation. I had inherited the title of Viscount, but my reputation at the time was less than sterling. I was known as a rake—a man with little discipline, unfit for the responsibilities of the title. Many believed I wasn't deserving of the inheritance, and there were whispers of stripping me of it altogether."

I listened intently, intrigued by the glimpse into their shared past. Jeremiah's expression grew more thoughtful as he continued. "Rupert was the one who saw past my reputation. He believed I could be more, that I could rise to the occasion if given the chance. He used his influence as Duke to support me—he spoke on my behalf, vouched for my character, and even arranged for me to be introduced to certain circles that were otherwise closed to me."

He paused, his gaze distant as he remembered. "Rupert's support was what turned the tide. He convinced others to give me a chance, and through his patronage, I was able to prove myself. I owe him a great deal, Your Grace. Without Rupert, I would not be the man sitting before you today."

I felt a lump form in my throat. It was just like Rupert to see the best in others, to extend his hand when no one else would. "He believed in people,"

I whispered. "He believed in you."

"Your husband was a good man," he said softly, his voice breaking the silence.

"Yes," I replied, my voice catching. "He was...steady. Dependable." I bit my lip, feeling the familiar twist of grief. "I hadn't expected him to go so soon. To leave me, to leave us..." My hand drifted instinctively to my abdomen, resting on my belly. The warmth beneath my palm reminded me that I wasn't alone, though some days I felt nothing but isolation.

Jeremiah met my eyes, his expression sincere. "And now, Your Grace, I'm here because of him. I'm here to help you, just as Rupert once helped me. I know what it feels like to be doubted, to be surrounded by those who would rather see you fail. You are not alone in this."

Jeremiah's gaze softened, following the movement of my hand. He seemed to understand without my having to explain, a relief in itself. I hesitated, wondering just how much I could trust him. But the vulnerability of the moment coaxed out words I hadn't spoken aloud before.

I took a deep breath, the tension in my shoulders easing ever so slightly. "Thank you, Jeremiah," I said quietly. "Since Rupert's passing, I've felt as though the walls were closing in. His family... they want control of the estate, they don't believe the child is his and they want to take my child's future away."

"I can see why they might try to sow doubts. Rupert spoke of his family's ambitions more than once." His expression darkening slightly. He leaned forward, resting his forearms on his knees. "Did they make these accusations openly?"

"Not outright," I replied, shaking my head. "But they whisper. In hallways, at gatherings, even to the staff. They seem eager to see me displaced, eager to be rid of me altogether. I believe some of them want control over the estate before my child is born. If...if my child is even allowed to remain."

The bitterness in my voice surprised me. I hadn't allowed myself to think so directly about the family's machinations; they had been background shadows, faceless whispers, but speaking them aloud brought them into harsh focus. It wasn't only the estate that was under threat—it was my place here, my child's claim to any semblance of security.

Jeremiah listened in silence, his expression unreadable, though his gaze never wavered. "They see you as an inconvenience," he said finally, his voice low but steady.

"Yes," I whispered. "As if I am nothing more than an obstacle, something to be dealt with."

I nodded, understanding immediately the threat that lay between her words. "If they succeed, you and the child will have nothing," I said plainly. "They would see you cast out."

"Yes, You're right," I whispered s while looking down and staring at my slightly growing belly.

For a moment, he said nothing, his gaze shifting to the window, as if he were processing the weight of what I had told him. I felt exposed, uncertain, my heart pounding as I waited for some sign of what he might say or do. Would he dismiss my fears as fanciful? Would he walk away, deciding that Rupert had overestimated my plight?

But instead, he leaned forward, his voice quiet but certain. "I won't let them harm you, or the child," he said, and though his words were simple, I felt them settle deep within me. "As long as I am here, I will do everything in my power to protect you and the Duke's heir. Rupert believed in me, and I will honor his trust."

His words, though earnest, left me with the strange, unfamiliar sensation of hope—a sensation I wasn't yet sure I was ready to trust. "Forgive me," I began, feeling the need to challenge him further, "but I hardly see how you—a man who has been gone from society and who...well, whose reputation has certain associations—"

"Can be of any help to you?" He finished for me, a faint smile tugging at the corner of his mouth. "I understand your doubt, Your Grace. I have lived a life that many would call unrespectable. But I am not here for society's opinion. I am here to keep you safe."

There was a finality in his tone, an assurance that held more weight than I expected. I could see that he meant every word, and it stirred something in me that I hadn't felt since Rupert had passed away—a sense that I might not be alone in this battle.

"I want to trust you, Jeremiah," I said softly, feeling as though the admission cost me something fragile and unguarded. "But you must understand—since my husband's death, I have had little to trust in."

He inclined his head, his expression softening. "That is fair, Your Grace. I would not ask you to trust me blindly." His gaze grew thoughtful, almost gentle. "But perhaps you might allow me to earn that trust?"

I nodded, unable to speak, my throat tight. It had been so long since anyone had offered to share the burden with me, since anyone had cared to even attempt to understand what it meant to be in my position. And here was Jeremiah, an unlikely ally, with a pledge that felt as strange as it was sincere.

There was a beat of silence between us, charged with an unspoken understanding, and it felt like the first real breath I'd taken in weeks.

"May I ask you something, Your Grace?" he said, breaking the silence, his voice low and hesitant.

"Yes, of course," I replied, surprised by his sudden hesitance.

"What are your plans?" he asked. "Once the child is born, once the dust settles—what do you hope for?"

The question took me by surprise, and for a moment, I didn't know how to answer. It was as if he had pulled back a curtain I hadn't dared to look behind.

"I...haven't allowed myself to think that far," I admitted, my voice barely a whisper. "All I've been able to focus on is surviving each day, keeping the whispers at bay, protecting what I can of my husband's memory." I glanced down, my hand instinctively returning to rest over my belly. "And protecting this child, as best I can."

When I looked back at him, his expression was contemplative, his eyes fixed on me with an intensity that felt almost intimate. "Surviving isn't enough, Your Grace," he said, his voice low. "Not for you. Not for the child."

I swallowed, his words settling over me like an unfamiliar warmth. He was right; I had been living as if survival were my only aim, but perhaps...perhaps there could be more. Perhaps there could be a future beyond these walls, beyond the accusations and doubts.

"I don't know what I hope for," I admitted, feeling the weight of the words as I spoke them. "But perhaps, with someone by my side, I could begin to imagine it."

His eyes softened, and he offered a slight nod. "Then we will begin there," he said simply, as though it were the easiest decision in the world.

In that moment, I felt a glimmer of relief, a tentative easing of the weight that had pressed on me since Rupert's passing. Jeremiah was not the ally I had expected, and perhaps he was not the ally I would have chosen, had I any other choice. But as I met his gaze and saw the quiet resolve there, I realized that he might be exactly the ally I needed.

"Thank you," I said softly, meaning it with a depth I hadn't anticipated. "Truly, Jeremiah...thank you."

He inclined his head, a faint smile playing at the corner of his mouth. "You needn't thank me, Your Grace. This is what I promised Rupert, and it's what I would do regardless. We are in this together."

The words lingered between us, a shared promise that, for the first time, felt as if it had the strength to hold me up. And as I sat there, in the quiet presence of this unlikely ally, I felt the faintest stirring of hope, a fragile but steady flame in the darkness.

7

Allies and Intruders

J eremiah's words lingered between us, their warmth a balm to wounds I had not dared to admit were still raw. I studied his face, the quiet confidence etched into his features, and for a fleeting moment, I allowed myself to believe that I was no longer alone in this fight.

But before I could fully grasp the fragile hope growing within me, a knock at the door shattered the moment.

Mary peeked in, her expression cautious. "Your Grace, Lords Frederick and Cedric Harland have arrived to see you."

Jeremiah raised an eyebrow, his posture straightening as if bracing for a confrontation.

I sighed, my hand instinctively brushing over my growing belly. "Send them in, Mary."

They're entered with all the grace and posturing that I had come to expect from Rupert's family. Frederick, a distant relative who had shown little interest in Rupert's life while he was alive, led the way. His cold gaze swept over the room before settling on me, his expression conveying nothing but disdain, as though my very existence were an affront to him.

Cedric followed, his charm as polished as the shine on his boots. He offered a low bow, his smile bright and seemingly genuine.

"Your Grace," he began, his tone warm and apologetic, "I must start by expressing my regret for my mother's insistence on my... assistance. It was never my intention to impose. I also wanted to inquire about your health, Your Grace, and that of the child. My mother has been quite worried since the poisoning incident. She sent a tonic to help with your recovery, and that is partly why I felt it important to visit you today."'"

I studied him, wary but polite. "Thank you for your concern, Lord Harland, but Lady Henrietta's words do not trouble me. I have no intention of dwelling on them."

Frederick moved towards the tea table, his eyes flicking over the cups. He took a seat, leaning back with an air of practiced casualness.

"Your Grace," he began, his voice polite but with an edge of formality, "it is good to see that you are recovering. We all wish for your health, of course, especially given recent events." He paused, letting the words hang in the air. "I hope you understand that our visit today is to ensure that the estate remains well cared for. Wakefield is a significant responsibility, and we must all do our part to protect its legacy."

I inclined my head. "I appreciate your concern, Lord Frederick. I assure you, everything is under control."

Frederick's expression shifted slightly, his lips curling in a thin smile. "Your confidence is admirable, Your Grace," he said, his tone dripping with condescension. "Though I must admit, it's difficult to see how such confidence translates into effective management of an estate as vast as Wakefield."

I forced a polite smile, my fingers tightening around the armrest. "Rupert believed in my ability to manage Wakefield," I said evenly, "and I intend to honor that trust."

Cedric stepped in smoothly, his voice light and conciliatory. "Come now, Frederick, there's no need for hostility. We're here to support Her Grace, not to cast doubt. Family must stand together in times like these."

Frederick gave a slight smirk, lifting his teacup as though in toast. "Of course, of course. We all want what's best for the family. Though, I do wonder if the late Duke's confidence in certain... capabilities wasn't misplaced."

The jab was veiled in civility, but it stung nonetheless. I held my ground, refusing to let his words provoke me. "The late Duke made his wishes very clear," I replied, my voice steady. "And I intend to fulfill them."

Cedric's smile widened, his eyes briefly meeting mine with what seemed like sympathy. "And we will do whatever we can to assist you, Your Grace. As family, we are only concerned for your well-being and that of the child."

Jeremiah, who had remained silent up to this point, shifted in his seat. His eyes were watchful, his voice calm but pointed as he spoke. "Her Grace is fortunate to have loyal family members like yourselves," he said. "Though I must admit, I am surprised to see such concern after recent events."

The room went quiet for a moment, the tension thickening. Frederick's eyes narrowed at the implied accusation, but Cedric remained unruffled, his smile unwavering as he placed his teacup down gently. "We are all deeply grieved by what happened," Cedric said smoothly. "And it is precisely because of those events that I offered my assistance. It is my duty to ensure that Her Grace can focus on her health and the child without unnecessary burdens."

The politeness was suffocating, each word carefully chosen to mask the underlying currents of tension. I took a deep breath, my gaze flicking between them. "I am grateful for your concern, Lord Harland," I said, my tone polite but firm. "However, I have already made arrangements for assistance. Allow me to introduce Lord Jeremiah Langley, Viscount of Ravenscroft. He has graciously agreed to help manage the estate, as per my late husband's wishes."

Jeremiah gave a polite nod, his eyes never leaving Frederick and Cedric. There was a flicker of something in Frederick's expression—annoyance, perhaps—but it quickly vanished, replaced by a thin smile. Cedric, on the other hand, softened his expression, nodding. "I see. That is... a relief. With someone as capable as Lord Ravenscroft here, you can focus on what truly matters, Your Grace."

Frederick, however, was less tactful. He set his teacup down with a deliberate clink, his gaze shifting to Jeremiah. "It's curious, isn't it?" he said, his tone dripping with false curiosity. "That you would place your trust in a stranger rather than family."

I felt the sting of the accusation, the barely concealed disdain in his words. But before I could respond, Jeremiah leaned forward, his voice calm but commanding. "The late Duke's instructions were clear. My presence here is to fulfill his wishes, nothing more, nothing less."

Frederick's lip curled slightly, but he said nothing further. He turned his attention back to me, his eyes cold. "I trust you know what you're doing, Your Grace," he said, his tone making it clear that he did not.

I kept my expression steady, refusing to let his words affect me. "I assure you, Lord Frederick, everything is under control," I replied with a calm smile.

Frederick shrugged, his demeanor slightly softening, though the coldness in his gaze remained. "It is simply our concern for the estate, Your Grace. Wakefield has a long history, and we all wish to see it thrive. It would be... unfortunate if any mismanagement led to difficulties."

Cedric stepped in, giving a slight nod. "Indeed, Frederick. We are all here to offer our support, Your Grace. After all, the estate is not just a matter of family pride; it also represents the well-being of all those who work under its banner."

He looked around the room, as if taking in the history of the house. "Wakefield has always been a beacon of stability. We simply want to ensure that continues."

I inclined my head politely. "I understand your concerns, Lord Harland, and I assure you both that my foremost priority is the prosperity and well-being of Wakefield. I have already taken measures to ensure everything is in capable hands."

Cedric nodded, his expression earnest. "I believe you, Your Grace. You have shown remarkable strength and resolve during these trying times, and I trust that Wakefield is in good hands with you. My offer is simply to assist in any way I can."

I smiled politely, my tone softening. "Thank you, Lord Harland. Family should indeed help one another in times of need, and I appreciate your willingness to support me. It means a great deal."

Cedric rose, his movement smooth and deliberate. He gave a courteous bow, his smile still bright. "Thank you for receiving us, Your Grace," he said. "If you need anything, please don't hesitate to call on me. My only goal is to ensure your comfort and safety."

Frederick followed suit, though his bow was noticeably stiffer. "We do hope for the best, Your Grace. I trust you will reach out if any... issues arise."

They're departed shortly after, leaving a silence in their wake that felt heavier than their presence. I let out a breath I hadn't realized I was holding, sinking back into my seat as Mary entered to clear the tea.

Jeremiah turned to me, his expression thoughtful. "Cedric is... polished," he said carefully. "But I would caution you against trusting him too quickly."

I raised an eyebrow. "And why is that?"

"Because men like him," Jeremiah said, his voice low, "know how to say exactly what you want to hear while quietly pulling the strings behind the curtain. His charm is a weapon, Your Grace, and I suspect he wields it well."

I considered his words, my mind drifting back to Cedric's easy smiles and soothing tone. There had been a moment—just a moment—when I had felt almost reassured by his presence, but now, in the quiet aftermath, Jeremiah's warning felt all too apt.

"Do you think they mean to harm me again?" I asked softly, my hand moving instinctively to my belly.

Jeremiah's gaze hardened. "I think they'll do whatever they believe is necessary to secure control. Whether that means harming you, the child, or simply pushing you out altogether... it's clear they see you as an obstacle."

His words sent a shiver down my spine, but they also solidified my resolve. I straightened, meeting his gaze. "Then we won't let them."

Jeremiah nodded, a faint smile tugging at the corner of his mouth. "No, we won't."

For the first time since Rupert's death, I felt a glimmer of control return to me. The road ahead was uncertain, the threats against me and my child far from over, but with Jeremiah by my side, I felt a strength I hadn't thought possible.

They wanted me to falter, to crumble under the weight of their schemes. But I would not give them that satisfaction.

Let them come. I would be ready.

ALLIES AND INTRUDERS

8

Building Fortresses

S ince that day, Jeremiah became a near-constant presence in my life. It was odd to think that only a short time ago he had been a stranger to me, a figure whispered about in London's drawing rooms and mentioned only in vague, disparaging terms by society's more respectable members. Now, he was something far more critical—a kind of anchor, a guide through waters more treacherous than any I had imagined.

Each morning he arrived in the drawing room, where I waited with a notebook, a pen, and a mix of anticipation and apprehension. We had grown accustomed to the routine quickly, as if we had been doing this for much longer than a handful of days.

Today, he was already settled into his favorite armchair by the window when I arrived. He glanced up and greeted me with a slight nod before diving right into his usual low, steady tone, his voice full of quiet confidence.

"Your Grace," he said as I took my seat, his low, steady tone cutting through my unease. "We've got work to do. There are two things you must secure if you are to withstand your husband's family: allies and a solid defense strategy. They may expect you to fold under pressure, but we'll make certain they find you far less pliable than they anticipated."

His confidence sent a flicker of resolve through me, though my voice wavered as I replied, "Allies. And who, pray tell, would side with me over the influence of Rupert's family?"

A shadow of a smile crossed his face. "Don't underestimate the power of your position. You are the Duchess of Wakefield, and that title carries weight. Stability appeals to many, and if they believe you can provide it, they will choose you over the uncertainty of Lady Henrietta, Lord Frederick, or Lord Cedric Harland."

The mention of Lady Henrietta sent a chill down my spine. She had resided at Wakefield before her marriage, long before I became Duchess. Her familiarity with the estate, its secrets, and its staff gave her an edge I could hardly ignore. Jeremiah's assessment had only confirmed my worst fears.

"Lady Henrietta is one to watch," he continued, his tone darkening. "She's the most dangerous of them all. Your husband's death has given her a chance to claim the power she's been denied for years. If anyone would move to unseat you, it's her."

I forced myself to sit straighter, letting his words settle over me like armor. "Then how do we defend against her?"

Jeremiah leaned forward, his expression grim. "Her strength lies in her influence over the estate's staff and her connections within the ton. She's had years to build loyalty here—among the servants, among Rupert's distant relatives. They see her as a steady presence, someone who has always been part of Wakefield's legacy."

My thoughts churned as I considered his words. Lady Henrietta's veiled smiles and biting remarks had always made me uneasy, but after the poisoning incident, I could no longer dismiss her as merely an overbearing relative. If she were behind the attack, she would not hesitate to try again.

"Lady Henrietta controls the staff," I murmured, my thoughts racing. "The poisoning...it's possible, isn't it? That it was her?"

Jeremiah's jaw tightened. "It's more than possible. She's the only one with the influence to ensure such silence. The staff remains loyal to her because she's been here longer than anyone, and they believe she'll outlast you. If she senses that you're gaining favor, she'll likely try to discredit you. But her influence can be used against her. If we're going to protect you, we need to start there."

"How?" I asked, my voice sharper than I intended.

"We show the staff and the ton that loyalty to you offers more stability than her empty promises. Lady Henrietta thrives on fear and manipulation, but if we undermine her authority, even a little, the cracks will start to show. People want to follow strength, not desperation."

"Start with the staff?" I repeated, surprised. "I always assumed they would remain neutral, that they would simply do their jobs regardless of the shifting alliances above them."

Jeremiah shook his head. "The staff sees everything, hears everything. They are the estate's lifeblood. If they're spreading lies about you, it's the staff who will carry those whispers. But if we can win their loyalty, or at least their respect, they'll be more inclined to defend you than to act as Lady Henrietta's spies."

I nodded slowly, a new understanding dawning. "Then how do I win them over?"

Jeremiah studied me for a moment, as if assessing my readiness to step into this unfamiliar role. "You show them that you are more than what Lady Henrietta paints you to be. Treat them well. Learn their names, ask about their families. Show them kindness and fairness, and they'll begin to see you as someone worth protecting. A loyal servant is more valuable than the wealthiest ally, especially in battles like these."

His words settled over me, heavy but not unwelcome. If this was what it would take to protect my child, to secure our future, then I would do it.

"And Frederick?" I asked.

Jeremiah's expression hardened. "Frederick is a distant cousin of Rupert's and one of Lady Henrietta's staunchest allies. He's ambitious and bold, a man who doesn't shy away from using cruelty to achieve his goals. He's already begun whispering about your child's legitimacy, and he won't stop there. His ultimate aim is clear: he wants control of Wakefield, and he'll do whatever it takes to get it."

I nodded, my grip tightening on the armrest of my chair. Frederick's cutting remarks at the last gathering were still fresh in my mind. He hadn't just questioned my child's legitimacy—he had all but declared it a scandal waiting to explode.

"And Cedric?" I prompted, my voice low.

Jeremiah hesitated, his brow furrowing slightly. "Cedric is...different. He's dangerous in a quieter way. Where Frederick wields blunt force, Cedric uses charm. He's disarmingly polite, warm even, but make no mistake—his ambition is no less potent. He's already begun making himself indispensable to you, hasn't he?"

I thought back to Cedric's easy smiles, his gentle reassurances. "He has," I admitted.

Jeremiah nodded grimly. "He's positioning himself as your ally, someone you feel you can rely on. But it's a calculated move. He wants to be close enough to influence you and, by extension, the estate. Don't trust his charm— it's his greatest weapon."

My stomach twisted at the thought. Frederick and Cedric were two sides of the same coin, each dangerous in his own way. And then there was Lady Henrietta, the puppet master pulling their strings.

Jeremiah shifted slightly, his eyes narrowing in thought. "There might be another approach we haven't yet discussed," he began cautiously, his gaze meeting mine. "What if we focused on the dynamics between Frederick and Lady Henrietta? Their alliance is strong, but not unbreakable."

I paused for a moment, then leaned forward, my voice growing more cautious. "There might be another way—a dangerous method, but it could be effective. If we can drive a wedge between Frederick and Lady Henrietta, their alliance could crumble."

Jeremiah looked at me, intrigued but wary. "Break apart their relationship? How would we even begin to do that?"

I took a deep breath, my gaze steady. "We need to make Frederick see that Lady Henrietta doesn't truly value him, that she would sacrifice him if it meant advancing her own position. We could start by planting small doubts, subtle hints that she sees him as expendable. If we can exploit his pride, make him question her loyalty, it could start to erode the trust between them."

Jeremiah's expression turned grim. "Frederick is ambitious, but he is also proud. If we can make him believe that Lady Henrietta is holding him back or

43

using him for her own ends, it might be enough to create tension. Your idea of planting small doubts is sound—we suggest that Lady Henrietta sees him as expendable, as merely a tool to further her own power."

A shiver ran down my spine. "That sounds incredibly risky. If it backfires, they could both turn against me even more aggressively."

Jeremiah nodded, his gaze steady. "It is dangerous, yes. But it might work. The key would be making Frederick doubt Lady Henrietta's loyalty to him. He needs to believe that she is willing to sacrifice him for her own gain. If we can do that, their alliance may weaken."

He hesitated, then added, "Are you sure you can do it, Your Grace? This will require subtlety, patience, and a certain ruthlessness. It will not be easy."

I swallowed hard, considering the weight of his words. The idea of manipulating Frederick, of planting seeds of distrust, was not something I had ever imagined myself doing. But then again, I had never imagined I would be fighting for my child's future against my own husband's family.

I straightened, meeting Jeremiah's gaze with determination. "I will try. If it means protecting my child, I will do whatever it takes."

Jeremiah gave me a long, searching look before nodding slowly. "Very well, Your Grace. Just remember, this path is fraught with risk. You must be careful—Frederick is not easily swayed, and Lady Henrietta will surely fight to maintain her control. But if anyone can do this, it is you. I will be here to help you navigate every step."

I nodded, absorbing his words. "Thank you, Jeremiah. I know it won't be easy, but I have to try." I paused, taking a deep breath. "What else do we need to prepare for?"

Jeremiah's expression grew serious. "There are forces outside these walls, Your Grace. Allies and adversaries both. We need to prepare for any outside interference—those who might be swayed by Lady Henrietta's influence, or even Frederick's ambitions. We need to know who among the ton and the influential families can be approached, and who might pose a threat. It will require careful planning, but we need to secure our standing beyond the estate as well."

"Who else can I trust?"

He leaned back, his gaze thoughtful. "Lord Winfield is a good start. He despises Lady Henrietta and has no love for Frederick. His word carries weight in the House of Lords, and he values loyalty above all else. Winning him over would be a significant step in securing your position."

I jotted the name down, feeling a flicker of hope. "Anyone else?"

"Lady Sinclair," Jeremiah added. "She's influential among the ton's matrons. If you can win her approval, the whispers about your child's legitimacy will begin to fade. She's cautious but fair, and she values strength in women. If she sees you as capable, she'll champion your cause."

The thought of interacting with such powerful figures made my pulse quicken. I had grown up in the countryside, far removed from the intricate web of London society. But if I were to protect Wakefield, I would have to learn to navigate these waters.

"You must become the Duchess they respect," Jeremiah said firmly. "Show them a woman who is strong, who holds her own. They need to see that you are not some timid girl from the country but a leader worthy of this title."

I met his gaze, his words settling deep within me. "And you think I'm capable of that?"

Jeremiah leaned forward, his eyes steady. "Yes, Your Grace. I do. You just haven't had a reason to believe it yet."

His words struck something within me—a fragile seed of confidence that, for the first time, felt as though it might take root. Lady Henrietta, Frederick, Cedric—they would not see me falter.

"Then let us begin," I said, my voice steady. "If I am to defend this estate, my child, and my title, then I will do it with everything I have."

Jeremiah's expression softened, a faint smile tugging at his lips. "That's the spirit, Your Grace. Together, we'll ensure they think twice before crossing you."

For the first time, I felt that this was a fight I might just be able to win.

9

Rallying Friends and Foes

As I stepped into the busy halls of London society, Jeremiah's words echoed in my mind, guiding me as I navigated the intricate dance of building alliances. It was strange, how quickly my life had shifted from secluded mourning to subtle negotiations. But as I thought of my child's uncertain future and the whispers that clung to me like shadows, I felt the resolve in me harden.

My first visit was to Lady Sinclair, a figure Jeremiah had assured me could lend both credibility and stability to my position. She was known for her sharp tongue, iron will, and a keen sense of decorum. If I could sway her to my side, it would be an undeniable step forward.

Her home was a proof to her power—a stately townhouse in Grosvenor Square, its entrance framed by elegant columns. I was ushered in and offered tea in a drawing room, decorated with the opulence only a woman like Lady Sinclair could manage without being considered ostentatious. She greeted me with a nod, her eyes watchful as they took me in.

"Your Grace," she began, her tone polite but with an unmistakable note of curiosity. "It is a pleasure to see you. Though, I must admit, I was a bit surprised by your request to call upon me. I'd thought you were still in mourning."

I returned her steady gaze, drawing from the strength I'd been cultivating in recent days. "Indeed, I am. But my circumstances have...changed. As you know, the Duke's passing has left me in a precarious position, especially with a child on the way. I felt it necessary to reach out to those who might understand my predicament."

Lady Sinclair's eyes softened just slightly at my words. She nodded thoughtfully, taking a sip of her tea before she spoke again. "You are wise to do so, Your Grace. The ton can be a merciless creature, especially for those left without protection."

"Yes," I replied, my voice steady. "And with that in mind, I hoped I might count on your guidance."

She considered me for a moment, her expression unreadable. "Guidance is one thing, my dear, but loyalty is another. Tell me, what do you intend to do if those loyal to your husband challenge your position? I imagine the Duke's family must have their own opinions on your...future."

I knew what she was really asking: how I would face the questions surrounding my child's legitimacy. I took a breath, letting Jeremiah's advice guide me. "I intend to protect my child's legacy, no matter what it requires of me. This child is the Duke's heir, and as his mother, I will defend that truth to my last breath."

Lady Sinclair's expression softened just a fraction, and I could see that she respected my resolve. She nodded, a faint smile breaking her stern facade. "Then you may count on me, Your Grace. I do not tolerate slander, and it is clear to me that you are more than capable of leading your family forward."

Relief bloomed in my chest, and I inclined my head. "Thank you, Lady Sinclair. Your support means more to me than you can imagine."

As I took my leave, I felt a surge of confidence. Jeremiah had been right—Lady Sinclair would stand by me, and her influence would help still some of the whispers around me. Yet, there were still others I needed to persuade.

The following afternoon, I arranged to call upon Lord Winfield. He was a kind man, known for his fairness and his steadfast loyalty to those he respected. Jeremiah had assured me that he would be inclined to lend his support, though I sensed it would take more than a simple plea to win him over.

Lord Winfield greeted me warmly, offering a seat by the fire and inquiring after my health in a way that felt surprisingly genuine. It was refreshing, in a way, to be in the company of someone who didn't seem to view me as a pawn or a threat.

"Your Grace," he began, "I must say, I'm impressed with the grace you've shown in recent days. I imagine it cannot be easy, facing such uncertainty."

I smiled gratefully. "Thank you, Lord Winfield. I confess, it has been difficult. But I am determined to protect my child's future."

He nodded, his gaze warm but thoughtful. "You have a noble cause, Duchess, and you have the will for it. But you must be prepared for what may come. The Duke's family can be...relentless."

"I am aware," I replied, a flicker of steel entering my tone. "But I am prepared to fight, if need be."

Lord Winfield smiled, seeming pleased by my response. "Then I will gladly lend you my support. It's clear to me that you are more than up to the task, and I believe your child has every right to inherit the legacy left by the Duke."

Relief washed over me, and I thanked him sincerely. It was another victory, another step toward securing my child's place in the world.

The following days were a blur of conversations and guarded glances, of tentative support and veiled questions. Most of the people I spoke to responded with a surprising warmth, offering their support or at least their sympathy. Yet, there were those whose loyalty was more elusive, whose polite smiles hid reservations and suspicions that I could sense beneath the surface.

One such encounter came at Lady Ashby's home. She was a woman of considerable wealth and influence, but as I quickly discovered, she had little regard for discretion.

"Your Grace," she began, her tone saccharine as she offered me tea. "It is so tragic, what you've endured. And to think, you must now bear this journey alone."

"Yes," I replied, keeping my tone neutral. "It has been challenging, but I am determined to carry forward my husband's legacy."

Lady Ashby gave me a sympathetic smile, though her eyes held a glint of something sharper. "Of course, of course. It is only natural to want to protect one's family. Though I must say, I have heard...concerns regarding the Duke's family's position. Surely you've been made aware of the whispers?"

I met her gaze, refusing to let my irritation show. "I am aware that certain individuals may question my child's place. But I assure you, Lady Ashby, those questions are both unfounded and undeserved."

Her smile grew slightly. "Of course. But, as you know, society can be merciless when it chooses. It would be wise, Your Grace, to consider all options."

I thanked her politely, though I left with a bitter taste in my mouth. Lady Ashby's words were a reminder of how quickly loyalties could shift in this world, and how fragile my position remained.

That evening, Jeremiah arrived at the estate to discuss my progress, his expression thoughtful as he listened to my recounting of the day's events.

"Lady Sinclair has offered her support, and so has Lord Winfield," I told him, the pride evident in my tone. "But Lady Ashby...well, she seemed less inclined to be of use."

Jeremiah's mouth twitched in a faint smirk. "That sounds about right. Lady Ashby is as slippery as they come. If she senses that you're gaining support, she may still align with you, if only to avoid being on the losing side."

"Do you truly think she would?" I asked, skepticism clear in my voice.

"People like her always follow power," he said, a hint of weariness in his tone. "For now, continue strengthening your alliances. With Lady Sinclair and Lord Winfield on your side, others may begin to view you as a viable leader in your own right."

I nodded, feeling a surge of gratitude toward him. Without Jeremiah's guidance, I wouldn't have known how to navigate these murky waters. But with his counsel, I felt capable—stronger than I had ever felt before.

"Thank you, Jeremiah," I said quietly, meeting his gaze. "I couldn't have done this without you."

His eyes softened, a warmth there that I hadn't seen before. "I'm merely keeping my promise, Your Grace. And it seems you're doing quite well on your own."

His words stirred something in me, a feeling I couldn't quite name. It was as if, for the first time since Rupert's passing, I felt the spark of something beyond survival—a hint of hope, a glimpse of a future I hadn't dared to imagine.

With allies beginning to rally to my side, and Jeremiah by my side as both a guide and a friend, I began to believe that I might just win this fight. And though the journey was far from over, I felt a glimmer of confidence that steadied me for whatever lay ahead.

10

Secrets Beneath the Surface

E velina was seated across from me in the dimly lit study, the fire crackling softly in the hearth, its light casting flickering shadows on the mahogany walls. Her brow furrowed in concentration as she traced her finger along the edge of a map spread out before us. Her determination was palpable, a quiet force that seemed to fill the room.

I leaned back in my chair, watching her as she considered our next move. It was difficult not to admire her resolve. The woman I had first met, shrouded in grief and uncertainty, had transformed into someone sharper, steadier—yet no less vulnerable.

I had come here tonight to discuss strategy, to help her solidify her alliances and weaken the grip of those who sought to destroy her. But I found myself distracted, my thoughts wandering to places they had no business being.

Evelina's hand moved absently to her belly, resting there in a gesture so natural I doubted she realized she was doing it. I caught myself staring, noticing for the first time how much her figure had changed. The slight curve of her pregnancy was now unmistakable, the gown she wore accentuating the growing life within her.

It wasn't the first time I'd noticed, of course. But tonight, something about the sight gave me pause. That small movement—protective, instinctual— tugged at something in me I couldn't quite name.

"Jeremiah?" Evelina's voice broke through my thoughts, pulling me back to the present.

"Yes?" I replied, leaning forward to feign attentiveness, hoping she hadn't noticed my lapse.

"I was saying that we need to prioritize Lady Ashby," she said, her tone measured. "She's too unpredictable. If we let her linger on the fence, she could sway others against me."

"True," I agreed, though my gaze lingered on her a moment longer than necessary. "But we should also focus on Frederick and Lady Henrietta. If we can fracture their alliance, it will weaken their influence over others in the ton."

She nodded thoughtfully, her hand still resting on her belly. "How do we do that? Frederick is...volatile, but he's not stupid. And Lady Henrietta is as calculating as ever. She won't let go of him easily."

"Frederick is ambitious," I said, choosing my words carefully. "He aligns himself with Lady Henrietta because it benefits him. If we can find a way to make her position less secure—something that threatens her more than it threatens you—he may reconsider his loyalty."

Evelina tilted her head, considering. A strand of hair slipped from the loose knot at her nape, brushing against her cheek. She pushed it back absently, her focus unwavering. "And how do we threaten Lady Henrietta without exposing ourselves?"

"By using the staff," I said, leaning forward, my elbows resting on the table. "You know as well as I do that the servants see everything. If there's discontent brewing among them—or if there's a trail leading back to her from the poisoning incident—we need to find it. And we need to do it quietly."

Her expression tightened at the mention of the poison. I regretted bringing it up so bluntly, but it was a reality we couldn't afford to ignore.

"You're right," she said softly, her fingers tightening slightly against her belly. "We can't let something like that happen again."

"We won't," I said, my voice firmer than I intended. "But we need their trust first. Right now, Lady Henrietta's influence runs too deep in this house. We have to root it out, starting with those closest to her."

She smiled faintly, the corners of her lips softening as she considered my words. "You make it sound easy."

"It won't be," I admitted. "But you have something she doesn't."

"What's that?"

"Hope," I said, the word slipping from me before I could stop it.

Her eyes flicked to mine, and for a moment, the room felt too quiet, too small. I cleared my throat, leaning back to break the tension. "And leverage," I added, a weak attempt to cover the slip. "If we find the right information, it'll be enough to make even her closest allies think twice."

Evelina turned back to the map, her focus returning to the task at hand. But I couldn't shake the momentary stillness that had passed between us. It was as though she'd seen through the facade I so carefully maintained, glimpsing something I wasn't ready to acknowledge.

She began outlining a plan to meet with the head housekeeper, her voice steady and clear as she detailed her approach. But as I watched her speak, her hands moving animatedly over the map, I found my attention drifting again.

The way she spoke—so sure of herself, so committed to protecting the child she carried—made me think of my mother. Of the nights she spent sewing by candlelight, her fingers raw from work but her resolve unshaken. She had fought tooth and nail to give me a life my father's family would have denied me, and I saw that same fire in Evelina now.

But it wasn't just admiration or respect that stirred in me. It was something deeper, something dangerous.

"Jeremiah?" Evelina's voice broke through my thoughts again, and this time there was a hint of concern in her tone.

"Yes?" I asked, straightening.

"Are you all right?" she asked, her brow furrowing slightly.

"I'm fine," I said quickly, though the tightness in my chest suggested otherwise. "Just...thinking."

She gave me a small, hesitant smile. "Well, don't overthink too much. I need your sharp mind in one piece if we're going to get through this."

Her words were light, but there was an unspoken gratitude in her eyes that nearly undid me.

"You'll have it," I said quietly, meaning it more than she could know.

As we continued planning, I forced myself to focus on the details—the meetings, the alliances, the quiet inquiries among the servants. But in the back of my mind, a single thought lingered, persistent and unwelcome:

Evelina wasn't just a duty anymore. She wasn't just a promise or an obligation. She was something far more dangerous.

And I wasn't sure how much longer I could pretend otherwise.

11

How to Win a War with Tea and Biscuits

Winning the loyalty of a household staff was, I quickly learned, not entirely unlike taming a pack of wolves—albeit ones armed with feather dusters and ladles instead of teeth. The staff of Wakefield Manor was a formidable force, and winning them over would require far more than titles or polite words. I approached the challenge with what I hoped was quiet determination, though I could not deny the unease gnawing at me. Winning over servants who had likely spent decades under Lady Henrietta's watchful, commanding eye felt about as achievable as shifting the very mountains surrounding the estate.

Wakefield Manor was a world unto itself, a great living machine with countless cogs—cooks, housemaids, footmen, stable boys, gardeners, and butlers—each working seamlessly to maintain its grandeur. And every single pair of eyes watched me. Some held skepticism, others suspicion, but the general air was one of expectation—waiting to see if I would crumble or falter, waiting to judge if I was merely an intruder, a temporary occupant destined to vanish as soon as Lady Henrietta's shadow grew too heavy.

Lady Henrietta had built a legacy here, not just in stone and splendor but in people. She knew their names and histories, their triumphs and tragedies. She had sat at their weddings, attended their christenings, and, in her quieter moments, ensured dowries and physician's fees were paid without fanfare. To the staff, she was more than the mistress of Wakefield—she was the bedrock of their existence, unshakable and omnipresent. By comparison, I was an uncertain figurehead, a new duchess whose claim hung precariously on the thin thread of my unborn child.

Jeremiah's words echoed in my mind as I prepared to begin: "Show them that you are more than what Lady Henrietta paints you to be. Treat them well, ask about their families, earn their respect, and they'll fight for you instead of against you." Easier said than done.

And so, on a gray and drizzling afternoon, I embarked on what I could only describe as a campaign—an effort to prove myself not through grand declarations, but through small, persistent acts. I moved through Wakefield Manor with deliberate purpose, my footsteps echoing against the polished floors as I descended into the bowels of the house where the true work took place.

The kitchens were my first stop. I had braced myself for what I imagined to be a war zone of heat and chaos, but nothing quite prepared me for the reality. The room was alive. The air pulsed with the rich smells of roasting meats, freshly baked bread, and something sweet that tugged at my senses. Fire blazed in the hearth, pots clanged, and servants darted through the haze of steam and shouted instructions. It was a symphony of labor, each person an instrument in perfect discordant harmony—until I stepped through the threshold.

The effect was immediate. All eyes turned to me. Mrs. Branagh, the head cook, a stout woman with flour-dusted hands and a gaze sharp enough to cut through bone, turned to face me. The clatter of a dropped onion echoed through the stillness as a young scullery maid scrambled to recover it, cheeks red with embarrassment.

"Your Grace," Mrs. Branagh said flatly, her tone void of warmth but brimming with professionalism.

I managed a steady smile, though I could feel the weight of every unspoken word pressing down on me. "Good afternoon. I hope I'm not disturbing your work."

Mrs. Branagh's brow lifted a fraction. "Not at all, Your Grace. What can we do for you?"

"I realized," I began carefully, clasping my hands to keep them from fidgeting, "that I've spent far too little time in this part of the house. And far too little time getting to know the people who keep Wakefield running so admirably."

A glance passed among the servants, silent but loud enough to hear. I could feel the unspoken words radiating from them: What is she doing here? Mrs. Branagh's face was unreadable, though I caught a flicker of curiosity in her sharp eyes.

"I thought I might sit for tea," I added, forcing a lightness into my tone, "and see for myself all the work that goes into this house."

The silence that followed was nearly unbearable. Then, mercifully, a footman—his sleeves rolled high, his face flushed from the heat of the ovens—pulled a stool from a corner. "Of course, Your Grace."

The stool was far too low, and the moment I perched upon it, I felt ridiculous. Still, I held my head high as Mrs. Branagh handed me a cup of tea—plain, black, and hot—watching me with the shrewd air of someone expecting criticism. I took a sip, ignoring how it burned my tongue, and smiled. "It's wonderful, Mrs. Branagh. Thank you."

Surprise flickered in her expression, quick as a blink but unmistakable. "You're welcome, Your Grace."

Encouraged, I pressed on, asking about the meal preparations. To my relief, one of the maids piped up, her voice tentative, "Roast lamb, Your Grace."

"I'm sure Rupert would have loved it—" The words left my mouth before I could stop them. The silence that fell felt as though the entire room held its breath. I swallowed hard and smiled faintly. "What I meant to say is...he always admired the work here. As do I."

Gradually, the clamor resumed, though at a quieter pace. The tension was still there, but I had cracked its surface. As I finished my tea, Mrs. Branagh's voice reached me, low but deliberate. "You've a hard job ahead, Your Grace. But the staff pays attention. You'll see."

And see I did. Over the following days, I became a presence in their world, not by command but by intent. It began with small, deliberate acts—the kind that spoke louder than any decree. I visited the stables, where the familiar scent of hay and leather mingled with the crisp morning air.

The stable master, Mr. Hargrove, was initially wary, his eyes narrowing as I approached. "Your Grace," he said, tipping his hat but not entirely welcoming.

I smiled and gestured toward Blackthorn, the Duke's prized stallion. "He's magnificent. Tell me about him."

The cautious expression softened as he launched into the horse's lineage and temperament. "Strong as an ox, clever too," he said, his voice tinged with pride.

"You must spend hours with him," I said, my voice light but curious. "He looks as though he trusts you completely."

Mr. Hargrove nodded slowly, his fingers brushing Blackthorn's sleek coat. "Trust comes with time, Your Grace. And patience."

"Patience," I echoed thoughtfully, watching the stallion's calm demeanor. "You've given him the best care, Mr. Hargrove. It shows."

The stable master's weathered face softened, and after a moment, a rare smile crept across his lips. "Not many notice the work behind the shine," he admitted, his voice tinged with quiet pride.

As he spoke, I glanced past Blackthorn and noticed little Will busily polishing a saddle in the corner, his small frame hunched over his task. "And what about you, Will?" I asked, stepping toward him. "Are you the one who keeps everything looking so pristine?"

Will froze, his eyes wide as saucers. "Y-yes, Your Grace," he stammered, clutching the rag in his hand. "I just... try to do my best."

"You're doing more than that," I said, crouching to his level. "Would you mind showing me how you manage such a perfect shine?"

His cheeks flushed as he nodded eagerly, his small hands demonstrating careful circular motions. "Like this, Your Grace," he whispered, his voice barely above a whisper. I mirrored his movements, eliciting a shy grin from the boy.

"You're a natural teacher, Will," I said warmly, catching Mr. Hargrove watching us with a soft expression. "With care like this, Wakefield is in good hands." Will beamed, and even the stable master gave a slight nod of approval, the beginnings of trust blooming between us all.

The gardens became another point of connection. I wandered there often, pausing to admire the vibrant roses and lush hedgerows. Mr. Ridge, the old gardener with calloused hands and a perpetually furrowed brow, initially regarded me with suspicion.

"Fine blooms this year, Mr. Ridge," I remarked one afternoon, kneeling to inspect a particularly fragrant rose. His gruff mutter came after a pause.

"The soil's good here. Been good since the Duke's time." His words carried an unspoken reverence for Rupert, and I nodded, respecting his sentiment.

In the kitchens, I found Mrs. Branagh, the housekeeper, orchestrating the staff with the precision of a general. I complimented the arrangement of the dining table, noting how the silverware gleamed under the chandelier's light.

"It's your standards that keep Wakefield's reputation intact," I told her sincerely.

She gave me a considering look before nodding slightly, the smallest crack in her formal demeanor.

The changes were slow, like the shifting of seasons. In the halls, the maids began to meet my gaze, their curtsies accompanied by faint smiles. I made it a point to acknowledge them in return, offering a kind word or asking after their families, small gestures that seemed to bridge the gap. The footmen's replies grew less clipped, and their posture softened when I addressed them. Once, while passing the library, I overheard two of them whispering about the improvements I'd made to their work schedules, their tone lacking the usual edge of skepticism that had once permeated such conversations.

Even Mrs. Branagh, whose nods were as measured as her steps, began to offer those subtle acknowledgments more frequently. Once, I found her in the pantry inspecting the inventory and took the opportunity to ask about her favorite recipe.

"You're curious about the kitchens, Your Grace?" she asked, her brow lifting slightly.

"Always," I replied. "After all, the heart of the household beats strongest where care is given most."

She seemed surprised by my answer but nodded, a faint but significant shift in her demeanor.

Every interaction, every exchange—no matter how small—was part of a plan I was carefully weaving. Lady Henrietta's presence still loomed over Wakefield, her years of influence casting long shadows that I could feel even in her absence. The staff's loyalty to her was deeply ingrained, but Jeremiah had been right—they were watching me, weighing me, testing to see if I was truly worthy of the title I bore.

One afternoon, as I passed Mrs. Branagh in the corridor, she paused, her sharp eyes studying me. "You're surprising them, Your Grace," she said, her tone measured. "Surprising us all."

I met her gaze, understanding the weight of her words. "Change takes time, Mrs. Branagh. But Wakefield is as much theirs as it is mine."

Her lips twitched, almost a smile. "A fair sentiment. One they're starting to believe."

It wasn't victory. Not yet. But as I ascended the staircase that evening, the fading sunlight casting golden hues across the stone walls, I allowed myself a small smile. Wars weren't always won with armies or banners. Sometimes, they were won in kitchens and gardens, with tea and quiet words, and the slow, steady rebuilding of trust.

Soon, Lady Henrietta's spies would have nothing to whisper about. Because soon, I would have more than just their obedience. I would have their loyalty.

12

A Midnight Conversation

The estate's gardens were hushed under the darkened sky, their beauty softened in the moonlight. It was late, far later than any respectable hour, but sleep had evaded me, leaving me restless, my thoughts tangled like the ivy that crept along the garden walls. I'd never thought a single task, a single promise, would consume me in the way this one had.

In truth, it wasn't just the promise I'd made to Rupert. It was Evelina herself—her quiet determination, the depth of her sorrow hidden behind layers of composure. She reminded me, uncomfortably, of all the things I'd once valued but had long left behind. And against every instinct I'd honed over the years, I found myself caring more than I should.

A soft rustle broke the silence, and I turned, half-expecting one of the servants. But instead, I saw Evelina stepping along the garden path, her dark shawl wrapped around her shoulders, her face illuminated by the soft glow of the moon. She hadn't noticed me yet, her gaze fixed on the ground, her steps slow and careful. Even now, she moved with a quiet elegance that felt out of place amid the clamor of scandal surrounding her.

"Your Grace," I called softly, and she started, her hand going to her chest. "Forgive me—I didn't mean to startle you."

She relaxed, a faint smile tugging at her lips as she stepped closer. "You don't have to call me that," she murmured. "Not here, at least."

I raised an eyebrow. "What should I call you, then?"

She hesitated, her gaze dropping to the ground. "Evelina. Just...Evelina." There was a vulnerability in her voice, as if the simplicity of her own name were a luxury she rarely allowed herself.

"Evelina, then," I said, tasting the name as if it were something new. I took a step back, gesturing for her to join me on the bench beneath a sprawling oak tree. She sat beside me, her hands folded in her lap, her shoulders tense despite the calm that surrounded us.

"Couldn't sleep?" I asked, though the answer was obvious in the faint shadows beneath her eyes.

"No," she admitted, her voice soft. "It seems there is...too much in my mind to allow it. I came out here hoping the quiet might settle my thoughts."

I nodded, understanding more than I cared to admit. "This estate has that effect," I said. "It's both a sanctuary and a prison, isn't it?"

She looked at me, her gaze sharpening slightly. "How do you mean?"

"There's a peace here," I explained, glancing around at the gardens, the hedges and blooms now shrouded in darkness. "A silence that feels safe. But it's a trap, too. The longer you stay, the more it convinces you that the world beyond these walls isn't worth the fight."

She considered my words, her brow furrowing. "You sound as if you've known that trap yourself."

A faint laugh escaped me. "Once, perhaps. The military felt the same way, back in the day. There was a clear sense of purpose, of loyalty. But it became easier, eventually, to stay in that narrow world. I think it's part of why I...earned the reputation I did, once I was free of it."

She was silent for a moment, and I felt her eyes on me, searching. "It must have been lonely."

I glanced at her, surprised by the insight in her voice. "It had its moments," I admitted, feeling the truth of it settle in my chest. "But loneliness becomes a habit, like anything else. Easier to bear than facing the past, perhaps."

Her gaze softened, a look of understanding crossing her face. "You and I have that in common, then," she said, her voice barely above a whisper. "Loneliness has been my companion as well. Even with Rupert, there were...

parts of my life I learned to keep hidden."

I watched her carefully, noting the way her hands trembled slightly, as if she were holding something back. "And yet here you are," I murmured. "Facing everything alone, with a strength most would envy."

She let out a soft laugh, the sound edged with bitterness. "Strength? I hardly feel strong. I feel..." She trailed off, her voice catching. "I feel as if I'm only surviving, like I'm barely holding onto what's left of my life."

Her words struck something deep within me, a pang of empathy I hadn't expected. I reached out, hesitating before letting my hand rest lightly on hers, a simple gesture of comfort that felt strangely intimate. "Surviving can be its own kind of strength, Evelina."

She looked up at me, her eyes shining with a vulnerability she usually kept so carefully hidden. "And what about you, Jeremiah?" she asked, her voice steady despite the softness in her gaze. "Why have you chosen to stay, to risk your reputation for a woman society deems unworthy?"

The question caught me off guard, and for a moment, I struggled to find the words. "It started as a promise," I admitted, my voice low. "But now...now it's because I believe you're worth more than what society says. You've shown more courage and grace than anyone I've met. And for reasons I can't entirely explain, I find myself caring about what happens to you. More than I should."

Her gaze held mine, and in that moment, it felt as if the world had narrowed to just the two of us, bound by an unspoken understanding that neither of us could name. She took a slow breath, her hand tightening slightly around mine.

"I think I understand," she whispered, a tremor in her voice. "It's strange, but...knowing that you're here, that you're willing to stand by me despite everything...it gives me hope. And for the first time since Rupert's death, I feel...less alone."

Her words, so simple yet so full of meaning, settled over me like a warmth I hadn't known I'd been seeking. I didn't know what to say, so I simply held her gaze, allowing the silence to fill the space between us.

In the quiet, I became acutely aware of her hand in mine, of the soft rise and fall of her breath, of the faint scent of lavender that seemed to cling to her even now. She was no longer just a duty, no longer just a promise made to a friend. She was Evelina—a woman of quiet strength, of grace and courage, a woman who had found her way past my defenses without even trying.

And as I looked at her, I felt a shift within me, something I couldn't quite name—a tenderness, a desire to protect her not out of duty, but out of something far more personal.

Her gaze drifted down, a faint blush coloring her cheeks as she looked away. "Forgive me," she murmured, withdrawing her hand from mine. "I didn't mean to burden you with my troubles."

"You're not a burden," I replied, my voice quiet but firm. "Not to me."

She looked up, and the vulnerability in her eyes stirred something deep within me, a need to shield her from the world's cruelty, to be the one she could lean on when no one else seemed to care. And in that moment, I knew that my promise to protect her had grown beyond a mere obligation.

We sat in silence for a while longer, the midnight air cool around us, the sounds of the garden soft and soothing. There was no need for more words, no need to explain what had passed between us. The connection we shared had been laid bare, a bond born not from obligation but from something deeper, something neither of us dared name.

Finally, she rose, her movements slow and graceful, as if reluctant to break the stillness of the moment. "Thank you, Jeremiah," she whispered, her voice filled with a quiet gratitude. "For being here. For...everything."

I stood as well, inclining my head. "Anytime, Evelina."

She offered a faint smile, and for a moment, I thought she might reach out to me again. But instead, she turned, walking slowly back toward the house, her figure disappearing into the shadows as she slipped away.

As I watched her go, a sense of loss settled over me, tempered only by the knowledge that I would be here when she needed me again. I had come to Wakefield for a promise, but I stayed now for something I couldn't quite define.

And as I turned to face the quiet garden, I felt the warmth of our midnight conversation linger, a reminder that sometimes, the most powerful connections were the ones forged in silence, in shared solitude.

13

The First Scandal

The rumor started as a low hum, as they always do—a whisper in the corner of a drawing room, a chuckle over a glass of brandy. But by the time it reached my ears, it had grown like wildfire, fueled by London's insatiable appetite for scandal. I could almost feel the heat of it as I made my way to Evelina's estate that morning, the familiar weight of London's judgment settling around me. Normally, I wouldn't give a damn. Scandal was as much a part of my reputation as my name was.

But this time, it was different.

The first hint of trouble came when I passed a cluster of ladies in Hyde Park on my way to the estate. I didn't know them personally, but I knew the look well enough—a collective glance, followed by a string of murmurs and titters, none of them subtle in their regard. And I understood, as I'd understood in so many drawing rooms and public spaces before, that my very presence invited suspicion. But in this case, it wasn't just my name they were savoring.

They were discussing Evelina. And her "indiscretion."

I clenched my jaw, the urge to turn and confront them curling in my chest like a slow burn. I knew, of course, that any such reaction would only fan the flames. Confronting rumors only makes them stronger, and I had no intention of adding fuel to an already vicious fire. Still, it was different— knowing that my own name was being whispered alongside Evelina's, that my visits to the estate were now being spun into a scandal of their own making.

My presence, it seemed, had become the perfect material for a salacious tale: *the Duke's widow openly cavorting with her "lover" under her own roof.*

I arrived at the estate with a grim resolve, my mind churning with how best to approach the matter with Evelina. She was due to face enough challenges without this kind of gossip clouding her name, threatening her standing, her child's future.

As I stepped inside, one of the maids glanced away quickly, avoiding my gaze with an expression that could only be described as apprehensive. The staff had likely heard the rumors as well, I realized. No doubt the servants' corridors were alive with the latest speculation, their whispers circling like crows around the family's name.

"Lord Ravenscroft," came a familiar voice, and I turned to find Evelina standing in the doorway, her face framed by the soft glow of the morning light. She looked calm, poised as ever, but I could see the tension in her posture, the way her fingers pressed together in a white-knuckled grip.

"Your Grace," I said, inclining my head, masking my own unease. "I had hoped we might talk in private, if you would allow it."

She hesitated, a flicker of something uncertain crossing her face. "Of course. The drawing room?"

I followed her inside, my mind already sorting through how best to broach the subject without alarming her. Yet, as I stepped into the drawing room and the door closed behind us, the silence that filled the room told me she already knew.

She turned to me, folding her hands together, a faint line of worry appearing between her brows. "Jeremiah," she began quietly, her voice steady but tense, "I've...heard the rumors."

It didn't surprise me, but hearing it from her brought a fresh sting. "I assumed you might have," I replied. "It seems the ton has found a new tale to entertain itself with."

Her expression tightened, and she lowered her gaze. "It is...unsettling. I expected whispers, but this..." She trailed off, pressing her lips together as though choosing her words carefully. "This is crueler than I anticipated."

I nodded, struggling to keep my own anger in check. "I'm sorry, Your Grace.

I've tried to be discreet, but it appears even that has done little to quell their tongues."

She looked up at me, her eyes reflecting a mixture of sadness and frustration. "I knew people would talk, Jeremiah. But to suggest...to suggest that you and I..." She shook her head, letting out a shaky breath. "They even question the child's paternity. As if it could be anything other than Rupert's."

The hurt in her voice was undeniable, and I found myself gripping the back of a nearby chair, steadying myself against the impulse to defend her right then and there. But the reality was clear. The rumors would spread regardless, and any attempt to confront them head-on would likely only worsen the situation.

"Your Grace," I began, keeping my tone measured, "the more we deny, the stronger they'll become. It's the nature of these things, as cruel as it may be. But I won't stand by and let them tear your name down. There are ways we can counter this without fueling their speculation."

She looked at me, her gaze wavering with the same uncertainty that had been gnawing at me since I first heard the rumors. "How?" she asked quietly, almost pleading. "How do I protect my reputation, my child's future, when every eye in London is watching, waiting for me to stumble?"

I took a steadying breath, sorting through the words in my mind, determined to give her reassurance. "We remind them who you are, Your Grace," I replied. "The Duchess of Wakefield. You are a woman of integrity, honor, and quiet strength. And those who matter—the allies you've gained and those who respect the title—will stand by you, if they see you hold your ground."

She nodded, though the sadness in her eyes remained. "And you, Jeremiah?" she asked softly, her gaze steadying on mine. "What about you? The rumors may damage you as well."

I let out a low laugh, though the sound lacked any real amusement. "My reputation, I assure you, has endured far worse. They expect scandal from me, but from you?" I shook my head. "They'll judge you much more harshly than they would ever judge me."

Her gaze held mine, a strange warmth flickering beneath her sadness. "And still, you choose to stay."

"Yes," I replied simply, meeting her gaze without hesitation. "I made a promise, and I intend to keep it."

For a moment, neither of us spoke, the weight of that promise settling between us. Her eyes softened, and she gave a slight nod. "Thank you, Jeremiah," she murmured. "I can't say how much it means to have someone... someone who is willing to stand by me."

The words hit me harder than I'd expected, filling me with a sense of responsibility I hadn't anticipated. She wasn't simply the Duchess I'd sworn to protect—she was a woman, vulnerable and determined, and something in me felt irrevocably bound to her cause.

"Always," I said quietly, a promise wrapped within the single word.

We spoke at length, strategizing ways to quietly counter the rumors, but my thoughts lingered on Evelina's determination. She told me about her efforts to win over the household staff, and I could see the weight of her vulnerability beneath her words. She described the small gestures—visiting the stables, gardens, and kitchens—acts she hoped would reveal her true nature. Listening to her recount how she engaged with them, despite the long shadow of Lady Henrietta's influence, I couldn't help but admire her resolve.

"This rumor shows that they're watching you," I said, breaking the silence that hung between us. "And that's a good thing. Winning their respect isn't about grand gestures—it's about consistency. Keep showing them who you are, and soon enough, they'll see it for themselves."

She nodded, but I saw doubt flicker in her eyes, a hesitance that weighed on me more than I cared to admit. "It's hard not to wonder if I'm doing enough," she said quietly. "The loyalty they had for Lady Henrietta feels insurmountable."

I stepped closer, meeting her gaze with as much reassurance as I could muster. "You're not Lady Henrietta, Your Grace, and that's not a weakness. It's your strength. You're building something new here—trust takes time, but I've no doubt you'll earn it. Just as you'll earn the loyalty of those beyond these walls."

She hesitated, but after a moment, her expression softened. The faintest glimmer of hope appeared, though tempered by the weight of her burdens.

Still, she nodded, and together we planned the next steps. Her gatherings would need to resume, a subtle but bold move to defy the scandal and remind her allies of her strength. Though initially hesitant, she agreed that visibility, not retreat, was the key to projecting the dignity her enemies sought to undermine.

14

Gossips and Glances

The murmur of voices swirled around me, punctuated by the clinking of glasses and the faint rustling of skirts. I stood at the edge of the gathering, allowing myself to be seen, to be present, even as every instinct urged me to flee. I had attended countless gatherings like this in the past, but this one felt different, tainted somehow. I was not here as the Duchess of Wakefield, Rupert's respected widow; I was here as a subject of scandal, a woman whose reputation hung by a thread.

A group of ladies nearby glanced in my direction, their expressions a curious blend of sympathy and disdain. I caught snippets of their whispered conversation as I passed, their voices lowered but laced with unmistakable intent.

"—such a shame, really. And to think, her husband only just passed—"

"Yes, and already she's entertaining another gentleman under her late husband roof!"

"Not just any gentleman," one of them murmured, her voice carrying a gleeful note. "Lord Ravenscroft. Imagine the nerve, flaunting their... connection, especially given her condition."

I felt the familiar sting of their words but kept my expression placid, refusing to let them see the impact. Instead, I lifted my chin, moving past them with a slow, deliberate step. Inside, my stomach twisted with shame and anger, each remark cutting deeper than I cared to admit.

The glances that followed me across the room were no less subtle, each one weighted with suspicion, with accusation. They all seemed to have accepted the rumors as truth—that I, the grieving widow, had already replaced my husband with another man, and not just any man, but Jeremiah Langley, a notorious figure in his own right. Worse, they dared to question whether the child I carried was Rupert's, as if my love and loyalty could be so easily undermined.

As I reached for a teacup, my fingers brushed the stem with a trembling hand. I reminded myself of Jeremiah's advice: *Stay visible. Show them your dignity, your resolve. They can only take your power if you give it to them.*

I forced myself to take a slow, steady breath, channeling every ounce of composure I could muster. It would have been easier to confront them, to defend myself, but I knew that any reaction would only fuel the fire. I was walking a narrow line, balancing between scandal and survival.

A sharp voice broke my concentration, the words cutting into the hum of conversation. "Your Grace, how lovely to see you out and come here."

Lady Marchmont approached me, her gaze as keen and calculating as a hawk's. She was known for her ability to read people with frightening accuracy, and I felt her assessing me, her eyes flicking briefly to my barely perceptible belly before settling on my face.

"Lady Marchmont," I replied evenly, inclining my head. "It is a pleasure."

She smiled, though the expression held no warmth. "How admirable that you continue to show such...resilience in the face of recent events. Not everyone would have the fortitude to bear it with such grace."

I felt the barb hidden within her words and met her gaze unflinchingly. "I find that resilience is often required of those in positions such as mine," I replied, keeping my voice calm, even if my heart pounded beneath my ribs. "I have a duty to my family and my husband's memory."

Her expression remained unchanged, though a glimmer of amusement flickered in her eyes. "Indeed. It must be a comfort to have such...dedicated friends by your side, especially now." She glanced meaningfully in the direction where Jeremiah stood, as though her point needed further clarification. "Lord Ravenscroft, isn't it?"

I sipped my tea, letting the warmth steady my nerves. "Yes, has been an invaluable friend," I said lightly. "My husband held him in the highest regard."

"And so, it seems, do you," she replied, her smile sharpening. "What a relief it must be to have such steadfast devotion. Particularly now."

The insinuation made my blood run cold, and I fought to keep my composure. I would not rise to her bait. "It is indeed a comfort to have allies who understand loyalty and respect," I replied smoothly, praying that my voice did not betray the tremor of anger beneath my words.

Lady Marchmont's smirk faded, replaced by a look of mild surprise, as if she hadn't expected me to respond with such control. She inclined her head, a glint of grudging respect in her eyes. "Of course, Your Grace. Loyalty is a rare quality these days." She paused, her gaze sweeping over me one last time. "Though I do hope, for your sake, that your loyalty is well-placed."

With that, she turned and drifted away, leaving me with the weight of her veiled accusation hanging in the air. I clenched my hands, feeling the sting of her words settle like thorns beneath my skin.

I let my gaze drift across the room, searching for something—someone—to steady me. And there he was, standing near the fireplace, watching me with a look that seemed to reach across the room and steady my nerves. Jeremiah's expression was calm, his eyes warm and unwavering, as if to remind me that I was not facing this alone.

The tension in my shoulders eased, and I felt the strength of his silent support wrap around me, grounding me. Somehow, knowing he was there made the whispers easier to bear, the glances less cutting. It was a relief I hadn't anticipated, the feeling of having someone on my side, someone who understood the cost of this charade and shared the burden without question.

Drawing strength from his gaze, I turned my attention back to the gathering, ignoring the sidelong glances, the thinly veiled smiles of pity and disdain. I would not allow them the satisfaction of seeing me flinch.

Another woman approached, her expression one of practiced politeness. "Your Grace, it is wonderful to see you," she said, though her tone held a note of insincerity. "I must say, your strength is truly inspiring. I don't know how you manage, especially...in your condition."

I resisted the urge to roll my eyes, recognizing her subtle attempt to bring my pregnancy into the conversation. "Thank you," I replied, keeping my tone light. "My strength comes from the knowledge that I am preserving my husband's legacy, something I take very seriously."

Her expression faltered, and I could see her quickly casting about for another line of questioning. "Yes, of course. And you must feel so fortunate to have the assistance of...Lord Ravenscroft, in these trying times."

My heart clenched at the mention of Jeremiah, though I forced my smile to remain steady. "Yes, he has been a great help to me. My husband trusted him implicitly."

"Indeed," she replied, though her gaze sparkled with thinly veiled delight. "And I'm sure he will continue to be...indispensable to you."

There was no mistaking her meaning, and I could feel the weight of the other women's gazes, watching, waiting for me to slip. But I held firm, refusing to let them see the pain or frustration that lurked beneath my calm facade.

From across the room, I saw Jeremiah's gaze sharpen, his expression turning serious as he took in the exchange. His eyes found mine, and though he said nothing, his steady gaze filled me with a reassurance I hadn't known I needed. He inclined his head, just slightly, as if to remind me that I was not alone in this room of jackals.

Taking a quiet breath, I met my questioner's gaze head-on. "Indeed. Loyalty, as Lady Marchmont mentioned, is a rare quality. I am fortunate to have found it."

The woman's eyes widened, clearly surprised by my unwavering tone. She gave a faint, forced smile, then turned away, clearly defeated in her attempt to unsettle me.

When I glanced again, Jeremiah was standing near the hearth with his arms crossed, his presence a quiet defiance against the whispers that had enveloped the gathering. His eyes met mine, and there was a steadiness in his gaze that calmed the storm raging beneath my facade. I couldn't help but feel a flicker of gratitude for his unspoken support.

"Your Grace," a smooth, familiar voice interrupted, pulling my attention away. Cedric Harland appeared at my side, his expression one of polite concern. "I trust you're holding up well this evening."

"Quite well, thank you," I replied, studying his handsome, perfectly composed face. "Though the evening has certainly offered its challenges."

He gave a sympathetic nod, his dark eyes glinting with a warmth that felt almost genuine. "The ton can be...unkind, especially to those they do not understand. But take heart, Your Grace. There are still those of us who see the truth of your character."

His words were soothing, a balm against the sting of Lady Marchmont's remarks. And yet, I couldn't shake the faint unease that stirred whenever Cedric spoke. His charm was undeniable, but it carried a practiced precision, a deliberate calculation that kept me wary.

"Your kindness is appreciated, Lord Harland," I said carefully, offering a measured smile. "Though I suspect such sentiment is a rare commodity here tonight."

He chuckled softly, his gaze sweeping the room. "It is rare, but not entirely absent. If you'll permit me, Your Grace, I would be honored to lend you my support. A woman of your grace and fortitude deserves nothing less."

Before I could respond, Lord Frederick Harland appeared, his sharp, cold eyes fixed on me with barely concealed disdain. "Fortitude?" he said, his voice dripping with mockery. "That's an interesting word for it, Cedric."

Cedric's smile didn't falter as he turned to his cousin. "And what word would you prefer, Frederick? Perhaps 'courage'? Or is that too foreign a concept for you?"

Frederick's jaw tightened, his gaze narrowing. "I merely meant that fortitude is wasted when applied to certain...circumstances."

The venom in his tone was unmistakable, and I felt the sting of his insinuation as clearly as if it had been a physical blow. But before I could respond, Cedric stepped in smoothly, his voice calm and measured. "I think we've heard enough opinions for one evening, cousin. Perhaps it's time you found someone else to entertain."

Frederick glared at Cedric, but after a tense moment, he turned on his heel and stalked away, leaving the two of us alone.

"Forgive him, Your Grace," Cedric said, turning back to me with an apologetic smile. "Frederick's manners leave much to be desired."

I inclined my head, forcing a polite smile. "Your intervention is appreciated, Lord Harland."

"It is my pleasure," he said, his voice warm. "You deserve better than the petty judgments of others. And if I may, Your Grace, you've handled yourself admirably tonight."

I nodded, murmuring a soft thanks, though my thoughts churned with unease. Cedric's words were perfectly crafted, his demeanor perfectly polished. And yet, there was something about his kindness that felt too precise, too deliberate.

As the evening wore on, I found myself gravitating toward Jeremiah's steady presence. His concerned gaze met mine as I approached, and I felt a sense of relief at the honesty in his expression—a sharp contrast to the calculated charm of Cedric's support.

"Your Grace," he said softly, his voice low enough that only I could hear. "You've endured enough for one evening. Shall we take our leave?"

I hesitated, glancing around the room at the lingering glances, the whispered conversations. "Perhaps," I murmured, my voice heavy with fatigue. "Though I'm certain the whispers will follow us regardless."

"They will," Jeremiah agreed, his tone calm but resolute. "But you've shown them your strength tonight. Let that be enough."

I nodded, allowing him to guide me toward the exit. As we passed Cedric, his gaze lingered, his expression unreadable. For a moment, I wondered what secrets lay beneath his polished exterior, what motives guided his seemingly sincere support.

"Your Grace," Cedric said smoothly as we passed, his voice light. "Do let me know if there's anything I can do to assist you."

I nodded politely, though the warning echoed in my mind. *Too perfect to be trusted.*

I took my leave, nodding politely to those who had watched me with such intense interest. And as I reached the door, I felt Jeremiah fall into step beside me, his presence as natural as breathing.

In the quiet carriage ride back to the estate, I allowed myself to exhale, the tension in my shoulders easing as the events of the evening faded behind us. Jeremiah sat across from me, his gaze steady, a faint smile tugging at the corner of his mouth.

"You held your ground well," he said softly, his tone filled with a quiet pride.

"Thank you," I replied, my voice barely above a whisper. "I couldn't have done it without...knowing that you were there."

His smile deepened, and for a brief moment, we simply sat in the comfortable silence, the weight of the evening replaced by a warmth that lingered between us. And as the carriage moved through the darkened streets, I realized that Jeremiah's presence had become more than just a comfort. It was a source of strength, a reminder that I was not facing this battle alone.

In that moment, I understood that whatever challenges lay ahead, whatever whispers or glances or accusations the world chose to throw at me, I would be ready.

Because Jeremiah was by my side. And somehow, that was enough.

15

A Promise Entangled in Feeling

The steady rhythm of the carriage wheels seemed louder in the quiet, each turn a reminder of the moments slipping away between us. Evelina sat across from me, her posture straight yet softened by exhaustion. Her head leaned slightly against the window, her expression unreadable in the dim light that filtered through the narrow curtains. The flicker of lanterns outside cast fleeting patterns on her face, highlighting the shadows beneath her eyes, the faint curve of her lips pressed into a determined line.

I told myself to look away, to focus on anything but the way the soft glow accentuated her quiet strength. But I couldn't. My gaze lingered, caught in a trap of my own making, one that had slowly closed around me since I first stepped foot on Wakefield soil.

This wasn't how it was supposed to feel. Not at all.

At first, it had been simple. A promise made to Rupert—a friend, a comrade, someone I respected as much as I envied. He'd entrusted me with his final wish: to watch over his wife and unborn child if the worst should happen. I'd given him my word, believing it to be a straightforward duty. I would step in, ensure the estate was secure, fend off any vultures, and then leave her to her life and her legacy.

But Evelina... had been nothing like I expected.

"Is something on your mind?" Her voice pulled me from my thoughts, soft but tinged with curiosity. She didn't look at me, her eyes fixed on the passing landscape, but I could sense the weight of her question. She always had a way of knowing when something stirred beneath my calm facade.

"Only that you've handled tonight far better than most could," I replied, choosing my words carefully. "You've proven your strength once again."

Her lips curved into the faintest of smiles, though it didn't quite reach her eyes. "Strength is easier to fake than most believe," she murmured, more to herself than to me.

"It's not fake," I countered, my voice firmer than intended. "What you've done tonight—what you've been doing for weeks—it's real, Your Grace. Don't let anyone tell you otherwise."

She finally turned to meet my gaze, her eyes searching mine as if trying to discern the truth of my words. I held her stare, feeling the heat rise in my chest. Damn it. This was getting harder by the day.

At first, I told myself it was sympathy. She was a young widow, thrown into a world of vipers, with nothing but her wit and a fading title to protect her unborn child. Who wouldn't feel for her? She reminded me of my mother in some ways—how she'd struggled to carve a space for herself in a family that never wanted her, raising me alone against impossible odds. I knew what it was like to be born into suspicion, to be seen as an inconvenience rather than a blessing.

But it wasn't just sympathy. It hadn't been for some time now.

Each day by her side had chipped away at the barriers I'd erected around my heart. I'd thought myself immune to this sort of thing—falling for someone so far out of reach, so tied to another man's memory. Yet, Evelina had a way of surprising me. Her quiet resolve, her sharp mind, the moments of vulnerability she tried so hard to hide—they were all pieces of a puzzle I hadn't expected to want to solve.

"You're too kind," she said softly, breaking the silence. Her voice carried a note of hesitation, as if she didn't quite believe my praise. "I'm only trying to survive."

"And you're doing more than that," I replied, leaning forward slightly. "You're standing against men like Cedric, against Lady Henrietta, against a society that wants to see you fail. That's not just surviving. That's fighting."

Her brow furrowed, and for a moment, she looked away. "It doesn't feel like fighting," she admitted. "It feels like flailing. Like I'm barely keeping my head above water."

I wanted to reach out, to take her hand, to offer some tangible reassurance, but I knew better. Instead, I kept my voice steady, my words deliberate. "You're not flailing, Evelina. You're doing what needs to be done—for yourself, for the child. And you're not alone."

Her gaze flicked back to me, something softening in her expression. "Jeremiah..." she began, but she trailed off, as though the weight of what she wanted to say was too much.

I felt the tension between us, the unspoken words hovering in the air like a delicate thread. "You don't have to carry all of this by yourself," I said gently. "I'm here. Whatever you need, I'll see it done."

Her lips parted, but no words came. Instead, she nodded, a single, hesitant motion that spoke volumes.

I leaned back, exhaling slowly as I tried to rein in the emotions threatening to surface. It wasn't just a promise to Rupert anymore. It wasn't just a sense of duty, or sympathy, or even admiration. It was her. The way she moved through a world determined to see her falter. The way she placed her hand protectively over her belly when she thought no one was looking. The way she met every challenge with a quiet defiance that made me want to tear apart anyone who dared to harm her.

God help me, I wanted to protect her from more than just Cedric or Lady Henrietta. I wanted to protect her from the world itself, from every cruel word and judgmental stare, from every whisper that questioned her worth or her child's legitimacy. And that scared me more than anything.

Because I knew these feelings had no place here. Not in this estate, not in this carriage, not in the life she was trying to rebuild.

But feelings, I'd learned long ago, were stubborn things. They didn't care about propriety or promises or the long shadows of late dukes. And as I sat there, watching Evelina struggle to hold herself together, I knew there was no turning back.

79

I didn't just want to protect her. I wanted to be the one she turned to when the weight became too much. I wanted to be the reason she smiled, the reason she felt safe.

But for now, I would settle for being her ally. For standing beside her in this war, no matter what it cost me. Because she deserved that much. And perhaps, selfishly, I needed to believe I could still be that kind of man.

The carriage slowed as we neared the estate, the soft crunch of gravel pulling me back to the present. Evelina straightened, her composure returning like a mask slipping into place. She glanced at me, offering a small, tentative smile.

"Thank you, Jeremiah," she said quietly. "For everything."

I nodded, my voice catching in my throat. "Always, Your Grace."

As the carriage came to a stop, I stepped out first, extending a hand to help her down. The feel of her fingers in mine was brief but grounding, a reminder of what I'd vowed to do.

For Evelina. For the unborn child. For the promise that had become something far more complicated.

As the night closed in around us, I knew one thing for certain: I would not fail her. Not now. Not ever.

16

The Reckless Kiss

The orchard was quiet that morning, the kind of silence that seemed to press against my ears, demanding to be filled. Sunlight filtered through the canopy above, dappling the ground with golden patches of light. The air smelled of ripened fruit, sweet and familiar, but it brought little comfort as I paced beneath the trees. My heart was heavy, weighed down by the endless whispers and judgment that seemed to follow me wherever I went.

I reached for the rough bark of a nearby tree, resting my forehead against it as I tried to steady my breathing. How had it come to this? How had my life unraveled into such a cruel tapestry of doubt and disgrace? My child's future, my husband's legacy—it all felt so fragile, so perilously close to shattering beneath the weight of society's disdain.

The snap of a branch behind me startled me, and I turned quickly, my heart lurching in my chest. But it was only Jeremiah, his expression softening as he took in my wide-eyed gaze.

"Forgive me," he said, his voice low. "I didn't mean to startle you."

I exhaled slowly, the tension easing from my shoulders. "It's all right," I murmured, though my voice trembled slightly.

He stepped closer, his presence grounding me in a way I hadn't expected. "I saw you leave the house," he said gently. "You seemed...troubled."

I gave a weak smile, brushing a hand over my hair. "When am I not troubled these days?" I replied, attempting to sound lighthearted, though the words fell flat.

He didn't answer, his gaze steady as he watched me. The weight of his attention made me feel exposed, as though he could see every fear, every doubt I tried so hard to conceal.

"I just needed some air," I admitted, turning away and walking deeper into the orchard. "Some space to think."

Jeremiah followed, his steps measured, his silence both reassuring and unnerving. When I stopped beside an old wooden bench, he took a seat, gesturing for me to join him.

I hesitated for a moment before sitting down, the distance between us both comforting and unbearable. The stillness stretched on, the only sound the faint rustle of leaves in the breeze.

"Evelina," he said finally, his voice soft but insistent. "You don't have to face this alone."

His words struck something deep within me, and I turned to him, my composure threatening to crumble. "But I do," I whispered. "Don't you see? I'm all my child has. If I falter, if I fail..." My voice broke, and I looked away, unable to meet his gaze.

"You won't fail," he said firmly. "You're stronger than you think."

I shook my head, tears stinging my eyes. "Everyone looks at me and sees weakness. They see a young widow, a foolish girl who can't possibly hold her own. And maybe they're right. Maybe I'm not enough."

His hand reached for mine, hesitating briefly before his fingers curled around mine. The warmth of his touch steadied me, and I looked up to find his eyes locked on mine, filled with a quiet intensity that took my breath away.

"They're wrong," he said simply. "You are enough. More than enough."

The sincerity in his voice brought the tears spilling over, and I turned away, embarrassed by my vulnerability. But Jeremiah didn't let go of my hand. He held it firmly, as if anchoring me to the moment.

"You're not alone, Evelina," he said quietly. "Not as long as I'm here."

His words hung in the air, heavy with meaning, and when I turned back to him, I saw something in his expression that mirrored the storm inside me—uncertainty, longing, and a fragile hope that neither of us dared to name.

"I'm scared, Jeremiah," I admitted, my voice barely above a whisper. "I'm scared of losing everything. Of losing myself."

He reached up, brushing a tear from my cheek with a tenderness that unraveled me completely. "You don't have to be scared," he murmured. "Not with me."

The air between us seemed to shift, charged with something unspoken yet undeniable. I felt his gaze drop briefly to my lips before returning to my eyes, seeking permission, searching for something I wasn't sure I could give.

And then he leaned in, his movements slow, hesitant, as though giving me every opportunity to pull away. But I didn't.

The kiss was soft, tentative, a whisper of connection that spoke volumes more than words ever could. His lips were warm against mine, a fleeting promise that sent my heart racing and my thoughts spiraling.

When he pulled back, his eyes searched mine, his expression a mixture of uncertainty and hope. I stared at him, my heart pounding, my breath shallow as I tried to process the depth of what had just happened.

"Evelina," he began, his voice barely audible, but I shook my head, unable to find the words to respond.

The moment hung between us, fragile and electric, before I stood abruptly, my hands trembling as I clasped them together. "I—I need to go," I stammered, my voice shaky.

He rose as well, concern etched into his features. "Evelina, wait—"

But I couldn't. I turned and walked away, my mind a whirlwind of emotions I couldn't begin to untangle.

As I left the orchard, I felt the imprint of his kiss lingering on my lips, a reminder of the connection we shared—a connection that, no matter how much I tried to deny it, had just become impossible to ignore.

17

A Flutter of Life

The room was quiet, save for the faint ticking of the mantel clock. I stood by the window, staring out at the sprawling grounds of Wakefield, but my thoughts were far from the rolling hills and manicured gardens. My hand rose unbidden to my lips, brushing them softly as the memory of Jeremiah's kiss flooded back.

It had been reckless. Foolish. And yet...

I closed my eyes, and the vivid memory of his touch rushed through me like a warm tide. The kiss had been soft, almost hesitant, as though he were testing boundaries neither of us had dared acknowledge before. His lips carried an urgency and tenderness that left me breathless, their warmth searing into mine as if branding me with something I couldn't ignore. His hand had slipped into my hair, his fingers threading gently but firmly, cradling me as though I were something fragile and irreplaceable.

A shiver ran through me as I recalled how his other hand had lightly brushed my waist, his touch grounding and yet electrifying at once. My knees had felt weak, and for a fleeting moment, I'd let myself lean into him, into the strength he offered without words. The scent of rain and pine that clung to him lingered in my memory, wrapping around me even now.

My heart fluttered wildly in my chest, each beat a betrayal of the composure I tried so desperately to maintain. I let out a shaky breath, rubbing my arms as if to dispel the phantom sensation of his touch. But it wouldn't fade. His gaze, intense and unyielding, haunted me. The way he'd looked at me, as if I were the only person in the world, left me feeling exposed and alive in a way I hadn't been since Rupert's passing.

How could I have let this happen? How could I have allowed it?

My hand drifted instinctively to my stomach, cradling the life growing within me. I was a widow—a pregnant widow. Whatever feelings Jeremiah's kiss had stirred in me, whatever flicker of hope or longing had sparked in my heart, it was utterly inappropriate. I had no right to feel this way, to entertain even the faintest notion of love again.

My child deserved better.

I let out a bitter laugh, though it was choked with unshed tears. "It's so unfair," I whispered to the empty room, my voice trembling. "It's all so unfair."

The weight of my responsibilities pressed heavily on my shoulders. Society had already branded me as a woman teetering on the edge of scandal, my every move scrutinized and judged. I was fighting to protect my child's legacy, to secure a future where they would not have to bear the whispers of gossip or the cruel judgment of those who had already dismissed me as unworthy.

But as much as I tried to focus on those battles, a part of me—the part that still ached for companionship, for solace—couldn't let go of the moment in the orchard.

The memory of his lips on mine sent another wave of longing through me. My hand rose once more to brush against my mouth, my fingers trembling. It wasn't just the kiss. It was everything that had come before it: the quiet moments of understanding, the strength he'd lent me when I felt weakest, the way he'd stood by me despite the risks. Jeremiah had become more than an ally, more than a friend. And that terrified me.

A soft flutter in my belly startled me, pulling me abruptly from my thoughts. I gasped, my hand flying to my stomach as a wave-like sensation rippled beneath my palm.

My baby was moving.

A rush of emotion overwhelmed me, tears spilling over as I pressed both hands to my belly, feeling the faint flutter of life within me. "Oh," I whispered, my voice catching. "Oh, my darling."

The movement was subtle but unmistakable, a quiet reminder that I wasn't alone. My child, the last piece of Rupert, was here, growing stronger every day.

I sank into the nearest chair, my hands never leaving my stomach as I whispered soft apologies to the tiny life within me. "I'm so sorry," I murmured, the words tumbling out in a rush. "I've been so foolish, letting myself think of things that don't matter. None of it matters, not as much as you."

The fluttering sensation stilled, but the warmth it left behind lingered, grounding me in a way nothing else could. I tilted my head back, staring at the ceiling as fresh tears streamed down my face.

"I'll fight for you," I promised, my voice steadier now, infused with the resolve I had nearly lost. "I'll fight for your future, for your legacy. You're all that matters."

As I wiped at my cheeks, my thoughts returned to Jeremiah. The kiss, the way he'd held me, the concern in his voice as he'd vowed to protect me—they were all distractions, I told myself. Lovely, dangerous distractions.

But as I pressed a hand to my heart, feeling its steady rhythm beneath my palm, I knew it wasn't that simple. Jeremiah's presence had become something more to me, and pretending otherwise wouldn't change the truth.

Even so, I couldn't let myself dwell on it. Not now. Not while my child needed me to be strong.

Rubbing my belly gently, I whispered one final promise to the little life within me: "No more foolish thoughts. It's you and me against the world, my love. I'll see this through—for both of us."

The sunlight streaming through the window seemed brighter now, its warmth settling over me like a quiet blessing. And as I sat there, feeling the first stirrings of my child within me, I allowed myself to hope—not for love, not for companionship—but for the strength to carry us both through whatever lay ahead.

18

A Secret Rendezvous

The garden was bathed in moonlight, the silvery glow casting long, soft shadows among the hedges and flowerbeds. The roses, usually vibrant in the sunlight, appeared muted and ghostly under the pale light. The stillness of the evening was broken only by the occasional rustle of leaves in the breeze and the faint chirp of crickets hidden in the foliage. I stood beneath the arbor, my fingers twisting nervously in the folds of my shawl, every sound setting my pulse racing.

All my determination to forget that kiss is still hard to do. This was foolish—reckless, even—but I couldn't bring myself to leave. Not yet.

When Jeremiah appeared, his tall frame emerging from the shadows like a figure conjured from my own thoughts, a sense of relief flooded through me. His shoulders, usually squared with confidence, were slightly slumped, the moonlight softening the sharp edges of his face. I hadn't realized how tightly I'd been holding my breath until I exhaled.

He approached slowly, his expression unreadable in the dim light, but his presence steadied me in a way nothing else could. His footsteps were near silent against the stone path, each step deliberate and measured.

"Evelina," he said softly, inclining his head in greeting. There was a pause before he added, almost hesitantly, "I owe you an apology."

I blinked, startled by the unexpected admission. "An apology?" I echoed.

He stopped a few paces from me, his gaze dropping briefly before meeting mine again. "This morning. I acted recklessly. I... I lost control. It was inexcusable." His voice, usually so composed, carried an edge of frustration—directed, it seemed, as much at himself as at the moment.

Heat crept up my neck as the memory resurfaced. The kiss—unexpected, charged, and impossible to forget—had lingered in my thoughts all day. "Jeremiah, I..." I began, but the words faltered.

"Please," he interrupted gently, his tone softening. "Let me say this. I... I care for you, Evelina. More than I should, more than is appropriate. But that doesn't excuse my behavior. You've endured enough without me adding to it."

His admission left me momentarily speechless. The weight of his words, coupled with the vulnerability in his expression, made my chest tighten. "You didn't hurt me," I said finally, my voice barely above a whisper. "But... we can't..."

"I know," he said quickly, his jaw tightening. "We can't. I just needed you to know that I regret putting you in that position." He hesitated, then added, "And I'll do everything in my power to ensure it doesn't happen again."

The sincerity in his tone was unmistakable, and though his words should have brought relief, they left me with a hollow ache instead. I nodded, my fingers tightening around my shawl. "Thank you," I murmured, unsure of what else to say.

For a moment, the silence between us was heavy, the unspoken truths hanging like mist in the cool night air. Finally, he gestured toward the bench nestled beneath a cluster of blooming wisteria. The flowers' fragrance was delicate but heady, their pale petals glowing faintly in the moonlight.

I followed him, sitting down with a mix of anticipation and trepidation, the wooden bench cool beneath me. The distance between us was a mere breath, but it felt like an ocean, the silence stretching taut and fragile.

"Do you ever wonder," Jeremiah said suddenly, his voice low and contemplative, "what life might be like if things were...different?"

I glanced at him, startled by the vulnerability in his tone. The usually stoic man now looked almost boyish, his expression tinged with a longing I hadn't seen before.

"Different how?" I asked cautiously.

"If there were no titles, no expectations," he replied, his voice growing softer. "No constraints forcing us to live within the narrow lines society has drawn."

My heart ached at the thought, the impossible dream of freedom tempting and cruel. "All the time," I admitted. "But wishing doesn't change anything, does it? We are who we are, bound by what we've been given and what's been taken from us."

He turned to me then, his gaze piercing yet gentle. "And yet," he said softly, "for just a moment, sitting here with you, it feels as though the rest of the world doesn't matter."

His words struck a chord deep within me, unraveling the carefully constructed walls I had built to protect myself. "Jeremiah..." I began, but the words caught in my throat.

He reached for my hand, his touch gentle yet firm, grounding me. His palm was warm, his calloused fingers wrapping around mine with a familiarity that felt both foreign and desperately needed. "You don't have to say anything," he murmured. "I just... I need you to know that you're not alone in this."

A lump formed in my throat, and I squeezed his hand tightly, drawing strength from his unwavering presence. "Thank you," I whispered, my voice trembling but sincere.

The conversation shifted, the words flowing between us like a hidden stream—quiet, steady, and profound. We spoke of dreams never voiced, regrets never confessed, and fears too deep to share in daylight. For the first time in what felt like forever, I allowed myself to be vulnerable, to let someone see the cracks in my armor.

But as the night deepened, reality crept back in, its cold fingers reminding me of the risks we were taking. "We can't keep doing this," I said softly, my voice tinged with regret. "The whispers, the rumors...they'll destroy us both."

Jeremiah's jaw tightened, but his eyes held mine. "I know," he said, his voice steady. "But I won't stop protecting you, Evelina. No matter what they say, no matter what they do, I won't let them hurt you or the child."

Tears stung my eyes, but I blinked them away, unwilling to let the moment end in sorrow. "Thank you," I said again, my voice steadier this time. "For everything."

We rose reluctantly, the night air cooler now, carrying with it the faintest hint of dawn. As we turned to leave, Jeremiah froze, his body tensing as his gaze flicked toward the shadows.

"Someone's watching," he murmured, his voice low but firm.

My heart leapt into my throat as I followed his gaze, my eyes scanning the darkness. The hedges and pathways appeared empty, but the oppressive stillness felt different now—charged, almost expectant.

"Are you sure?" I whispered, barely daring to breathe.

He nodded, his jaw tightening. "I've had my suspicions for some time. Someone in the estate has been reporting back to the Duke's relatives. This confirms it."

A chill ran down my spine, and I wrapped my shawl tighter around me. "What do we do?"

"I'll handle it," he said firmly, his tone brooking no argument. "But you must be careful, Evelina. Don't trust anyone."

I opened my mouth to protest, to insist that I could help, but the intensity in his gaze stopped me. "Please," he said, his voice softening. "Promise me."

Reluctantly, I nodded. "I will."

As we parted ways, I couldn't shake the feeling of being watched, the weight of unseen eyes pressing heavily on me. Jeremiah's words echoed in my mind, and with each step, the sense of urgency grew.

The danger surrounding us was more insidious than I had realized, and for the first time, I truly understood the precariousness of our position. Whatever happened next, I knew one thing for certain: time was running out.

19

Protection and Pretense

The dining hall buzzed with the subtle tension that only a gathering of the Duke's family could produce. Every look, every word, seemed barbed, dipped in a polite cruelty that only high society could achieve. I felt the weight of each gaze on me, the glances lingering just a little too long, as though I were a curiosity—or worse, an interloper. But I forced myself to walk into the hall, my chin held high, with Jeremiah at my side.

The whispers had not been kind. Attending this dinner was my statement, my way of proving that I belonged here, that my position was not so easily dismissed. I would not allow them to push me aside, to erase my presence as though I were nothing more than a mere inconvenience. And as we entered, I felt the eyes of the entire room settle on us, the murmurs momentarily stilled.

"Your Grace," a sharp voice called, and I turned to see Lord Frederick, Rupert's cousin, watching us with barely concealed contempt. His gaze lingered on Jeremiah for a moment, as though calculating, before he turned his full attention to me. "I must say, I'm surprised to see you here. It's hardly the place for...delicate company."

I bristled, the implication not lost on me. "Delicate or not, I am the Duchess of Wakefield," I replied calmly, keeping my voice steady. "This is exactly where I belong."

A murmur rippled through the room, a mix of surprise and thinly veiled disapproval. I could see Frederick's expression tighten, his mouth pulling into a thin, mocking smile.

"Of course, Your Grace," he replied, his tone carrying a hint of derision. "It's simply that...well, we have heard such disturbing rumors of late. And yet, you arrive here tonight, accompanied by Lord Ravenscroft, no less." He looked pointedly at Jeremiah, a challenge simmering in his eyes.

I felt a rush of anger, sharp and hot, but before I could respond, Jeremiah stepped forward, his voice low but firm. "The Duchess requested my presence," he said, meeting Frederick's gaze without a hint of hesitation. "And I was honored to accept. I assure you, my purpose here is simply to ensure her comfort in what must be a trying evening."

Frederick raised an eyebrow, clearly unimpressed. "A trying evening indeed," he murmured, his eyes sliding back to me. "Your Grace, forgive me, but I can't help but wonder...do you believe that bringing a companion of Lord Ravenscroft's reputation will ease the concerns of the family? Or, perhaps, might it only add fuel to the fire?"

I met his gaze head-on, refusing to be intimidated by his thinly veiled accusations. "I have nothing to defend, Lord Frederick," I replied, keeping my voice steady. "My presence here is not dependent on your approval, nor on the approval of those who would prefer I disappear."

Frederick's smile was thin. "Of course. But one cannot help but wonder if such responsibilities might be...better suited to someone with more experience."

Before I could respond, Cedric interjected smoothly. "And who would that be, Lord Frederick?" he asked, his tone light but edged with steel. "Yourself? I hardly see how a man who has spent more time in London than on any estate is better equipped than Her Grace."

Frederick's jaw tightened, and I couldn't suppress a flicker of gratitude for Cedric's intervention. "I was merely suggesting that the estate's interests might benefit from...additional oversight," Frederick said tightly.

"How generous of you to volunteer," Cedric replied with a faint smile, leaning back in his chair. "But I think we can all agree that Wakefield has flourished under Her Grace's stewardship. It would be a shame to upset the balance she's so carefully maintained."

The table fell silent for a moment, the tension palpable.

I allowed myself a small sip of tea, using the moment to collect myself. "I appreciate the concern, Lord Frederick," I said, keeping my tone steady. "But I assure you, the estate's affairs are well in hand."

Frederick looked as though he might retort, but Cedric's raised brow silenced him. It was an impressive display of control, one that did not go unnoticed by the other guests. Cedric's ability to redirect the conversation, to smooth over tensions while subtly asserting his influence, was nothing short of masterful.

Another voice chimed in, softer but no less barbed. Lady Henrietta, watched me with an expression of distaste she barely bothered to hide. "It's so... admirable," she said, her tone laced with condescension, "that you've found such a...reliable friend in Lord Ravenscroft. I imagine it must be quite the relief, especially given the...delicate circumstances of your condition."

I felt the blow of her words like a slap, but I forced myself to maintain my composure, though my hands tightened in my lap beneath the table. I would not let them break me.

"Indeed, I am fortunate," I replied, my voice calm but firm. "Lord Ravenscroft has shown me nothing but respect and loyalty, qualities I value deeply." I glanced briefly at Jeremiah, feeling a surge of gratitude for his presence, for the strength he lent me with his mere presence. "And as the Duchess of Wakefield, I have every right to determine who I choose to rely upon."

Lady Henrietta raised an eyebrow, clearly displeased with my response. "Of course, my dear," she replied with a cool smile. "But one can't help but wonder...is it wise to align oneself with a man whose reputation is...well, somewhat less than pristine?"

Beside me, Jeremiah's jaw tightened, and I felt a rush of indignation on his behalf. He had shown nothing but loyalty, had stood by me without question, and yet here they were, casting stones from their own glass houses.

"Lord Ravenscroft's reputation is not yours to judge, Lady Henrietta," I said, my voice cold and unwavering. "He has been a true friend to me in my time of need, a quality I find far more valuable than the fickle opinions of society."

A silence fell over the room, the weight of my words settling heavily. I could see the shock in their faces, the surprise that I would dare speak so openly, so defiantly. And in that moment, I felt a surge of pride—a pride not just in myself, but in the alliance I had forged with Jeremiah, an alliance they could not break with their whispers or their stares.

As the evening wore on, Cedric continued to charm and defend, his words weaving a narrative of support that left me feeling unexpectedly reassured. He offered suggestions for the estate, framed as helpful advice rather than criticism, and praised my handling of recent challenges with an enthusiasm that seemed entirely genuine.

"Her Grace has shown remarkable resilience," Cedric said at one point, raising his glass in a small toast. "I dare say, Wakefield has never been in better hands."

The room murmured its agreement, though I noticed Frederick's tight expression and Lady Henrietta's carefully neutral smile. Jeremiah, seated across from Cedric, watched the exchange with a quiet intensity, his gaze sharp and assessing.

The rest of the dinner passed in tense silence, the conversations muted, strained. I kept my focus on the food before me, though I barely tasted it, aware of the glances that darted in my direction, the murmured words that slipped just beyond my hearing. But I held my ground, my shoulders squared, my gaze steady.

And through it all, Jeremiah remained beside me, his presence a steady comfort, a reminder that I was not alone in this battle. When the dinner concluded, I rose with him at my side, determined to leave with the dignity they sought to strip from me.

As we made our way out of the dining hall, Frederick approached once more, his expression unreadable. "Your Grace," he said, his voice low. "I hope you understand the...difficulties your actions create for the family. We are merely concerned for the legacy Rupert left behind."

I met his gaze, unflinching. "And yet, it was Rupert who placed his trust in me, his wife. That trust is the only legacy I am concerned with."

Frederick's expression darkened, his mouth tightening, but he offered no further response. Instead, he inclined his head, a thinly veiled dismissal that only strengthened my resolve. Without another word, Jeremiah and I left, the weight of the evening lifting with each step we took toward the carriage.

Once inside, the silence between us lingered, a shared relief, a shared sense of defiance. Finally, Jeremiah turned to me, his gaze warm and steady.

"You handled yourself remarkably well," he said quietly, a faint smile softening his features.

"Thank you," I replied, allowing myself to exhale, the tension easing from my shoulders. "I...I couldn't have done it without you."

His smile deepened, and he reached out, his hand settling briefly over mine. "You could have," he said softly. "But I'm glad you didn't have to."

A warmth spread through me at his words, a feeling I hadn't expected, a sense of gratitude and something more, something unspoken that lingered between us. I met his gaze, and in that moment, I felt a connection stronger than any I had known—a bond forged in shared struggle, in quiet strength.

"Your Grace," he began, his tone low but firm, "I hope you'll forgive my boldness, but I feel it's necessary to speak plainly."

I raised a brow, intrigued. "Of course. What's on your mind?"

"Cedric," he said simply, his gaze steady. "He's clever. Too clever. And while his words may seem kind, his actions speak of a man with ambitions of his own."

I hesitated, my brow furrowing. "You think he has ulterior motives?"

"I do," Jeremiah replied, his voice unwavering. "I can't say what they are, not yet. But his influence is growing, and it's isolating you from others— potential allies who may fear offending him."

His words sent a ripple of unease through me. Cedric had been nothing but supportive, yet Jeremiah's warning struck a chord. "Do you think he means to harm me?" I asked softly.

Jeremiah's expression softened, though his eyes remained serious. "I think Cedric is playing a long game, Your Grace. One that may not include your best interests."

I nodded slowly, the weight of his words settling over me. "Thank you, Jeremiah. I will...consider what you've said."

"Good," he replied, inclining his head. "Because I've no intention of letting anyone manipulate you—not Cedric, not Frederick, not Lady Henrietta. You deserve allies, not puppeteers."

I met his gaze, feeling a flicker of gratitude for his unwavering support. "Thank you," I said again, my voice quieter this time. "I'm fortunate to have you by my side."

Jeremiah offered a faint smile, but his watchful eyes lingered, as though he were already planning his next move. As the carriage rolled onward, I leaned back, Cedric's polished charm and Jeremiah's steadfast warning warred in my mind, leaving me with a lingering sense of unease.

20

The Accusation

T he air in the ballroom was suffocating, heavy with perfume, judgment, and the low hum of gossip. Everywhere I turned, eyes followed me—some curious, others pitying, and still more filled with thinly veiled disdain. I held my head high, willing my spine to remain straight, but the weight of their stares bore down on me like a physical burden. My presence here was no accident, no mere gesture of civility. I had come to show them all—the nobility, the gossips, the vultures circling for weakness— that I would not cower.

A widowed, pregnant Duchess in attendance at such a grand event was, of course, scandalous to many. It was unseemly, they whispered, for a woman in my condition to make an appearance at all, let alone without the arm of a husband to steady her. But that was precisely why I was here. I refused to let them see me as weak or diminished, a fragile creature to be pitied or dismissed. This ball was more than a social gathering; it was a stage, and I intended to command it.

Jeremiah lingered nearby, his presence steady and grounding, though I could feel the tension in him, the restraint it took to remain silent under the scrutiny. I had asked him to keep his distance, to let me handle the whispers, but his loyalty would not allow it.

As I moved through the crowd, polite nods and strained smiles met me, a stark contrast to the murmurs I could still hear beneath the genteel façade.

"Such a scandal, don't you think?" a woman whispered behind her fan.

"Indeed. To entertain a man like that, and in her condition?" another replied.

The words were barbed, each one slicing through the fragile armor I had constructed. My pulse quickened, but I kept walking, determined not to give them the satisfaction of seeing me falter.

It wasn't until I reached the refreshment table that the true blow came. A noblewoman—a figure I recognized all too well, Lady Danforth—approached with a feigned air of concern. Her glittering eyes betrayed the malice behind her carefully measured tone.

"Your Grace," she began, her voice low but calculated, loud enough to draw the attention of those nearby. "Forgive me for intruding, but I fear there is a matter of some delicacy that must be addressed. Rumors have surfaced, and I felt it my duty to bring them to your attention."

The room seemed to freeze, the quiet hum of conversation vanishing as heads turned toward us. My breath caught in my throat, the accusation hanging in the air like a noose.

"I beg your pardon?" I managed, my voice trembling despite my effort to remain composed.

Lady Danforth's lips curved into a faint, pitying smile. "It is said that you and Lord Ravenscroft were seen together... shall we say, intimately, on the grounds."

A ripple of whispers spread through the crowd like wildfire, and I felt the heat of their judgment, their disbelief, their satisfaction. My vision blurred momentarily, and I clutched the edge of the table to steady myself.

"Enough," Jeremiah's voice cut through the murmurs like a blade, cold and commanding. He stepped forward, placing himself between me and the growing circle of onlookers. "This is slander, and you know it."

The room's attention shifted to him, and his presence seemed to silence even the boldest whispers. Jeremiah's gaze burned with quiet fury as he addressed Lady Danforth. "To levy such accusations against the Duchess without evidence is not only shameful but dangerous. You do realize the weight of your words, do you not?"

Lady Danforth raised an eyebrow, unfazed. "I merely repeat what has reached my ears, my lord. The ton, as you know, is a curious creature, and such rumors can be... disruptive to a household."

"Then you've been told lies," Jeremiah snapped, his tone sharp enough to make her flinch slightly. "Spread by those who seek to harm Her Grace for their own gain."

"Is it true, Your Grace?" a voice called from the crowd, its owner hidden among the throng. "Does the child belong to Lord Ravenscroft?"

The question struck like a blow to the chest, and for a moment, I couldn't breathe. My hand instinctively moved to my belly, the small curve that held my future, my hope, my love for Rupert.

"The child is the Duke's," I said, my voice firm despite the quiver in my heart. "Anyone who dares to say otherwise insults his memory and his name."

The room quieted, the weight of my words settling over them. But I knew it wouldn't last. The ton thrived on scandal, and this one would not fade so easily.

Jeremiah stepped closer, his voice low and steady as he addressed me. "We should leave, Your Grace. You don't need to endure this."

I turned to him, seeing the fury in his eyes, the barely restrained urge to defend me further. His presence was a comfort, but it was also a reminder of how deeply the rumors had entangled him in my scandal.

"Thank you, Lord Ravenscroft," I said, forcing a smile for the benefit of the watching crowd. "But I will not be driven away by baseless lies."

He hesitated, searching my face as though trying to decipher my true thoughts. Slowly, he nodded, his jaw tightening. "As you wish."

I turned back to the crowd, meeting their stares with as much composure as I could muster. "I trust the rest of you will enjoy the evening," I said, my voice carrying through the room. "I would hate for baseless rumors to spoil such a lovely gathering."

With that, I moved toward the exit, my steps measured and deliberate, though my heart thundered in my chest. The whispers followed me, nipping at my heels, but I refused to let them see my pain.

Jeremiah followed at a distance, his presence a silent shield against the tide of judgment. As we stepped outside into the cool night air, the weight of the evening pressed down on me, and I let out a shaky breath.

"They won't stop," I said quietly, my voice breaking. "No matter what I say, no matter what I do...they'll never stop."

Jeremiah stepped closer, his expression fierce with determination. "Then we'll find another way. Together."

I looked up at him, my resolve wavering. "I don't know if I can do this," I admitted. "It feels...impossible."

"It's not," he said, his voice firm. "You've already proven your strength tonight, Evelina. You stood tall when they tried to tear you down. And you'll do it again."

His words should have comforted me, but instead, they left me feeling hollow. Because as much as I wanted to believe in my own strength, I couldn't help but feel the cracks forming beneath the weight of it all.

And I couldn't ignore the whisper of doubt Cedric had planted—the question that lingered in the back of my mind.

Was Jeremiah truly here to help me? Or was he, as Cedric suggested, another threat I had failed to see?

21

The Society's Cruelty

On another occasion, I attended a gathering at the grand salon of one of the upper-class aristocrats—a space where noble families mingled, their interactions as much about politics as they were about social etiquette. The invitation was not simply an opportunity for diversion; it was a battlefield disguised in silk and candlelight. I was here to demonstrate my strength, to show them that I would not fade quietly into the shadows, and to ensure that my child's future remained untarnished by their venomous whispers.

The moment I stepped into the salon, the shimmering light of crystal chandeliers reflected off the polished marble floors, and a ripple passed through the crowd. Conversations faltered, fans fluttered, and a wave of whispers swelled like a tide cresting on the shore. Every head turned toward me, their expressions a mixture of curiosity, pity, and judgment.

"She dares to show herself," came a sharp voice from a group of elegantly clad women gathered near the gilded fireplace. Lady Marchmont, resplendent in a gown of emerald silk, leaned closer to her companions, her lips curving into a smile that failed to reach her cold blue eyes. "Grieving widow or scheming usurper? One can never tell these days."

The words sliced through me like a blade, but I did not falter. My spine remained rigid, my chin held high, and a faint, serene smile graced my lips. I had learned to wear my composure like armor, each whispered cruelty becoming fuel for my resolve.

"Poor Rupert," another voice chimed in, its owner—Lady Pembroke—shaking her head with exaggerated sorrow. "If only he'd known the full truth about his wife. These rumors... they do cast such an unfortunate shadow."

I moved through the room with deliberate grace, the black silk of my gown trailing behind me like the sweep of a storm cloud. My every step was measured, every glance calculated. The murmurs followed me like a shadow, their cruel words weaving a web of doubt and suspicion.

"Her child," a hushed voice whispered from a nearby corner. "If it even is his. Have you noticed how eager she is to secure her place? It makes one wonder what she's truly hiding."

Heat rose in my chest, but I quelled it, my gloved fingers tightening slightly on the delicate lace fan in my hand. As I swept my gaze over the room, my eyes landed deliberately on the cluster of women whose voices had carried to me. Lady Marchmont and her companions froze under my scrutiny, their masks of false concern slipping for the briefest moment.

"Lady Marchmont," I said, my voice a melody of grace and steel, "how lovely to see you tonight. I trust the evening finds you well?"

Lady Marchmont's smile faltered but recovered quickly. "Your Grace," she replied, dipping into a shallow curtsy. "You honor us with your presence. It must be such a comfort to be among friends in such... trying times."

I tilted my head, my smile unwavering. "Indeed. True friends have a way of revealing themselves, especially when one's circumstances change. Don't you think?"

The tension between us thickened, and the murmurs of the crowd grew quieter as others strained to listen. Lady Marchmont's expression stiffened, the subtle challenge in my words unmistakable.

"Of course," Lady Marchmont said, her voice cool and measured. "And it is in such times that clarity becomes paramount. For example, ensuring the future of a title as esteemed as Wakefield—a matter that requires... absolute certainty."

Her words hung in the air, heavy with implication. My grip on the fan tightened, but my composure did not waver. "Certainty, my lady, is built on integrity and truth," I said smoothly. "Qualities that are often revealed in actions rather than words. Wouldn't you agree?"

A murmur of approval rippled through the onlookers, subtle but unmistakable. My calm strength had drawn them in, turning the tide of the conversation. Lady Marchmont's smile grew brittle, her eyes narrowing ever so slightly.

As I turned away, a familiar voice at my side startled me. "Well done," Jeremiah said, his tone low and steady. He had appeared beside me like a shadow, his presence grounding me in a way I had not expected.

"They will not stop," I murmured, my voice barely audible over the hum of the room. "But neither will I."

Jeremiah inclined his head, a faint smile playing at the corner of his lips. "Good. Let them underestimate you. It will make your victory all the sweeter."

I allowed myself a brief glance at him, his unwavering confidence a balm to my frayed nerves. Then I turned back to the room, the weight of its scrutiny bearing down on me. This gathering was no ordinary party; it was a proving ground. If they wanted to question my place, my strength, or my resolve, I would answer them in kind.

If society wanted a battle, I would meet them on the field—and I would win.

22

The Ball of Betrayal

The carriage rolled to a halt in front of Lady Henrietta's grand estate, its imposing facade glittering with the light of a hundred chandeliers. The sight of it stirred unease in my chest, but I straightened my shoulders, determined not to let the fear show. This was not a night for weakness; it was a night to remind them all who I was—the Duchess of Wakefield, not some timid widow to be swept aside.

Jeremiah's warnings echoed in my mind as I stepped from the carriage, the chill of the evening brushing against my bare shoulders. *"Don't go,"* he'd said, his voice firm with concern. *"It's a trap, Your Grace. You know it is."*

And yet, here I was. Because not going would have been worse. I had to know what they were planning because Jeremiah didn't find anything that night. Besides, I had to come because of the rumors circulating between myself and Jeremiah. To retreat now would have been to confirm their whispers, to hand them the very power they sought.

The ballroom was dazzling, its gilded walls and sparkling crystal chandeliers a testament to Lady Henrietta's wealth and taste. But beneath the beauty, there was an undercurrent of tension, a sense that every smile was a weapon, every laugh a barb.

I entered with my head held high, my steps slow and deliberate. Eyes turned toward me, the ripple of whispers following in my wake. I felt their gazes, sharp as daggers, but I met them with a steady gaze of my own.

"Your Grace," Lady Henrietta greeted me, her smile cold and calculating as she swept forward to meet me. She was a vision of elegance, her gown a deep, regal blue that only underscored the authority she wielded in this room. "How delightful of you to join us."

"Lady Henrietta," I replied evenly, inclining my head. "Thank you for the invitation."

Her eyes flickered over me, her smile tightening. "It is only fitting, of course, that we celebrate unity within the family. I trust you are...comfortable here?"

I returned her gaze with a faint smile of my own. "As comfortable as one can be in the company of such gracious hosts."

She hesitated, a flicker of something dark crossing her expression before she composed herself. "Enjoy the evening, Your Grace," she said, stepping aside to allow me further into the room.

The ball unfolded as such gatherings always did—dances and idle chatter, glances and whispers exchanged under the guise of civility. But I could feel the trap closing in around me, the tension winding tighter with every passing moment.

The first blow came when the servant stepped forward, his voice trembling but clear as he addressed the room. "Pardon, Your Grace, my lords, and ladies," he began, his eyes darting nervously around the crowd. "I—" He hesitated, as if summoning courage. "I have seen something...indiscreet."

The room fell silent, the attention of every guest snapping to him like hounds scenting blood.

Lady Henrietta's voice was calm, measured, but there was a gleam in her eyes. "Speak plainly, man. What have you seen?"

He hesitated again, his gaze flicking to me. My stomach twisted with unease.

"I saw Her Grace," he said at last, his voice gaining strength, "with Lord Ravenscroft. In the east wing of the estate. They were...embracing."

A gasp rippled through the crowd, the weight of the accusation crashing over me like a tidal wave.

"That's absurd," I said, my voice steady but loud enough to carry. "I've done no such thing."

The servant's gaze dropped, his hands wringing together. "I swear it's true, Your Grace. I saw it with my own eyes."

The whispers began immediately, a torrent of scandalized murmurs sweeping through the room. My throat tightened, but I refused to let the panic show. I stood tall, meeting the eyes of those who dared to look at me with judgment.

"Lies," I said firmly, my voice cutting through the noise. "This man has been bribed to discredit me. I will not stand for such baseless accusations."

Lady Henrietta stepped forward, her expression a mask of concern. "Your Grace," she said, her voice dripping with feigned sympathy, "surely you must see how troubling these allegations are. It would be best to address them openly, for the sake of clarity and decorum."

"I have nothing to address," I snapped, my composure fraying under the weight of their stares. "This is nothing but an attempt to ruin me. Surely you can see that."

But their faces told me otherwise. The seed had been planted, and already it was taking root.

At that moment, the doors swung open, and Jeremiah strode into the room. His presence commanded attention, the murmurs quieting as he crossed the floor with purposeful strides.

"Enough," he said, his voice low but resonant, cutting through the tension like a blade.

He turned to the servant, his gaze sharp and unyielding. "Do you swear on your honor that what you've said is true?"

The man faltered, his gaze darting nervously around the room. "I—I do, my lord."

"Interesting," Jeremiah said coolly, stepping closer. "Because I was not even in the estate on the night you claim to have seen this...indiscretion. So tell me, sir, how is it that you saw me in a place I could not possibly have been?"

The servant's face drained of color, and he stammered, "I—I must have been mistaken, my lord. It was dark, and—"

Jeremiah cut him off with a withering glare. "Mistaken, indeed. Or perhaps paid to fabricate such a tale?"

The room erupted into murmurs once more, the tide of judgment shifting as suspicion turned on the servant.

Lady Henrietta's expression hardened, but she quickly composed herself. "I'm sure there's been some misunderstanding," she said smoothly, though her eyes betrayed her frustration.

"I'm sure there has," Jeremiah replied, his tone biting.

He turned to me then, his gaze steady and filled with unspoken reassurance. "Your Grace," he said, extending his hand, "shall we?"

I hesitated, my pride warring with my need for escape. But the warmth in his eyes, the silent promise of his support, broke through my defenses. I placed my hand in his, and together we left the ballroom, the whispers of the crowd fading behind us.

Once outside, I exhaled a shaky breath, the weight of the evening pressing down on me.

"Thank you," I said softly, my voice trembling with a mixture of gratitude and exhaustion.

Jeremiah squeezed my hand gently. "You don't have to face them alone, Evelina," he said. "Not ever."

His words settled over me like a balm, and for the first time that night, I felt the faint stirrings of hope. But deep within, I knew the battle was far from over.

23

The Whispers and Shadows

Although I tried to be calm and unflappable while attending every gathering, but the rumors had grown sharp, ravenous teeth, gnawing at my resolve with each passing day. What had begun as whispers had swelled into a cacophony, threatening to drown me in its relentless tide. It clawed at my reputation, turning even the smallest gesture into fuel for their fire.

The accusations and slander with the false witnesses in the last ball made me really not understand, why are they so cruel?!

I paced the drawing room, the morning post scattered across the table. Each letter felt like a thorn in my side, but one in particular caught my eye—its seal marked with Lady Henrietta's precise hand. I should have ignored it, let its contents remain a mystery, but curiosity—or perhaps masochistic impulse—compelled me to open it.

Your Grace,

The tongues of London wag ceaselessly, and while I am loath to believe such vile gossip, I implore you to consider the optics of Lord Ravenscroft's presence at Wakefield. It is for your own protection, of course.

The elegant parchment crumpled beneath my fingers as anger flared in my chest. *Protection.* How kind of her to disguise her cruelty as concern. It was as though she had taken a dagger and wrapped it in silk before driving it home.

Mary entered with her usual quiet efficiency, carrying a tray of tea. She hesitated when she saw my expression, her gaze flicking to the crumpled letter in my hand.

"Your Grace?" she asked softly.

"Nothing of consequence," I replied, though the tremor in my voice betrayed me. I set the letter aside, turning to face her fully.

Mary placed the tray down carefully, her hands folding in front of her as if bracing herself. "If I may, Your Grace...there are rumors. In the village."

The air seemed to shift around us. I stiffened, my gaze narrowing. "What kind of rumors?"

Her hesitation was brief but heavy. "They're saying dreadful things. That the child isn't the Duke's." She lowered her voice further, as though afraid to speak the words aloud. "They're saying it's Lord Ravenscroft's. They also say that Lord Ravenscroft is helping you for the sake of making his son the heir to Wakefield."

The room tilted slightly, the air thickening around me. I gripped the back of a chair to steady myself.I've often heard mockery about the child in my belly not being my husband's child. Some even said to my face that this child was the result of my affair with Jeremiah.

But, I didn't expect that the rumors were no longer spread among the nobles alone, but had spread to the people living in the villages. I sighed heavily, perhaps the goal was to make the people in Wakefield doubt the duke's family— more precisely to make them doubt me.

"And they believe this?" I asked, though the answer was written in Mary's pained expression.

"Some do," she admitted, her voice barely above a whisper. "Others...they don't know what to think. But the more it's repeated, the more...plausible it seems."

"Plausible," I echoed bitterly. The word sat heavy on my tongue, its taste acrid.

Mary nodded, her gaze dropping. "People love a scandal, Your Grace. And Lord Ravenscroft...well, his reputation doesn't help matters. The fact that Lord Ravenscroft is unmarried does make for more scandals."

Her words struck true, a blade of unwelcome honesty. Jeremiah's presence had been a steadying force for me, but in the hands of the gossips, it had become a weapon aimed at my undoing. Mary's words weren't wrong. Jeremiah's status was indeed a risk. Not being married, not even having a fiancé made the situation worse. Their accusations were also terrible and hard to refute.

"The worse things, Your Grace. They even said that you were power-hungry and rushed to get pregnant with lord Ravenscroft for the sake of ruling Wakefield."

A bitter laugh escaped my lips. "A child who hasn't even been born yet is already being made the center of a scandal and showered with false accusations. These people really have an incredible imagination. They don't know how much Rupert wanted this baby and tried so hard to live to see our baby," I said as I looked down and clutched my belly.

"I hope you don't think too much about those rumors, Your Grace. You're pregnant and your health is most important."

I turned away, walking to the window. The glass was cool beneath my fingers as I stared out at the gardens, their serenity a cruel contrast to the turmoil within me. "Thank you, Mary," I said after a long pause, my voice soft but firm. "I didn't know that the scandal that broke out in the ball had become so widespread. I would rather know than be left in the dark."

Mary hesitated, then spoke with quiet conviction. "Lord Ravenscroft won't let them speak ill of you for long. He'll put a stop to it."

A faint, bittersweet smile tugged at my lips. Jeremiah would defend me, I had no doubt, but his involvement would only stoke the fire. He was already a target, and his name entwined with mine only added fuel to the blaze.

As the weight of the rumors settled over me, I felt the strain more acutely than ever. My hand drifted to my stomach, cradling the life growing within me. This child was Rupert's—the last piece of him I had left—and yet it seemed the world was determined to rip that truth away.

A sudden, sharp pain lanced through my abdomen, stealing the air from my lungs. I gasped, clutching the windowsill as the room swam around me. A hot, sickly sensation coursed through my body, and I felt a dampness between my legs. My heart sank, terror gripping me as I glanced down to see a faint smear of crimson staining my dress.

"Your Grace!" Mary's voice was distant, muffled by the roaring in my ears. I turned toward her, but my vision blurred, the edges darkening as panic set in.

My knees buckled, but before I could hit the ground, strong hands caught me, steadying me. "Easy, Your Grace."

The voice was familiar—Cedric's. I blinked up at him as his face came into focus, his usual charm replaced by an expression of genuine concern. His grip was firm but gentle, his arm supporting my weight as he helped me to the nearest chair.

"Fetch the physician," he ordered Mary, his tone firm but calm. His commanding presence seemed to galvanize her, and she dashed from the room without hesitation.

Cedric knelt beside me, his hand still supporting my arm. "You should have someone watching over you, Your Grace. This stress..." His gaze flicked briefly to my stomach, his lips pressing into a thin line. "It's not good for you. Or the child."

I wanted to argue, to assert my strength, but the pain had sapped me of all bravado. My breathing was shallow, each gasp a struggle against the stabbing ache in my abdomen. "Thank you," I murmured instead, my voice weak and trembling.

The physician arrived swiftly, his face grave as he assessed my condition. His examination was brisk but thorough, his hands deft as he checked for signs of further bleeding. After a moment, he prepared a tincture, mixing laudanum with a mild sedative to ease the pain and calm my nerves. "This will help you rest," he explained. "The bleeding is minimal, but it's imperative to keep it that way."

He instructed Mary to apply a cool compress to my forehead and prepared a mild herbal infusion to stabilize my condition. "She'll need to drink this twice daily," he said, handing the mixture to Mary. "It will help soothe the body and prevent further complications."

When he finally spoke directly to me, his tone was stern, leaving no room for protest. "Your Grace, you must rest completely. No exertion, no stress.

You'll remain in bed for the next few days at minimum, and we'll monitor the bleeding. Any further strain could lead to a miscarriage."

The weight of his words pressed down on me, a suffocating cloud that left me feeling helpless. "How serious is it?" I managed, my voice barely above a whisper.

The physician's eyes softened slightly, though his expression remained firm. "The bleeding is minor for now, but it's a warning. If you push yourself any further, the consequences could be dire. Your body needs time to recover, and the child's life depends on it."

Mary, who had returned with a basin of cool water and a cloth, dabbed at my forehead with a trembling hand. "You'll see to it, won't you, Your Grace? You'll rest?" Her voice was laced with worry, her eyes shimmering with unshed tears.

I nodded faintly, the enormity of the situation sinking in. The fight I had been waging against the rumors, against the cruelty of the ton, would have to wait. My child's life depended on it.

After the physician left, Cedric lingered, his presence a quiet reassurance. He stood by the chair, his hands clasped behind his back as if unsure of his welcome. "You shouldn't have to bear this alone," he said softly, his gaze meeting mine. "If there's anything I can do..."

For a moment, I hesitated. Cedric's charm was disarming, his concern seemingly genuine, but doubt crept into the corners of my mind. Still, in this moment of vulnerability, I had no choice but to accept his help. "Thank you," I said again, my voice steadier this time.

He inclined his head, a flicker of something unreadable passing over his face. "Your Grace, I'll ensure everything is handled. Rest, and don't worry about the household for now."

As he left the room, Mary knelt beside me, her hand resting lightly on mine. "You'll be alright, Your Grace," she whispered, though the tremor in her voice betrayed her uncertainty.

I squeezed her hand gently, drawing what little strength I could from her presence. The battle against the rumors and the ton's cruel judgment would resume another day. For now, my focus had to be on the life within me. And for that, I would do whatever was necessary.

24

A Life Worth Fighting For

The halls of Wakefield were silent, an oppressive stillness settling over the estate as I strode through its familiar corridors. The news of Evelina's collapse had reached me in town, each word cutting through my composure like a blade. Bleeding. Fainting. The physician's warnings of a miscarriage. My chest tightened with every step, my breath shallow as if the very air conspired to stifle me.

When I entered her room, the sight before me stopped me cold. Evelina lay pale and motionless against the sea of white linens, her dark hair a stark contrast against the pillows. Her hands rested lightly on her rounded stomach, and the sight of her swollen belly—so much more pronounced than the first time we'd met—struck something deep within me.

A wild thought tore through my mind, unbidden and impossible to ignore: *If only the child she carried were mine.*

The weight of it nearly staggered me. If it were my child, I would never have let her suffer like this. I would shield her from every whisper, every careless slight, every danger that dared to touch her. But the truth was painfully clear: the child was not mine, and I was not the man she needed. I was just a viscount, a man whose own legitimacy had been questioned since the day I drew breath. A man who had made a promise to a dying friend and was now helplessly watching the woman he vowed to protect endure a pain I couldn't take from her.

My fists clenched at my sides, a futile attempt to suppress the surge of frustration and guilt. I approached the bed cautiously, as though afraid to disturb the fragile peace she seemed to have found in sleep.

As I drew nearer, Evelina's eyes fluttered open, her lashes damp and her gaze unfocused. She blinked a few times, and recognition dawned. "Jeremiah," she whispered, her voice faint but tinged with relief.

I dropped to one knee beside her bed, bringing myself to her eye level. "I'm here," I said softly, unable to keep the edge of worry from my voice. "Don't try to move, Evelina. You need to rest."

She shifted, attempting to push herself upright, but I placed a firm hand on her shoulder, stopping her. "No," I said gently but firmly. "Stay as you are. The physician's orders were clear—you need complete rest."

"But the estate—" she began, her voice trembling as she glanced toward the window, as though the weight of her responsibilities lingered there.

"Let it wait," I interrupted, my tone steady.

"But..."

"Evelina... just rest, your baby is more at stake..." I took a breath and tried to calm her down. "And your fight will mean nothing if you lose this child."

The words were out before I could temper them, and for a moment, silence hung between us. I regretted their harshness, but not their truth.

Evelina's eyes welled with tears, and she turned her face away, her hand instinctively moving to her belly. "I don't want to lose my baby," she whispered, her voice breaking.

The rawness of her admission shattered something in me. I reached out, hesitating only for a moment before covering her trembling hand with mine. "You won't," I said, my voice low and resolute. "You won't lose this baby, Evelina. Not while I'm here."

She looked at me then, her tears spilling freely down her cheeks. The vulnerability in her gaze was a stark contrast to the strength she had shown in public, and it pierced me in a way I hadn't expected.

"I've tried so hard," she said, her voice shaking. "I've done everything I could, but it's never enough. They hate me, Jeremiah. They want to take everything—my child, my place, Rupert's memory." She drew a shuddering breath, her hand tightening over mine. "I can't let them win. I can't let them take this from me."

"You won't," I repeated, leaning closer. "But you have to trust me, Evelina. Resting isn't surrender. It's part of the fight. You can't protect your child if you push yourself to the brink."

Her lips trembled, and her hand moved again to cradle her belly. "I'm so afraid," she admitted, her voice barely audible.

I reached up, brushing a stray tear from her cheek with my thumb, the motion unthinking, instinctive. "I know," I said softly. "But you're not alone in this. I won't let them hurt you—or the baby. I swear it."

For a moment, she simply looked at me, her gaze searching mine as though trying to find the truth in my words. Whatever she saw there must have reassured her, because she nodded faintly, her shoulders sagging with exhaustion.

"Rest now," I urged, adjusting the blanket over her as she sank back against the pillows.

"Jeremiah," she said, her voice soft and hesitant.

"Yes?"

Her gaze lingered on me, her expression unreadable. "Thank you," she murmured.

The simple words were a balm against the storm raging within me, and I nodded. "Always," I replied, meaning it more than she could ever know.

As her breathing evened out and sleep claimed her, I remained by her side, watching the faint rise and fall of her chest. The shadows in the room grew longer, the firelight casting flickering patterns on the walls.

I couldn't stop the thought that returned, unbidden but relentless: *If only the child were mine.*

But it wasn't. And yet, as I looked at Evelina—her strength, her vulnerability, the fierce determination that defined her—I realized that my feelings for her were no longer bound by duty or a promise made long ago.

They were something deeper, something far more dangerous.

25

The Sweet Deception

The days after the hemorrhage blurred into one long, restless haze. The physician's orders were strict: complete bed rest, no exertion, and minimal stress. Jeremiah's stern insistence left no room for argument, but it did little to quiet my restless mind. My body may have been confined to the bed, but my thoughts wandered relentlessly—to Wakefield, to my child, and to the enemies circling closer with every passing day.

My hand drifted to my stomach, fingers splaying over the gentle curve that had become more pronounced in recent weeks. "It's just us, little one," I whispered, my voice barely audible over the crackle of the hearth. "But we'll manage. We have to."

The knock on the door was soft but firm, and I stiffened instinctively. Before I could answer, Mary opened it slightly, her expression hesitant. "Your Grace, Lady Henrietta has come to see you."

The name sent a jolt of unease through me, but I nodded. "Show her in."

Lady Henrietta entered like a ship cutting through calm waters, her dark gown and imposing demeanor as sharp as ever. Her gaze swept over me, taking in my pale complexion and the untouched stack of correspondence on the bedside table. "Your Grace," she began, her voice clipped but not unkind. "You look better than I expected."

I inclined my head, my fingers curling into the blanket. "Thank you for your concern, Lady Henrietta. What brings you to Wakefield today?"

She sank gracefully into the chair beside my bed, smoothing her skirts with precise movements. "I came to offer my assistance. And to propose a solution to... your current predicament."

The words hung in the air, and a knot formed in my stomach. My hand drifted to rest there again, the gesture as much for comfort as protection. "What predicament do you mean, exactly?"

Lady Henrietta's eyes gleamed with a calculating light. "Your condition, of course. The bleeding, the physician's orders—these are all signs that you must prioritize your health, dear child. You cannot possibly oversee Wakefield's operations in your state."

"I have Jeremiah—Lord Ravenscroft—to assist me," I replied carefully, watching her reaction.

Her lips thinned, and she sat straighter, her disapproval clear. "Jeremiah Langley is a capable man, I'll grant you that, but he is an outsider. Wakefield is a Harland estate, Your Grace. It is not a place for strangers to meddle."

I opened my mouth to protest, my fingers tightening on the blanket, but Lady Henrietta continued, her voice softening just enough to feign concern. "Cedric has offered to step in while you recover. It's the logical solution. He knows the estate, the tenants trust him, and he is family. Surely you can see the wisdom in this arrangement."

The air in the room felt heavier, pressing down on me as I considered her words. Cedric's charm and apparent willingness to help had always come with an undertone of calculation. But Lady Henrietta had positioned this as an act of familial duty, and any objection I made would be seen as paranoia or ingratitude.

My hand moved again, fingers circling gently over my stomach as if to soothe the unease twisting there. "I appreciate Cedric's offer," I said slowly, "but—"

"Your Grace," Lady Henrietta interrupted gently, her tone firm. "You must think of your child. Your duty is to your health and your heir, not to the day-to-day matters of the estate. Cedric can handle the responsibilities until you are well enough to resume them."

The implication was clear: if I refused, I would be seen as jeopardizing my child's well-being. My free hand moved to cover the other, my fingers interlocking tightly as I fought the swell of frustration rising in my chest.

In the end, I nodded, forcing my voice to remain steady. "Very well. If Cedric is willing to assist, I will allow it. But only temporarily."

Lady Henrietta's smile was triumphant, though she tried to mask it with a veneer of politeness. "A wise decision, Your Grace. I'll inform Cedric immediately."

As she rose and left the room, I exhaled slowly, the knot in my stomach tightening further. My agreement felt like a concession, a surrender of a piece of my autonomy.

Mary returned, her brow furrowed with concern as she set a fresh pot of tea on the bedside table. "Are you alright, Your Grace?" she asked softly.

I nodded faintly, my hand drifting back to my belly. "I'm fine, Mary."

But I wasn't fine. Not truly. Cedric's involvement felt like another thread unraveling from the tenuous hold I had on Wakefield, and I couldn't shake the feeling that I had just handed him another weapon to use against me.

As I lay back against the pillows, my fingers still resting protectively over my child, I closed my eyes and whispered the silent vow I had made countless times before.

I will protect you, little one. No matter what it takes.

26

A Devil's Bargain

The morning sunlight streamed through the curtains, golden and warm, yet I felt none of its comfort. Instead, I sat in my bedchamber, wrapped in a shawl, the physician's warning echoing in my mind. Rest. No exertion. No stress. As if such a thing were possible when the world seemed determined to devour me whole.

The rumors had grown like weeds, choking the remnants of my peace. They were everywhere—whispered in drawing rooms, murmured in the streets, and now, if Mary's observations were correct, even spreading among the staff. Each whisper cast a shadow over my child, over Rupert's legacy.

Jeremiah's name was at the center of it all, tangled with mine like an unshakable snare. Every glance, every pointed remark, was another barb, another reminder that society had already decided who and what I was.

I traced my belly absently, the faint flutter of life within a fragile solace. My child was the only thing that mattered now, yet even that seemed uncertain.

A knock at the door drew me from my thoughts, and I turned to see Cedric entering, his usual charm softened into something gentler.

"Your Grace," he said, his voice quiet but warm. "How are you feeling today?"

"Well enough," I replied, though the tension in my shoulders betrayed me. "The physician's advice to rest has been...difficult to follow."

Cedric gave a small smile, pulling a chair closer to my bedside. "That doesn't surprise me. You've never been one to shrink from a challenge, have you?"

I managed a faint laugh, though it felt hollow. "Perhaps, but this challenge feels insurmountable. The rumors...they grow worse by the day."

Cedric's expression darkened slightly, a flicker of anger passing through his otherwise composed demeanor. "I've heard them," he admitted, his tone grim. "And I share your outrage. It's appalling, the lengths people will go to twist the truth."

I nodded, my throat tight. "They question the paternity of my child," I said softly, the words bitter on my tongue. "Rupert's child. How can they be so cruel, so eager to tarnish his name and mine?"

Cedric's gaze softened, his expression one of perfect understanding. "Because scandal sells," he said simply. "And because they're jealous, envious of your strength, your position. It's easier for them to tear you down than to celebrate your resilience."

His words struck a chord, their logic undeniable. Yet they offered little comfort.

"I don't know how to stop it," I confessed, my voice trembling. "Every denial only fuels their whispers. And Jeremiah..." I hesitated, unsure how to finish the thought.

Cedric's brows lifted slightly, his expression sharpening. "Jeremiah is a liability, Your Grace."

The bluntness of his statement startled me, and I stared at him, unsure of how to respond. "A...liability?"

"He's a good man," Cedric allowed, his tone measured, "but his reputation precedes him. The ton will never see him as anything other than a rake and a scandal waiting to happen. His presence here—no matter how well-meaning—only gives them more to talk about."

I frowned, the weight of his words settling heavily on me. "But he's done nothing wrong," I protested weakly.

Cedric leaned forward, his gaze steady and earnest. "Perception is often more powerful than truth, Your Grace. You know that as well as anyone. And right now, Jeremiah's presence is casting doubt where there should be none.

It's not fair, but it's the reality of the situation."

The truth of his statement stung, though I hated to admit it. Jeremiah had been my rock, my protector, yet his very presence had become a weapon in the hands of my enemies.

Cedric hesitated, his expression softening further. "If I may offer a suggestion..."

I nodded slowly, my curiosity outweighing my apprehension. "Go on."

"Send him away," Cedric said gently, though his words felt like a blow. "Not permanently, but for now. Distance yourself from him publicly, and the rumors will lose their footing. Let the ton see that you are above reproach, that you don't need anyone—least of all a man with Jeremiah's reputation—to secure your position."

I stared at him, my mind reeling. The thought of asking Jeremiah to leave felt unbearable, a betrayal of the trust and loyalty he had shown me. Yet Cedric's argument made an uncomfortable kind of sense.

"But he's here because of Rupert," I said, my voice barely above a whisper. "He made a promise. How can I ask him to break that?"

"You wouldn't be breaking his promise," Cedric countered. "You'd be protecting it. His presence is only giving your enemies more ammunition. If he truly wants to help you, he'll understand that this is the best way to do so."

The logic was sound, yet it felt like a knife twisting in my chest. I looked away, my gaze falling to my hands, which rested protectively over my stomach.

Cedric reached out, his touch light but reassuring. "Your Grace, you have to think of the child. This is bigger than Jeremiah or anyone else. It's about preserving Rupert's legacy, your legacy. If you don't act now, the rumors will only grow, and they will taint everything you've fought to protect."

His words hung heavy in the air, their weight pressing down on me. I wanted to argue, to dismiss his advice, but the truth was undeniable. The rumors had already begun to overshadow everything—my marriage, my reputation, and even my child.

"I'll consider it," I said finally, my voice hollow.

Cedric smiled faintly, his relief evident. "You're doing the right thing, Your Grace. And you won't face this alone. I'll be here to support you every step of the way."

I nodded, though the ache in my chest remained. Cedric's logic was sound, his intentions seemingly noble, yet a faint voice in the back of my mind whispered a warning.

For now, though, I silenced that voice. My child's future was at stake, and I would do whatever it took to protect it. Even if it meant pushing away the one person who had been my greatest ally.

27

The Shadows We Cast

The road to Wakefield felt interminable, every turn of the carriage wheels grinding against my nerves. The rumors had reached me days ago, spreading like wildfire through the social circles of London, but Evelina's fragile condition had pushed me into action. I had debated the consequences of my presence at the estate, aware that my visits only fanned the flames of gossip. Yet, how could I stay away when she needed me most?

The estate emerged from the horizon, its grandeur muted by the tension that clung to it like a storm cloud. As the carriage came to a halt, I stepped down quickly, ignoring the dust that clung to my coat. My thoughts were sharp, ready for whatever confrontation might await.

I hadn't made it far before I was intercepted.

"Lord Ravenscroft."

Frederick's voice carried the chill of the late afternoon air, his tone devoid of courtesy. He stood rigid on the gravel path, his expression as unwelcoming as ever. There was no pretense of civility, only thinly veiled hostility.

"Lord Frederick," I replied, my voice steady despite the irritation simmering beneath the surface. "I'm here to see Her Grace."

"So I assumed," he said, a humorless smile curving his lips. "The rumors have preceded you, as I'm sure you're aware."

I exhaled slowly, already weary of his games. "I have no interest in entertaining gossip," I said, stepping past him.

But Frederick moved to block my path, his hand resting on the pommel of his cane. "No interest? That's rather convenient, considering the gossip centers on you."

I met his gaze with an icy stare. "If you have something to say, Frederick, say it plainly. I have no time for theatrics."

His expression darkened, his tone sharpening. "Very well. The ton believes you're the father of the Duchess's child."

The accusation landed like a blow, though I refused to let it show. "And do you share their belief?"

Frederick hesitated, his gaze flickering toward the house before returning to mine. "I don't," he said finally, though his tone remained clipped. "But I won't pretend to know the truth. What I do know is that your presence here is making things worse for her."

"Then perhaps you should direct your energy toward uncovering the source of these rumors instead of confronting me," I shot back. "Or would that force you to examine your own family too closely?"

Frederick's jaw tightened. "Do not mistake me for an ally of Henrietta or Cedric," he said coldly. "I've no love for their scheming, and I've made it clear that I will not harm the child."

I studied him, my irritation giving way to curiosity. "Why now, Frederick?" I asked, my tone calm but probing. "You've never been one to champion Evelina's cause. What's changed?"

His expression hardened for a moment before he sighed, glancing toward the house. "Because I've seen what Cedric is capable of," he said quietly. "Henrietta's machinations I've grown used to, but Cedric? He's a predator, Ravenscroft. He doesn't just want control of Evelina; he wants to break her. And that child...it's the last thing tying her to Rupert. If she falls into Cedric's hands, I shudder to think what will become of her—and the child."

His vehemence gave me pause, though I kept my expression guarded. "If that's true, then why confront me at all?"

"Because you're blind to the damage you're causing by being here," Frederick snapped. "The staff is watching you, the villagers are whispering about you, and every visit gives Henrietta and Cedric more ammunition to undermine her."

His words stung, not because they were false, but because they echoed my own fears. Still, I refused to let him dictate my actions.

"If you truly care about Her Grace and the child," I said, stepping closer, "then act. You claim to oppose Henrietta and Cedric, but where is your proof? Your intervention?"

Frederick's shoulders stiffened, his gaze darkening. "Her Grace won't listen to me," he admitted bluntly. "Not while Cedric has her ear. If you want to help her, tread carefully. The more you push, the more you'll drive her into his arms."

I stepped closer, my voice hardening. "And what is your alternative, Frederick? That I stand aside and watch as Cedric manipulates her into ruin? You speak of careful action, but all I've seen from you is hesitation and empty warnings. The Duchess and the child need protection, not platitudes."

Frederick's jaw tightened, but he did not flinch. "You think you're the only one who can protect her?" he asked, his tone edged with disbelief. "Your very presence is what's drawing the wolves to her door."

"Perhaps it is," I shot back, my voice low but firm. "But I would rather draw their attention and take the blows myself than leave her defenseless. Evelina's strength is unmatched, but no one can face this storm alone. And until someone else steps forward with more than words, I will stand by her side."

Frederick's face darkened, his grip tightening on his cane. "You think you're a savior, don't you?" he snapped. "You're the reason they're tearing her apart. You're not helping—you're making her life harder."

I stepped closer, my gaze unwavering. "And what are you doing, Frederick? Standing on the sidelines, wringing your hands? Don't pretend this is about Evelina or the child. You're here because you're worried about yourself. Your benefit. Your standing. Don't insult me by pretending otherwise."

His expression twisted into a scowl, anger flashing in his eyes. "You dare accuse me of selfishness? At least I'm not the one giving the gossips their ammunition."

"No," I said coldly. "You're just the one who stands by while Cedric sinks his claws into her. If you truly cared, you'd put off this act and do something. Evelina and the child need action, not your thinly veiled concern."

Frederick's jaw clenched, his nostrils flaring. "Your arrogance is astounding, Ravenscroft."

"And your inaction is damning," I retorted, stepping past him. "Now get out of my way. Unlike you, I have work to do."

Without another word, I brushed past Frederick, my thoughts racing as I entered the house.

In the drawing room, Evelina sat by the fire, her pale complexion and weary eyes a stark reminder of her fragile condition. Despite her exhaustion, her expression softened when she saw me.

"Jeremiah," she said, her voice tinged with relief. "You came."

"Of course," I replied, taking the seat across from her. "I heard about your condition, and..." I hesitated, the weight of the rumors hanging between us. "I've also heard the whispers."

Her smile faltered, and she glanced down at her hands. "You know they're baseless," she said quietly. "But that doesn't stop them from spreading."

"Your Grace," I said gently, leaning forward, "you are stronger than they know. But I'm worried. The stress, the judgment—it's not just affecting you. It's affecting the child."

She nodded, her gaze distant. "It feels like I'm being suffocated," she admitted. "Cedric says..."

I straightened, my tone sharpening. "What has Cedric said?"

Evelina hesitated, her hands twisting in her lap. "He says that if you were to...distance yourself, the rumors might lose traction. That my reputation could be salvaged."

The implication struck deep. "And you believe him?"

"I don't know what to believe," she said, her voice breaking. "I want to trust you, Jeremiah, but the more I hear, the more I wonder if your presence is doing more harm than good."

Her doubt was a knife to the heart, a painful reminder of Cedric's growing influence. I reached for her hand, my voice steady despite the storm within me. "You know me, Your Grace. You know why I'm here, why I've stayed. Don't let Cedric twist that."

Tears filled her eyes, but she pulled her hand back, turning away. "I just want to protect my child," she whispered. "Is that so wrong?"

"No," I said softly. "It's not. But protecting your child doesn't mean pushing away those who care for you."

Her silence cut deeper than any words could. Rising from my seat, I cast one last look at her, a silent vow forming in my heart. Cedric's grip on her would not hold. I would find a way to break through before it was too late.

"And I hope you don't let Cedric cloud your judgment and made you push me away," I said when Evelina didn't answer.

At the mention of Cedric, Evelina stiffened, her expression tightening. "Cedric has been... helpful," she said cautiously, her tone measured as if testing the waters.

"Helpful," I repeated, unable to keep the skepticism from my voice. "Or manipulative?"

She hesitated, her eyes narrowing slightly. "He's offered me solutions," she countered. "He's been a calming presence when I needed it most."

I leaned forward, my gaze fixed on hers. "A presence that isolates you from others," I said pointedly. "Including me."

My words struck a nerve. I saw it in the flicker of pain that crossed her face. Cedric had driven a wedge between us, encouraging her to see me as a threat. Yet sitting here now, I could sense that my presence—steady and unwavering—still held some weight with her.

"You think Cedric has ulterior motives," she said, her gaze sharp as she searched mine.

"I don't think, Your Grace. I know," I replied, my voice unwavering. "Cedric thrives on being seen as indispensable. He's charming, yes, but that charm is his weapon. He will wield it to ensure you trust him above all others."

Her eyes didn't leave mine as she asked, "And what of you, Jeremiah? What makes you any different?"

The question caught me off guard, though I quickly masked my reaction. "Because I have nothing to gain from your trust, Your Grace," I said, my tone softening. "Only your safety."

For a moment, the tension between us hung heavy in the air. I could see the conflict in her eyes, the war between her instincts and the doubts Cedric had sown. I wanted to reach her, to pull her back from the edge before it was too late.

"I don't know who to trust anymore," she admitted, her voice breaking slightly. The vulnerability in her words hit me like a blow.

I leaned closer, willing her to see the sincerity in my eyes. "Then trust yourself. You've survived this far, despite everything they've thrown at you. That is no small feat, Your Grace."

She nodded slowly, my words seeming to steady her, though the tension in her posture didn't fully ease. "I will think on what you've said," she murmured, rising from her seat.

I stood as well, watching her carefully. "Do not wait too long, Your Grace. Cedric is not the only one plotting against you. The longer you hesitate, the greater the risk to you and your child. And don't trust anyone."

Her brow furrowed, and she hesitated before asking, "Even you?"

"Yes," I said without hesitation. "Even me."

Her expression faltered, but she nodded before leaving the library. I watched her go, her silhouette disappearing into the dimly lit corridor. My words lingered in the air, heavy with truth and warning. Cedric's influence had taken root, but I could see that she was still fighting—still questioning.

I exhaled slowly, running a hand through my hair. Evelina's survival, and that of her child, depended on her ability to navigate the labyrinth of deceit closing in around her. And though she might not trust me fully, I vowed to remain by her side, ready to act when the time came.

The shadows were gathering, but I would not let them consume her. Not without a fight.

28

The Outsider

Wakefield had changed.

The estate, once lively with the quiet hum of loyal staff and the steady rhythm of Evelina's careful oversight, now seemed steeped in an unfamiliar tension. Conversations hushed as I passed, glances darting toward me before quickly looking away. Even the air felt heavier, like the weight of unspoken words clinging to every corner.

I had arrived that morning, as I often did, ready to check on Evelina. Her hemorrhage had been a stark reminder of how precarious her condition was, and though I trusted her strength, the image of her pale and trembling haunted me. The thought of her confined to bed, vulnerable and isolated, gnawed at me.

When I reached the grand hall, the butler greeted me with a polite but strained expression. "Lord Ravenscroft," he said, his tone neutral, "I'll inform Her Grace of your presence. If you'd please wait here."

I nodded, though the request was unusual. Evelina had always welcomed me without ceremony; the delay was unsettling.

I didn't have to wait long to find out why.

Cedric Harland strolled in, his entrance deliberate, his gaze locking on me with a faint smirk that made my hands curl into fists. His polished boots clicked against the marble floor, the sound echoing through the hall as though he relished every step.

"Lord Ravenscroft," he drawled, his tone dripping with mock civility. "What an unexpected pleasure."

"Lord Harland," I replied, matching his tone with careful neutrality. "I've come to see Her Grace."

Cedric's smirk deepened, his dark eyes gleaming with something sharp and malicious. "Have you now? Unfortunately, I'm afraid you'll have to wait for an invitation next time." He gestured toward the butler, who had retreated a few steps but remained within earshot. "You see, Wakefield is no place for... outsiders to come and go as they please."

The word *outsider* hit its mark, but I refused to rise to his bait. Instead, I inclined my head slightly, keeping my voice calm. "I wasn't aware that offering assistance to Her Grace required an invitation."

Cedric's chuckle was low, laced with condescension. "Well, things have changed. With Her Grace resting, it's important to ensure she isn't disturbed unnecessarily." He stepped closer, his gaze narrowing. "She needs proper care, after all. And proper guidance."

I met his gaze evenly, though my jaw tightened. "Her Grace is more than capable of determining what she needs."

"Is she?" Cedric's tone sharpened, the facade of civility cracking. "Because from where I stand, it seems she's had quite a few... distractions lately. Distractions that do little for her health or the estate."

"If you're implying something," I said coolly, taking a deliberate step forward, "I suggest you say it outright."

Cedric's smirk returned, his confidence unshaken. "Why, Lord Ravenscroft, I would never dream of being so crass. I'm merely pointing out the obvious. Wakefield is a Harland estate, and it's high time its affairs were handled by family."

"Family," I echoed, my voice steady but sharp. "Or those who see an opportunity to seize control?"

His eyes flashed with something dangerous, but his tone remained smooth. "You're quick to accuse, Ravenscroft. Perhaps you should consider why you're so eager to involve yourself in matters that don't concern you."

"Evelina's well-being concerns me," I said firmly, my fists clenching at my sides. "And I won't stand by while she's manipulated."

Cedric stepped closer, his smirk vanishing. The tension between us crackled like a storm ready to break. "Careful, Ravenscroft," he said, his voice low and dangerous. "You're walking a fine line. One misstep, and you'll find yourself on the wrong side of Wakefield's gates."

I held his gaze, refusing to back down. "And you'll find that Evelina is stronger than you think. She doesn't need your interference or your schemes."

The silence between us was heavy, the air charged with unspoken threats. Finally, Cedric stepped back, his smirk returning like a mask. "As I said, Lord Ravenscroft, things have changed. Perhaps it's time you adjusted to that."

"I'll return tomorrow," I said evenly, turning on my heel. "We'll see if anything has truly changed by then."

Cedric's laugh followed me as I walked away, cold and mocking. "A bold claim. Do try not to disappoint us, Langley."

The moment I stepped outside, the cool air biting at my face, I let my facade drop. My fists clenched at my sides, my jaw tight as the weight of Cedric's interference settled over me.

Evelina wasn't just resting—she was being cornered, cut off from allies and surrounded by those who sought to control her. Cedric was positioning himself as her confidant, her protector, and if he succeeded, it would be all the easier for him to tighten his grip on Wakefield.

As I mounted my horse, the distant silhouette of the estate loomed against the horizon, its grandeur now tinged with a sense of foreboding. Cedric might have kept me from Evelina today, but this wasn't over.

I would return tomorrow, as I'd said. And when I did, I'd make sure to find a way to reach Evelina, no matter how many obstacles Cedric put in my path.

For now, though, I needed to regroup. Whatever Cedric was planning, he wouldn't stop until he had total control. And I wouldn't stop until I unraveled his schemes and freed Evelina from his grasp.

29

Unlikely Alignments

After being forcibly evicted from Wakefield and Evelina's refusal to meet, I thought of many bizarre things. The first peculiar thing is Frederick., his sudden shift in demeanor gnawed at me like a persistent ache. This was the same man who had sneered at Evelina's abilities, who had openly questioned the legitimacy of her child and her place in Wakefield. Yet now, he seemed determined to play the role of protector, warning me against Cedric's intentions as though he were Evelina's greatest ally.

It didn't add up.

As the morning light spilled over the estate's grounds, I found myself pacing in the small sitting room. The fire crackled faintly in the hearth, its warmth doing little to soothe the restless energy that coursed through me.

Why had Frederick changed so suddenly? And why had Evelina so readily embraced Cedric's poisonous charm?

The answer to the latter question was simple enough: Cedric was clever. His affability was his weapon, his ability to read people and tailor his behavior to their needs almost unnerving in its precision. Evelina, under siege from every direction, had latched onto his assurances like a lifeline. In her isolation, he offered what appeared to be support, even as he quietly tightened his grip.

But Frederick? That was a puzzle of a different sort.

The man who barged into the room barely five minutes later had the same haughty air I'd grown used to, but there was something sharper in his movements, a tension I hadn't seen before.

"Frederick," I said, keeping my tone neutral. "To what do I owe the pleasure?"

He ignored the chair I motioned to and stood near the fireplace instead, his stance rigid as he stared into the flames. "I'm not here to exchange pleasantries, Ravenscroft," he said curtly.

"No, I didn't imagine you were," I replied, folding my arms. "What is it, then? Come to issue another warning, or perhaps a veiled threat?"

Frederick turned to face me, his expression taut with something I couldn't quite place—anger, perhaps, but also something deeper. Resentment? Guilt? It was hard to tell.

"You think me your enemy," he said bluntly. "And perhaps I've given you every reason to think so."

"That's putting it mildly," I said dryly.

He let out a sharp breath, his gaze narrowing. "Do you think I don't see what Cedric's doing?"

The question caught me off guard, and for a moment, I said nothing.

"He's worming his way into her trust," Frederick continued, his voice low but fierce. "He's charming her, isolating her, making her question everyone who might truly help her. And when the time comes, he'll strike. He'll ruin her—and the child—for his own gain."

I studied him carefully, my skepticism warring with the truth in his words. "And you suddenly care about Evelina's well-being?"

Frederick's jaw tightened, his gaze flickering back to the fire. "You don't know me, Ravenscroft. You don't know my history with this family." He hesitated, his voice dropping lower. "I never wanted the title. The estate. Any of it. But I grew up under Lady Henrietta's thumb, and I've seen what ambition like hers can do. She used to talk about Wakefield as if it were hers—resenting Rupert for taking what she thought she deserved."

The bitterness in his tone was genuine, and for the first time, I saw a crack in his carefully constructed arrogance.

"And Cedric?" I pressed. "What's his role in all this?"

135

"Cedric," Frederick spat the name like a curse, "has always been her favorite. Her golden child. But make no mistake—he's no innocent in this. He plays the fool, the affable charmer, but he's just as ruthless as she is. And now that Rupert's gone..." He trailed off, shaking his head.

"They want the estate," I said quietly, the pieces falling into place.

"They want control," Frederick corrected, his eyes meeting mine. "Cedric has no interest in the day-to-day drudgery of managing Wakefield, but he'll happily take the power that comes with it. And Evelina is an obstacle. One that can be removed, if they play their cards right."

A chill ran through me at his words, and I felt my hands clench into fists. "Why tell me this, Frederick? You've spent weeks undermining her, questioning her at every turn. Why the sudden change?"

Frederick's expression hardened, his voice edged with frustration. "Because I see now that I was wrong. She's not the weak, simpering country girl I thought she was. She's fighting, and for that, she has my respect. But Cedric..." He trailed off, his gaze darkening. "He won't stop until he has everything."

The sincerity in his voice was unexpected, and for a moment, I allowed myself to consider the possibility that Frederick might not be the enemy I'd thought him to be. But trust was a dangerous thing, especially here.

"So what now?" I asked, my tone cautious.

Frederick straightened, his expression resolute. "Now, we work together. You want to protect Evelina, and so do I—for different reasons, perhaps, but our goals align. If we don't stop Cedric, he'll destroy her, and then he'll destroy Wakefield."

The thought of working alongside Frederick was hardly appealing, but his words carried weight. Cedric's manipulations were growing bolder, his influence over Evelina stronger with each passing day. Alone, I might not be able to counter him. But with Frederick's insight and connections...

"And what's in it for you?" I asked, narrowing my eyes.

Frederick's lips curled into a faint, humorless smile. "Let's just say I have no interest in seeing Cedric or Henrietta take what isn't theirs. My motivations are my own, Ravenscroft. But for now, we have a common enemy."

I nodded slowly, the uneasy alliance settling over me like an ill-fitting coat. "Very well. But if I so much as suspect you're playing your own game—"

"I won't," Frederick interrupted, his tone clipped. "This is bigger than either of us, Ravenscroft. And for Evelina's sake, we can't afford to fail."

As he turned to leave, the realization struck me with the force of a blow. Frederick wasn't just here to warn me about Cedric—he was here because he recognized the danger Cedric posed to his own ambitions. Cedric's growing influence over Evelina threatened not only her position but also Frederick's tenuous claim to relevance within Wakefield.

Whatever his reasons, Frederick's alliance was born of necessity, not altruism. And yet, for Evelina's sake—for the child's sake—I would take whatever advantage I could find. Cedric's web was tightening, and time was running out. If we didn't act soon, it might be too late.

Whatever my misgivings about Frederick, I couldn't ignore the urgency of the situation. For Evelina's sake—for the child's sake—I would do whatever it took to stop Cedric. Even if it meant trusting the devil I knew.

30

A Performance of Trust

The morning light filtered through the drawing room windows, illuminating the worn papers strewn across the desk. My fingers hovered over the estate ledger, the weight of its contents pressing heavier on my chest than any number ever could. Cedric stood beside me, gesturing to a proposed adjustment in the tenant leases, his voice measured and smooth.

"You see, Your Grace," he explained, tracing the figures with a gloved finger, "adjusting the terms slightly will allow for a more equitable distribution of resources while ensuring loyalty among the tenants. It's all about appearing just, even if the numbers ultimately favor the estate."

He pointed to the details, showing how the rents would increase marginally for wealthier tenants while offering modest reductions to smaller holders. "This approach," he continued, "not only ensures their gratitude but also solidifies your reputation as a fair and benevolent leader. The tenants will feel cared for, while the estate's coffers remain strong."

I nodded, furrowing my brow in feigned consideration. "You make a compelling point, Lord Cedric. I'll review it more closely before making a decision."

He smiled, his charm effortless. "Of course, Your Grace. Take all the time you need. You've shown remarkable acumen for these matters—far beyond what anyone could have expected."

The compliment, though innocuous on the surface, carried a subtle edge, one I ignored as I gestured for Mary to collect the papers. Cedric lingered a moment longer, his presence a constant reminder of the performance I'd committed to.

"Additionally," he added, "there's the matter of implementing annual lease reviews. It will give the appearance of ongoing care and involvement while allowing flexibility to make adjustments that benefit the estate further. The tenants will appreciate the attention, and any inefficiencies can be corrected incrementally."

"An interesting proposal," I replied, my tone neutral. "I'll consider it carefully."

When Cedric finally excused himself, I allowed myself a brief moment to breathe, though the weight on my chest remained. This charade was necessary—I had convinced myself of that time and time again. But every moment spent in Cedric's orbit felt like a betrayal, not just to Jeremiah but to myself.

A knock at the door pulled me from my thoughts, and before I could respond, Jeremiah stepped inside. His expression was a mixture of frustration and something deeper, something raw that made my stomach twist.

"Your Grace," he said, his tone formal but edged with urgency, "we need to talk."

I straightened, clasping my hands in front of me as if the gesture could steady me. "Of course, Lord Ravenscroft. What is it?"

Jeremiah glanced at the desk, the ledgers and notes still scattered there, before returning his gaze to me. "It's about Cedric. I've seen enough to know that his influence here is growing dangerously. He's charming, yes, but his motives are anything but noble. You must see that."

I swallowed hard, forcing myself to maintain the icy composure I had adopted so often in recent days. "I appreciate your concern, but Cedric has been nothing but helpful. His guidance has been instrumental in managing the estate."

Jeremiah's jaw tightened, his frustration evident. "You can't be serious. He's manipulating you, using your position to further his own agenda.

Whatever loyalty you think he's shown is a facade."

The words struck like arrows, each one finding its mark. But I couldn't let him see the truth—not yet. "Lord Ravenscroft," I said, my voice sharp and unwavering, "I have made my decisions with the best interests of the estate in mind. Cedric has proven himself trustworthy, and I will not allow baseless accusations to undermine his contributions."

Jeremiah's expression darkened, hurt flickering in his eyes before he masked it with a steely resolve. "If you can't see the danger, then I'll have to show you. But make no mistake, Your Grace—this is a mistake you'll regret."

I turned away, unable to meet his gaze any longer. "Thank you for your input, Jeremiah. But I'll manage this as I see fit."

His footsteps were heavy as he left, the sound echoing through the room like a judge's gavel. Once the door closed, I sank into the chair, my hands trembling as I pressed them to my temples. The effort to push him away, to drive that wedge between us, had taken more out of me than I expected.

The guilt gnawed at me like a persistent ache, the memory of Jeremiah's hurt expression searing itself into my mind. But this was the only way. If Cedric believed he had my trust, if he saw me distancing myself from Jeremiah, he might lower his guard.

Hours later, Cedric found me in the parlor, his presence as calculated as ever. "I saw Lord Ravenscroft leaving," he said lightly, settling into the chair opposite me. "He seemed...displeased. Did something happen?"

I forced a small, weary smile, feigning reluctance as I replied. "He's concerned about your involvement, suggesting I shouldn't rely on you so heavily."

Cedric's expression was a masterclass in wounded sincerity. "I'm sorry to hear that, Your Grace. I only wish to support you in whatever way I can. Lord Ravenscroft...he means well, I'm sure, but perhaps his emotions cloud his judgment."

The words were like honey dipped in poison, sweet but dangerous. I nodded, letting out a heavy sigh. "It's been difficult, balancing everything. I appreciate your support more than I can say."

Cedric reached for my hand, his touch gentle but deliberate. "You are not alone in this, Your Grace. Together, we will protect your child and your legacy."

His words, though crafted to reassure, sent a shiver down my spine. I pulled my hand away under the guise of reaching for my teacup, avoiding his gaze.

That night, as I lay awake in my chambers, the silence pressed heavy around me. The distance between Jeremiah and me felt unbearable, a chasm I wasn't sure I could bridge once this was over. And Cedric's hold on the estate, on the staff, on me—it tightened with every passing day.

But the most crushing weight of all was the knowledge that I was walking this path alone, my actions alienating the one person who might truly understand the battle I was fighting. The cost of my deception loomed larger with each passing moment, and I could only hope it wouldn't destroy me entirely.

31

The Serpent's Smile

Cedric's voice rang out in the drawing room, a smooth cadence that commanded attention without effort. He stood beside me, gesturing to the plans laid out on the desk—a blueprint of Wakefield's future, or so he called it. The staff hovered nearby, nodding in deference as he outlined his grand vision for the estate.

"Your Grace," Cedric began, offering one of his practiced smiles, "your foresight in granting me the opportunity to assist has been most fortuitous. Under your enlightened leadership, Wakefield is poised to enter a new era of prosperity."

He pointed to specific areas on the map, his finger tracing a pathway to what he called "progress." The construction of a new guest wing, the restructuring of the stables, and a larger, more secure granary were just a few of the initiatives he proposed.

"Imagine, Your Grace," he continued, "the estate not only thriving but becoming the envy of every household in the county. We will modernize Wakefield while preserving its heritage. The staff morale will soar, the villagers will benefit from increased trade, and you, of course, will be celebrated as the visionary behind it all."

I nodded, meeting his smile with one of my own, though it felt as hollow as the promises behind his words. Cedric's schemes were wrapped in charm and flattery, but his ambitions had always carried a weight of self-interest.

"You paint a compelling picture, Lord Harland," I said evenly, allowing the title to linger with an edge of detachment. "Your expertise in these matters has been invaluable."

Across the room, Jeremiah stood stiffly by the window, his arms crossed tightly over his chest. His expression was a stark contrast to Cedric's polished demeanor. The sharp lines of his jaw and the dark fire in his eyes betrayed his growing frustration. He had said little since the meeting began, but his silence was louder than any words.

"Perhaps," Jeremiah said now, his voice deliberate and controlled, "it would be wise to consider the long-term implications of such rapid changes. Stability, after all, is paramount in a time of transition."

Cedric turned toward him, his brow arched in polite curiosity. "Are you implying, Lord Ravenscroft, that these improvements pose a risk? I assure you, every decision I've proposed is calculated to benefit Her Grace and the estate."

Jeremiah's gaze didn't waver. "Calculated they may be, but sudden shifts can expose vulnerabilities. Progress isn't worth the cost of security."

Cedric's smile tightened. "And yet, Her Grace has trusted me to oversee these changes. Surely, we should respect her wisdom in choosing the best course for Wakefield." He turned to me, his expression softening. "Your Grace, you have shown remarkable leadership in navigating these challenges. Together, we are ensuring Wakefield's future remains bright."

"Thank you, Lord Harland," I said, my voice steady as I glanced at Jeremiah. "Your insights have indeed been invaluable."

Jeremiah's jaw tightened, and I saw the conflict flicker in his eyes. "As you wish, Your Grace," he said curtly, stepping away from the window.

Cedric turned his attention back to the plans. "The expansion of the granary will ensure that the estate is self-sufficient for years to come," he explained. "Furthermore, the guest wing will allow Wakefield to host influential gatherings, strengthening its position among the nobility. Visibility is key, Your Grace, and Wakefield must adapt to remain relevant."

I nodded, though his words settled uneasily within me. "You have clearly thought this through, Lord Harland. And the staff?"

"Morale will only improve," Cedric assured me. "I propose establishing additional roles to oversee these changes—new responsibilities that will elevate their sense of purpose. With time, loyalty to you will deepen."

Across the room, Jeremiah made a sound low in his throat, though he remained silent. His disapproval was palpable, and though I didn't meet his gaze, I could feel the weight of his judgment.

That evening, I sat alone in my chambers, the plans Cedric had presented spread out before me. My hands rested on my belly, now more rounded and heavy with the child I carried. The effort of the day had left me exhausted, my breath coming slower, and a dull ache settling in my back.

Mary entered quietly, carrying a tray of tea. Her sharp eyes immediately took in my weariness, and her brow furrowed in concern. "Your Grace," she said softly, "you've been working late again. You need to rest. This pregnancy has already made you faint once; I'm worried it might happen again if you push yourself too hard. Please, at least take some chamomile to ease your mind."

I offered her a faint smile, though her words struck deeper than I let on. "Thank you, Mary. The estate's future requires careful thought," I said, trying to sound resolute, but the fatigue in my voice betrayed me.

Her brow furrowed slightly, and she hesitated before speaking again. "If I may, Your Grace...Lord Ravenscroft seemed troubled earlier. He's always had your best interests at heart."

I looked away, her words striking a chord I couldn't ignore. "Jeremiah's advice is always valued," I said carefully. "But Lord Harland's contributions have been significant as well."

Mary pursed her lips, clearly wanting to say more, but she nodded and left me to my thoughts. I sipped the tea, staring out the window as the gardens below swayed in the breeze.

Jeremiah's warnings replayed in my mind, each one layered with a conviction that Cedric's charm masked something far darker. Yet Cedric's plans were practical, even visionary. The balance between trust and suspicion weighed heavily on my shoulders.

For now, I had to play this game carefully. Cedric's influence needed to remain unchecked, at least publicly, until I could understand his true motives. Jeremiah's distance was painful, but necessary. The cost of failure was far greater than the discomfort of my doubts.

With a sigh, I closed the plans and extinguished the lamp. Tomorrow would bring another day of decisions, and I needed every ounce of strength to navigate the serpents coiled around me.

32

A Whisper of Danger

The gardens at Wakefield had always been my sanctuary, a refuge from the weight of titles and the ever-present whispers that shadowed my every step. This morning, however, even the vibrant blooms seemed subdued, their colors muted beneath the overcast sky. The crisp air carried the faintest hint of rain, and I strolled along the gravel path, my thoughts swirling like the restless wind. Rumors, the growing unease within the household, and my fragile trust in those around me pressed heavily on my mind.

The soft scrape of stone reached my ears, subtle but distinct. I paused, glancing around the gardens before instinctively looking upward. On the balcony above, a terracotta pot teetered on the edge, its weight shifting as though pulled by an invisible force. For a moment, time slowed, and I stood frozen as its descent began.

A sudden grip yanked me backward, strong and unyielding. The pot shattered against the gravel where I had stood, shards scattering like jagged teeth across the path.

"Your Grace!" Frederick's voice rang out, sharp with panic. His arm steadied me, his fingers still firm on my elbow. "Are you hurt?"

I stiffened at the sound of his voice, the shock of his touch making the moment even more surreal. We had never been close—far from it, in fact. His relentless criticism and calculated barbs had often made me feel more like a rival than an ally. Yet now, his concern seemed genuine, and it left me unsettled.

My breath came in shallow gasps, and I instinctively placed a hand on my abdomen. The life within me was safe, but my heart raced uncontrollably. "I think I...I'm all right," I managed, though my voice trembled.

Frederick's expression was a mixture of fury and concern as he glanced upward toward the balcony. A shadow moved briefly, its presence unmistakable.

"Stay here, Your Grace!" he ordered, his tone brooking no argument.

Before I could protest, he strode purposefully toward the house, his figure disappearing through the doorway. My legs felt weak, and I sank onto a nearby bench, the shattered pot's fragments a stark reminder of what could have been. Someone had tried to harm me.

The minutes stretched endlessly until Frederick returned, his jaw tight and his expression grim. "The servant responsible for the balcony..." he began, his voice clipped, "was recently hired. On Cedric's recommendation."

The name hit like a blow. "Lord Harland? Are you certain?"

Frederick nodded, his frustration barely contained. "I intend to confront him immediately."

The thought of Frederick storming into Cedric's chambers filled me with dread, but it also stirred something else—suspicion. Why was he suddenly so invested in my safety? We had always been at odds, our relationship defined by barbs and calculated slights. His uncharacteristic concern felt almost unnatural, and it set my nerves on edge.

"Wait," I pleaded. "We don't know for certain. It could have been an accident—"

"An accident?" Frederick interrupted, his voice rising. "Your Grace, that pot was placed deliberately. If I hadn't pulled you back—"

He stopped abruptly, running a hand through his hair in an effort to temper his anger. "This isn't coincidence. Someone wants you out of the way, and Cedric is involved."

I wanted to believe him. The fear in my chest told me he was right, yet the image of Cedric's affable demeanor and his easy charm made me hesitate.

"He's been nothing but kind to me," I said softly, though the words felt hollow even as I spoke them.

Frederick's eyes narrowed, his tone turning sharp. "That's precisely why he's dangerous, Your Grace. He hides his true intentions behind a mask of civility. Don't let him fool you."

I pressed my hands together, willing the tremor in them to subside. The awkwardness between us lingered in the air like an unspoken accusation, and I found it difficult to meet his gaze. His actions seemed too sudden, too convenient, and my mistrust refused to fade. "Let me speak to him first. I need to hear his side."

Frederick's expression darkened, but he said nothing, the set of his jaw revealing his displeasure. Before I could say more, a voice interrupted us.

"Is everything all right?"

Cedric's voice was smooth as always, though his gaze was sharper than usual as he approached. His posture exuded casual confidence, but his eyes took in the scene with precision. He stopped a few paces away, his gaze flicking to the shards of terracotta at my feet before shifting back to me. "Your Grace, you look pale. Are you hurt?"

I hesitated, glancing toward Frederick, whose glare was cold enough to freeze the very air. "I'm fine," I said, injecting as much firmness into my voice as I could muster.

Cedric's brow furrowed, and he stepped closer. "What happened?"

Frederick answered before I could. "A flower pot fell from the balcony, nearly striking Her Grace. The servant responsible was hired on your recommendation."

For a moment, Cedric's expression remained unreadable before he let out a soft laugh, devoid of humor. "Surely you're not accusing me of orchestrating this?"

Frederick's tone turned glacial. "I'm stating facts. Make of them what you will."

Cedric's eyes narrowed, his calm demeanor giving way to a simmering anger. "How convenient for you, Frederick," he said, his voice dripping with suspicion. "You appear out of nowhere, in the garden without any apparent reason, just in time to save Her Grace. And now you stand here, accusing me? Perhaps we should question your motives instead."

Frederick stiffened, his glare intensifying. "You're deflecting, as always. Typical of someone with something to hide."

Cedric raised his hands in a placating gesture, though his tone was laced with condescension. "Frederick, I understand your concern, but this is absurd. The servant seemed competent, and I recommended him in good faith. To suggest anything else is insulting. If anyone's actions seem questionable here, it's yours."

The ease with which he deflected made my stomach churn. "Cedric," I said, my voice quieter now, "you must admit it looks suspicious."

His gaze softened as he turned to me, his expression open and almost wounded. "Your Grace, I would never do anything to harm you. Surely you know that. I care deeply about your safety."

Frederick let out a derisive snort. "Convenient words from someone whose recommendations lead to near-disasters."

Cedric's expression hardened as he faced Frederick. "Perhaps your time would be better spent addressing the whispers about your own actions rather than inventing conspiracies about mine."

The tension crackled between them, sharp and unrelenting. Their animosity was a storm brewing in the air, and I felt trapped between their opposing forces.

"Enough," I said firmly, cutting through the hostility. Both men turned to me, their eyes wary. "Lord Frederick, I appreciate your concern, but I don't want this to escalate further."

Frederick's jaw tightened, but he inclined his head. "As you wish, Your Grace."

Cedric stepped closer, his tone soft and soothing. "You've been through enough, Your Grace. Rest now. Let me handle this matter quietly."

I nodded, exhaustion washing over me like a tide. "Thank you, Lord Harland."

Frederick said nothing, though his disapproval radiated from him. As Cedric led me back toward the house, I glanced over my shoulder, meeting

Frederick's gaze one last time. There was something in his eyes—an urgency, a warning—but I turned away, unwilling to confront it.

33

The Whispered Trap

The shadows of Wakefield felt heavier than ever, as though the estate itself mirrored the tension winding through its walls. I stood by the drawing-room window, my gaze fixed on the fading sunlight that painted the gardens in hues of gold and crimson. Somewhere out there, Evelina was likely walking with Cedric, her hand resting lightly on his arm as though he were her closest confidant.

The image was one I could scarcely bear to imagine, let alone witness.

I turned away from the window, pacing the length of the room as frustration gnawed at me. Cedric's presence felt like a tightening noose around the estate, his influence seeping further with every passing day. Evelina—damn her stubbornness—seemed blind to his machinations. Or was she?

That question had haunted me ever since Evelina pushed me away. Her demeanor had changed abruptly after that evening in the garden, the night I had been reckless. The kiss I had stolen lingered in my mind like an echo, both a torment and a balm. It had been a moment of weakness, a betrayal of the boundaries I had sworn to uphold. Yet it had also been honest, a reflection of the care I bore for her, a care I could no longer suppress.

"You've done enough, Jeremiah," she'd said the next morning, her voice colder than I'd ever known it to be. "Cedric understands the estate's needs. I trust him to guide me."

Those words had cut deeper than any blade, leaving me questioning everything—her trust in Cedric, her dismissal of me, and most painfully, the possibility that my actions had driven her into his arms. Had I been too forward, too careless? Did she see me as another threat, no better than the men she sought to protect herself and her child from?

The door creaked open behind me, breaking my thoughts. I turned to see Mary, Evelina's maid, hovering hesitantly in the doorway. Her usually composed demeanor was replaced by unease, her hands wringing as her gaze darted nervously around the room.

"Lord Ravenscroft," she began in a low voice. "May I have a word?"

"Of course." I gestured for her to enter, watching as she closed the door softly behind her. The way she glanced over her shoulder sent a chill down my spine.

Mary stepped closer, her voice dropping to a whisper. "It's about His Grace—about Lord Cedric, I mean. There are things happening, my lord, things I can't explain. And Her Grace... she's not herself."

I stiffened, my frustration sharpening into a focused edge. "What things, Mary? What's going on?"

She hesitated, her hands trembling. "It's small things, at first glance. Staff being replaced or reassigned without notice. Rooms locked or opened at odd hours. And Lord Cedric... he's always there, whispering in Her Grace's ear. She... she trusts him implicitly now. Too much, if you ask me."

Her words struck a chord of both dread and vindication. Cedric wasn't merely insinuating himself into the estate; he was tightening his grip, weaving a web designed to isolate Evelina and control everything around her.

"Why haven't you brought this to Evelina's attention?" I asked, though I suspected the answer.

Mary's face crumpled with frustration. "I've tried, my lord. She won't hear it. She says Lord Cedric's actions are for the good of the estate. And now..." She faltered, her voice breaking.

"Now what?" I pressed, my patience thinning.

"There have been accidents, my lord," Mary whispered. "Dangerous ones. Her Grace and her child have been at risk more times than I can count.

The falling pots in the garden—that wasn't the first time. The horse that disengaged itself during a ride, nearly throwing her. The carriage whose wheels suddenly broke apart, leaving her stranded. Even the stairs in the carriage... they weren't installed properly. If one of us hadn't checked them, Her Grace could have slipped. Imagine a fall like that for a woman in her condition."

My blood ran cold as she listed each incident, her words painting a chilling picture of Cedric's calculated schemes. Evelina's life, and the life of her unborn child, hung precariously in the balance, and Cedric seemed to have orchestrated every subtle attack with ruthless precision.

"Yesterday, one of the footmen said something—a comment about Lord Cedric. By evening, he was gone. No warning, no explanation. Just... gone."

My jaw tightened, fury rising at Cedric's audacity. He wasn't just maneuvering for power; he was silencing dissent, eroding Evelina's support from within.

"Thank you for telling me, Mary," I said, my voice steady despite the storm brewing inside me. "You've done the right thing."

Mary nodded, though her worry remained etched in her features. "Please, my lord," she whispered. "Do something. Her Grace needs someone she can trust."

Her words echoed in my mind long after she slipped out of the room. Trust. That was the crux of it, wasn't it? Evelina no longer trusted me, and without that trust, my ability to protect her was limited.

I returned to the window, staring out into the darkening gardens. Cedric's game was becoming clearer, but his endgame remained elusive. Did he want control of the estate? The child's inheritance? Or something more insidious?

As I stood there, my thoughts circled back to that night in the garden. My reckless kiss had fractured something between Evelina and me, and perhaps Cedric had seized upon that rift to wedge himself further into her confidence. Yet, I couldn't regret my actions entirely. That kiss had been more than a moment of passion; it had been a declaration, however poorly timed, of the depths of my care for her.

Could Evelina's distance be her way of protecting herself? Or had my mistake convinced her I was no different from the threats she sought to guard against?

I clenched my fists, vowing to uncover Cedric's true intentions. I could not afford to fail, not when Evelina's future—and that of her child—hung in the balance. Whether she trusted me or not, I would protect her, even if it meant working from the shadows.

As the moonlight spilled over the estate, I made my decision. Cedric's schemes would not stand. And Evelina... she would see the truth, even if it cost me everything. For her sake—and the future of Wakefield—I could not afford to fail.

"For her," I murmured to the empty room. "For the child. For Wakefield. I won't let them fall."

34

A Shadow's Vigil

The morning air was crisp, laden with the earthy scent of damp leaves. I had spent hours tucked among the trees at the edge of Wakefield's grounds, my horse tethered nearby, its rhythmic grazing the only sound breaking the quiet. From my concealed vantage point, the estate sprawled before me like a serene painting, its deceptive calm masking the turbulence that brewed within. Servants moved briskly about their duties, their subdued chatter carrying the weight of unspoken tension.

I had thought my departure would extinguish the flames of gossip. Instead, it had fanned them. The whispers had evolved, twisting into cruel accusations: that I had abandoned Evelina, leaving her and her child to fend for themselves. Even the rogue Viscount Ravenscroft, they said, had his limits.

The reins in my hand creaked as my grip tightened. Words could be weapons, and these were aimed with precision. They weren't just meant to discredit me but to isolate Evelina further, eroding her standing until she was defenseless. And in the void my absence created, Cedric Harland had stepped in, his polished veneer hiding motives I did not trust.

"Too perfect by half," I muttered under my breath, my gaze sweeping the estate. Cedric's seamless charm and timely interventions had never sat well with me. Men like him didn't act without an agenda, and his recent actions were far too convenient to be altruistic.

A faint rustle behind me shattered my thoughts. My hand instinctively moved to the hilt of my knife as I turned, muscles taut. Relief washed over me when I saw Mary emerge from the shadows, her movements careful and deliberate. She had become an invaluable ally, her loyalty unwavering despite the risks she faced.

"Lord Ravenscroft," she whispered, her voice low and cautious. Her eyes darted toward the estate as though the walls themselves had ears. "I've brought news."

I gestured for her to come closer, my pulse quickening. "What is it?"

She extended a folded letter, her hands trembling. "I found this in Lord Harland's study. He left it out on his desk. It's... troubling, my lord."

Taking the letter, I unfolded it carefully, my eyes scanning the elegant script. The correspondence was addressed to a solicitor in London, requesting a "review and reassessment" of the recent additions to Wakefield's holdings. On the surface, it seemed benign, even helpful. But the undertone was unmistakable: Cedric was undermining Evelina's authority, positioning himself as the estate's savior while casting doubt on her competence.

"He's setting her up," I muttered, anger flaring as I reread the letter. "He's planting seeds of distrust, making it appear as though she can't manage the estate."

Mary's expression was grim. "It's worse than that, my lord. He's been meeting with the staff—the newer hires especially. They act differently, like they answer to him, not Her Grace."

A cold knot formed in my stomach. Cedric wasn't merely maneuvering for influence; he was building a network within the estate, a web designed to ensnare Evelina completely.

"I won't let this stand," I said, folding the letter and slipping it into my coat. My mind raced with possibilities, each one more precarious than the last.

Mary hesitated, her brow furrowing. "What will you do, my lord? If you confront him outright, he'll twist it to his advantage. And Her Grace... she might not believe you."

Her words struck a nerve. Evelina's request for me to leave had been born of a desire to quell the rumors, to protect her child and the estate. But my absence had given Cedric the space to tighten his grip.

"She doesn't trust me right now," I admitted, the confession heavy in my chest. "But I won't let him destroy her or what she's built."

Mary's voice dropped even lower. "There's more. The staff say Lord Harland's been... charming Her Grace, advising her on estate matters. Some believe he's positioning himself for more than just control."

"Positioning himself?" The words tasted bitter. "For what? Influence over the estate? Over the child?"

Mary's silence was answer enough, her downcast gaze speaking volumes.

I exhaled slowly, suppressing the fury that threatened to boil over. "Thank you, Mary. You've done more than enough."

She nodded, though her worry was evident. "Just... be careful, my lord. Lord Cedric's dangerous, even if he hides it well."

"Don't worry about me," I said, my tone softening. "Men like Cedric underestimate people like me. That's their first mistake."

As she disappeared back into the trees, I turned my gaze once more to the estate. Cedric's machinations were cunning, but he had underestimated one crucial thing: I wasn't just a rogue or a soldier. I was a strategist, and I knew how to dismantle a plan from within.

I retrieved the letter, studying it with renewed focus. The solicitor's name leapt out at me, sparking an idea. If I could intercept their correspondence, I might uncover something irrefutably damning—evidence that would shatter Cedric's facade.

But for now, I faced a decision. I could take the letter to Evelina, risking her mistrust in the hope she would see the truth. Or I could remain in the shadows, unraveling Cedric's schemes until I had enough to expose him fully.

The latter was safer, but it left Evelina vulnerable. Alone in that house, surrounded by enemies disguised as allies, she couldn't hold them off indefinitely. She was strong, yes, but even the strongest needed someone to guard their back.

The estate's stillness belied the battles yet to come. I lingered a moment longer, letting the weight of my choice settle over me. Then I murmured, "Soon, Evelina. I'll find a way to end this. And Cedric will regret the day he ever tried to take what's yours."

With that, I mounted my horse, vanishing into the shadows once more. Protecting her from the dark was a duty I would carry—even if she never knew.

35

The Blindfolded Duchess

Wakefield's halls were unnervingly quiet as I was led toward Evelina's drawing room. The footman avoided my eyes, his shoulders hunched as though reluctant to play his part in facilitating my visit. Cedric's presence weighed heavily here, his influence palpable in every carefully placed glance and measured word among the staff.

The letter burned in my pocket—a damning piece of evidence I hoped would pierce through the veneer of Cedric's polished facade. Yet as I neared Evelina's door, doubt crept in. Would she even listen?

The footman knocked lightly, and her familiar voice called out from within, "Enter."

I stepped inside, my gaze immediately finding her seated near the window, a delicate teacup in her hands. The soft light framed her in a way that made her seem almost ethereal, a fragile figure cloaked in layers of composure and quiet strength. But even from across the room, I could see the weariness in her eyes, the subtle slump in her shoulders.

"Jeremiah," she greeted, her tone caught between surprise and something harder to place. "I wasn't expecting you."

I inclined my head, choosing my words carefully. "Your Grace, I apologize for coming unannounced, but I've come across something I felt you needed to see."

She set her cup down, her fingers brushing her lap as she gestured for me to sit. I hesitated, the weight of what I carried pressing against my chest, before stepping closer and retrieving the folded letter from my coat.

"This was found in Cedric's study," I said, handing it to her. "It's addressed to a solicitor in London."

Her brow furrowed as she unfolded the letter, her eyes scanning the elegant script. Then she looked up sharply, suspicion flaring in her gaze. "Jeremiah, how did you get this? Were you in Cedric's study?"

I met her eyes steadily, carefully measuring my words. "No, Your Grace. It was given to me by someone who has grown increasingly concerned about Cedric's actions. They thought it was important that you see it."

Her expression softened slightly, though a hint of doubt lingered. "I see," she murmured, glancing back at the letter. "And this person, do they have a name?"

"For their safety, I think it's best I not say," I replied smoothly. "But I can assure you, their only concern is for you and the well-being of Wakefield."

When she finished reading, she folded the letter neatly and placed it on the table beside her. Her expression remained calm, almost maddeningly so.

"Jeremiah," she began, her tone measured, "I appreciate your concern, but I think you've misunderstood Cedric's intentions."

Her words struck me like a physical blow, my chest tightening as frustration surged. "Misunderstood?" I repeated, keeping my voice low but firm. "Your Grace, he's positioning himself to undermine you. This letter is proof of that."

She shook her head, a faint sigh escaping her lips. "I don't see it that way. Cedric has been nothing but supportive since I fell ill. He's taken on responsibilities that I couldn't manage while I've been confined to rest. Everything he's done has been for Wakefield."

"Supportive?" I couldn't help the edge creeping into my voice. "But He's charming the staff, meeting with solicitors behind your back, and laying the groundwork to paint you as incapable. How is that supportive?"

Her eyes hardened, a flicker of something defensive flashing across her face. "You're seeing shadows where there are none, Jeremiah. Cedric is ensuring that Wakefield remains stable. I asked him to step in while I recovered, and he's done exactly that."

I stared at her, disbelief coursing through me. How could she not see it? The evidence was right there, tangible and damning, and yet she dismissed it as if it were nothing more than paranoia on my part.

"Your Grace," I said carefully, trying to temper the frustration in my voice, "I'm not asking you to accuse him outright. All I'm asking is that you remain vigilant. Cedric is calculating—he wouldn't make his moves so openly if he didn't think he could manipulate the narrative."

Her expression softened slightly, but the tension between us remained. "Jeremiah," she said quietly, "I know you mean well. I know you're trying to protect me. But Cedric has given me no reason to doubt his loyalty."

I wanted to speak then—to tell her of the dangerous incidents that had plagued her, the falling pots, the faulty carriage wheels, the horse that disengaged itself, and the improperly installed steps that could have led to a devastating fall. But the guarded look in her eyes stopped me. Evelina wouldn't listen. Not now. Not while Cedric's influence shielded him from her scrutiny.

A bitter taste filled my mouth, and I forced myself to swallow the sharp retort threatening to spill out. "I only hope you're right," I said instead, my voice tinged with resignation. "But please, for your sake—and the child's— don't trust anyone too easily."

Her hand moved instinctively to her stomach, her fingers brushing over the gentle curve that seemed more pronounced now. The sight sent a pang through me, a reminder of everything at stake.

"I'll be careful," she said, her tone soft but dismissive. "Thank you for bringing this to my attention, Jeremiah."

The conversation was over. She had drawn the line, and I knew pushing further would only widen the rift between us. Rising from my seat, I gave her a curt nod, the weight of unspoken words pressing heavily against my chest.

As I turned to leave, I paused at the door, glancing back at her. She had picked up the letter again, her brow furrowing slightly as she studied it. A flicker of hope stirred within me—perhaps she would see reason after all.

"Your Grace," I said softly, my voice barely above a whisper. "Be careful."

She didn't look up, her attention fixed on the letter. "I will," she murmured.

The door closed behind me, and I stood in the hallway for a moment, my fists clenched at my sides. Evelina's trust in Cedric was blinding her, but I couldn't abandon her now—not when the storm was closing in.

As I walked away from the drawing room, my resolve hardened. If she wouldn't see the danger Cedric posed, I would have to find a way to expose him myself. Even if it meant working in the shadows, even if it meant standing alone—I would protect Evelina and her child, no matter the cost.

36

The Truth Beneath the Lie

I took another long swig of whisky, the burn tracing a familiar path down my throat as I stared into the low flicker of the hearth. The flames seemed to dance with mocking clarity, their movements an echo of the chaos swirling in my mind. My hair was a tangled mess from restless hands running through it, and the tension in my shoulders had knotted into a dull, unrelenting ache.

Evelina's distance gnawed at me, a sharp reminder of how easily the ground could shift beneath my feet. At first, I thought it might have been the kiss— that reckless, impulsive moment in the garden. But no. Evelina wasn't one to cower in the face of vulnerability, even her own. If anything, she'd likely write it off as a passing folly, a distraction amidst the storm of responsibilities she bore.

And yet, she had sent me away.

Why?

The question dug into me like a thorn I couldn't remove. Evelina knew— she knew—that Lady Henrietta was behind the poisoning, and she was fully aware of Cedric's machinations. How could she trust him, much less allow him so close, let alone push me away as if I were the outsider?

I reached for the whisky again, my fingers tightening around the glass as frustration surged. Nothing about her behavior made sense. She wasn't careless. She wasn't blind. Evelina was shrewd in her own quiet way, and she knew how to read people. Trusting Cedric completely? Dismissing me at his suggestion? None of it fit.

The memory of her words echoed in my mind. "I need you to leave, Jeremiah. It's best for both of us." The way she'd said it, the deliberate weight in her voice, had been wrong somehow. Forced. Controlled. As I handed her the letter found in Cedric's room—the one sent to the solicitor requesting a "review and reassessment" of Wakefield's recent holdings—I couldn't help but notice the way Evelina's gaze flicked around the room. It was subtle, the occasional turn of her head, the faintest narrowing of her eyes as if she were scanning for unseen threats. Her fingers brushed mine briefly when she took the letter, but her focus was elsewhere, her unease radiating in waves I could almost feel. What was she looking for? Or... who?

I swirled the whisky in my glass, watching the amber liquid catch the firelight. Slowly, like a puzzle falling into place, the scattered pieces began to connect.

Evelina wasn't obeying Cedric.

She was playing him.

The realization hit me like a bolt, sharp and electrifying. Frederick had stopped aligning himself with Lady Henrietta shortly after Cedric became Evelina's "confidant." Evelina had seen through Lady Henrietta's schemes before—had even whispered to me once about the subtle battle lines drawn within the estate.

And now she had seemingly welcomed Cedric into her trust, despite knowing the danger he posed.

What a fool I'd been.

The glass in my hand trembled as I set it down on the table, my pulse quickening. Evelina wasn't some naive woman taken in by Cedric's charm. She was deceiving him, drawing him into a web of her own making. She was playing a dangerous game, and I'd failed to see it for what it was.

I leaned back in the chair, exhaling sharply as the truth settled over me. Evelina was smarter than any of us had given her credit for—smarter than I had given her credit for. She'd orchestrated this entire charade, sacrificing her reputation and even our tenuous partnership to set Cedric up for the fall.

And here I was, sulking like a fool, blind to her strategy.

But even as understanding dawned, a fresh wave of unease rose to meet it. Evelina was walking a razor-thin line, and Cedric wasn't a man to underestimate. His charm was a weapon as much as his cunning was. If he realized Evelina's true intentions before she had the chance to expose him...

I stood abruptly, the chair scraping against the floor as I moved. I couldn't sit idly by while Evelina waged this war alone. Whether or not she'd intended to push me away for the sake of her ruse, I wasn't about to let her carry the weight of it without support.

But I couldn't charge in, either. If Cedric suspected that I'd seen through his act, he'd tighten his grip on her—and the estate. No, I'd have to be careful, deliberate.

I moved to the small desk in the corner of the room, pulling out a sheet of paper. My handwriting was sharp and precise as I drafted a letter to an old contact—a man whose loyalty could be counted on in situations like these. If Evelina's plan was to expose Cedric, then she'd need more than her word against his. She'd need incontrovertible proof, evidence that could silence even the most vicious tongues in the ton.

As I wrote, my mind returned to Evelina—her face as she stood in the library, her hand unconsciously rubbing her stomach, her expression caught between determination and exhaustion. I'd noticed then, as I had every time we were together, how her belly had grown since we first met. She was no longer just a duchess carrying a title or a widow mourning her husband.

She was a mother.

And with that realization came a sudden, wild thought—one that I'd tried to bury but which now surfaced with startling clarity.

If that child were mine, I would never let her endure this.

The thought startled me, its intensity cutting through the haze of whisky and weariness. It was absurd, of course. The child was Rupert's, and I was just a viscount with a questionable lineage, a man whose name often walked the fine line between respect and scandal.

But the thought lingered, unwelcome and undeniable.

Because somewhere, deep in the recesses of my heart, I knew that my concern for Evelina had grown into something more. Something I couldn't afford to feel.

I set the pen down, folding the letter carefully before sealing it. There would be time later to sort through the mess of emotions churning within me. For now, my focus had to be on Evelina and the storm she was walking into.

With her courage and my cunning, we'd see this through. And if Cedric thought he could play the puppeteer with her life, he was about to learn the cost of underestimating those who refused to be his pawns.

37

The Resolve

Wakefield loomed before me, its grand facade cloaked in the muted light of the overcast sky. The estate was as imposing as ever, its walls steeped in the weight of its legacy. The towering windows glinted faintly, like silent sentinels guarding secrets too dark to reveal. What once filled me with a sense of duty now stirred something closer to dread. Evelina's plan—whatever shape it had taken—was in motion, and Cedric's grip was tightening around her.

The rhythmic thud of my horse's hooves against the gravel driveway punctuated the uneasy silence that hung over the grounds. Even the usually cheerful sparrows flitting in the hedgerows seemed muted, their chirps drowned by an air of quiet unease. The servants at the entrance regarded me with cautious expressions, their polite nods unable to mask the wariness in their eyes. Something had shifted here—an undercurrent of tension as sharp as a blade.

I dismounted, handing the reins to a young footman who approached with visible hesitation. His stiff posture and darting eyes told me all I needed to know.

"Lord Ravenscroft," he said, his tone strained. "The Duchess is resting. Lord Cedric has instructed that no visitors be admitted without his consent."

I resisted the urge to scoff. Cedric's audacity knew no bounds, but to use Evelina's health as a barrier against me? That was a new low, even for him.

My jaw tightened as I regarded the footman.

"Rest assured," I replied coolly, my voice steady but sharp, "the Duchess will determine whether she receives visitors—not Lord Harland."

The footman hesitated, glancing nervously toward the corridor as though expecting Cedric to appear at any moment. "If you'll wait in the hall, my lord, I'll inform Lord Cedric of your arrival."

"Do that," I said, my irritation barely concealed.

Stepping inside, the familiar scent of polished wood and faint floral arrangements greeted me, but beneath it lingered something heavier— a tension that wrapped around the walls and crept through the air. The grandeur of the entryway felt hollow, its beauty unable to mask the rot festering beneath the surface.

I didn't have to wait long. Cedric appeared with his usual calculated precision, his strides measured and his expression exuding self-satisfied control. Dressed impeccably, his polished boots clicked against the marble floor, each step deliberate. His charm was a weapon, sharpened to a fine edge, and every detail of his appearance was tailored to disarm.

"Lord Ravenscroft," he said smoothly, his tone as insincere as the smile curling his lips. "What a...persistent visitor you are."

"Lord Harland," I replied, matching his tone with a measured calm. "It's always a pleasure to see you."

He ignored the jab, crossing his arms as he regarded me with mock patience. "I trust you're here for another futile attempt to see the Duchess? I've told you before—her health is delicate, and we cannot risk undue stress. Surely even you understand the importance of her rest."

"Spare me the pretense of concern," I said, stepping closer, my voice low and firm. "I'm here to see Her Grace."

His smile tightened, his eyes narrowing as a flicker of irritation broke through his polished facade. "I've tolerated your comings and goings out of respect for the late Duke, but my patience is wearing thin. Perhaps it's time you returned to your own estate, Viscount. Wakefield is no place for an outsider."

The word "outsider" was a deliberate barb, meant to remind me of my precarious position—a viscount with a reputation for scandal and whispers surrounding my lineage. But I didn't flinch. His games no longer held power over me.

"Let's be clear, Lord Harland," I said evenly, my gaze locked onto his. "I don't need your permission to see Her Grace. She's the Duchess of Wakefield—the one with actual authority here. If she decides she doesn't wish to see me, I'll leave. Until then, your opinions are irrelevant."

His jaw tightened further, a faint tic betraying his irritation. "And if the Duchess decides she's better off without your meddling?"

"Then I'll hear it from her lips, not yours."

The tension between us crackled, a silent battle waged in the space of a few breaths. For a moment, it seemed he might escalate the confrontation, but then he stepped back, his smile returning—a sharp, predatory thing that did little to conceal the venom beneath.

"As you wish," he said with a slight bow, his voice dripping with false civility. "But don't say I didn't warn you."

He turned, gesturing for the footman to lead me upstairs. As I climbed the grand staircase, Cedric's parting words lingered in my mind, their ominous tone a mixture of warning and threat.

The higher I ascended, the more the air seemed to shift. The grandeur of the estate felt oppressive, the weight of its history pressing down on me. Yet with each step, my resolve hardened. Evelina needed me—even if she wouldn't admit it outright, even if she'd tried to push me away. Whatever Cedric was plotting, I would uncover it. And I would protect her, no matter the cost.

38

An Act of Defiance

The library was quiet, the air thick with the scent of aged paper and candle wax. My desk, once a place of order, was now a battlefield of chaos. Ledgers, estate records, and correspondence lay scattered across its surface, their contents revealing more questions than answers. My head throbbed as I tried to make sense of the mounting irregularities. Numbers that didn't add up. Payments I hadn't authorized. Purchases that didn't seem to exist.

I pressed my fingertips to my temples, willing the ache behind my eyes to subside. The estate wasn't just struggling—it was hemorrhaging, and I was no closer to finding the cause. Worse, I was alone in this fight, having pushed away the one person whose insight I desperately needed.

Jeremiah.

A soft knock at the door startled me, and before I could answer, the door creaked open. I straightened in my chair, my heart lurching as his familiar silhouette filled the doorway.

"Jeremiah," I said, more sharply than I intended. "What are you doing here?"

He stepped inside, closing the door behind him with a quiet click. "We need to talk," he said, his tone low but firm.

"I thought I made myself clear," I replied, my voice laced with weariness. "I don't need your help."

He arched an eyebrow, crossing the room in measured strides. His presence was as commanding as ever, a steady force that refused to be ignored. "You don't need my help?" he repeated, his voice edged with incredulity. "Because from where I stand, Evelina, it looks like you're drowning."

I bristled at his bluntness, my pride prickling. "How dare you—"

"How dare I care?" he interrupted, his voice rising before he reined it back in. "Evelina, I know why you pushed me away. But let me ask you something. Did you think I wouldn't see it? That I wouldn't figure out what you've been doing?"

His words cut through my defenses, and I stiffened, my fingers curling over the armrests of the chair. "What are you talking about?" I asked, though my voice betrayed my unease.

He stepped closer, his piercing gaze fixed on me. "The plan," he said simply. "The lies. Evelina, I need to hear it from you. Did you orchestrate all of this to frame Cedric?"

I faltered for a moment, the weight of his question settling heavily in the air. Instead of answering immediately, I turned toward the window, staring out into the dimly lit gardens. The flickering shadows of the branches mirrored the chaos in my mind. Finally, I turned back to him and took a deep breath, steadying myself.

"Before I answer," I said softly, "I need you to understand something. Everything I've done has been to protect this estate, to protect my child, and yes, to protect you. If that meant making choices that others might misunderstand, so be it."

Jeremiah's eyes narrowed, his frustration evident. "Protecting the estate is one thing, Evelina. But did you truly think keeping me in the dark would make things better?"

"It wasn't just about keeping you in the dark," I countered, my voice trembling. "It was about staying one step ahead of Cedric. If he had any inkling that I wasn't the naive, overwhelmed duchess he thinks I am, he would have acted sooner. I needed him to think I was vulnerable so that he'd grow overconfident."

Jeremiah's expression softened slightly, though the tension in his shoulders remained. "And did that work, Evelina? Did his overconfidence give you what you need?"

I hesitated, then gestured to the scattered ledgers and correspondence on the desk. "I don't know yet," I admitted. "But I've found discrepancies. Patterns. And if I can piece them together with your help, we might just have enough to expose him."

Jeremiah's expression sharpened, his frustration clear. "You shouldn't have had to do this alone, Evelina," he said firmly. "You could have asked me for help. I would have been there. You know that."

For a moment, silence stretched between us, heavy and unrelenting. Then, I let out a shaky breath, my hands trembling as they gripped the edge of the desk. "You don't understand," I whispered. "This was never about deceiving you—it was about protecting you."

His eyes narrowed, his disbelief evident. "Protecting me? Evelina, if you think keeping me in the dark does anything but erode trust, you're wrong."

"I didn't want your name dragged through the mud!" I snapped, my voice trembling with emotion. "If anyone suspected you were involved in any of this, your reputation would be ruined. And you've already sacrificed so much just by standing by me."

"You think it's to protect me, to protect my reputation. And instead of letting me stand by you, you trapped Cedric alone and pushed me away, just to protect my reputation?"

"Yes."

"Why would you go to such lengths?"

"Because I didn't want you to become a target," I admitted, my voice barely above a whisper. "The rumors, the whispers...they're cruel, Jeremiah. If you stay, they'll only drag you down with me."

"Dammit, Evelina. I don't need to be protected."

The raw emotion in his voice stunned me into silence. He stared at me, his eyes blazing with a mixture of frustration and concern that cut through my defenses.

"You're the one who needs protecting," he continued, stepping closer. "You and the child."

The weight of his words crashed over me, breaking through the wall I'd so carefully constructed. My shoulders sagged, and I sank back into my chair, suddenly feeling every ounce of the exhaustion that had been dragging me down.

He knelt beside me, his face level with mine, his expression softening. "Do you really think I care what they say about me?" he asked, his voice quieter now. "Evelina, I've been a target my entire life. Scandal is the one constant I've always been able to count on. But you? You don't deserve this. You've done nothing to deserve this."

Tears pricked my eyes, and I quickly looked away, staring at the scattered papers on the desk. "It's not just the rumors," I murmured. "It's the estate. It's the child. Everything feels like it's slipping away."

"Then let me help you," he said, his voice steady and sure. "Don't push me away because you think it's the noble thing to do. Cedric is dangerous and you don't have to fight this alone."

"I just don't want to put you in danger. You can live quietly without getting into trouble here."

"You're not putting me in danger, Evelina."

"But, still, I'm going to get you in trouble, Jeremiah," I shook my head.

Jeremiah reached out, his hand brushing mine in a gesture so simple yet so grounding that it brought tears to my eyes. "We'll figure it out," he said gently. "Together."

I looked at him, searching his face for any sign of doubt or hesitation, but there was none. Only resolve.

"Do you mean that?" I asked, my voice trembling. "Even if it means risking your reputation?"

"Evelina," he said, his tone firm but gentle, "my reputation has never mattered to me. What matters is you. And the child."

A tear slipped down my cheek, and I quickly brushed it away. "I need your help," I admitted, the words feeling both like a defeat and a relief. "I can't do this alone."

He nodded, rising to his feet. "You won't have to," he said simply. "Not anymore."

His words struck something deep within me, unraveling the last threads of my resistance. "I found more irregularities," I confessed, gesturing toward the mess on the desk. "Payments I didn't authorize. Expenses that don't make sense. It's as though someone's deliberately trying to undermine the estate, and I can't..." My voice broke, and I pressed a hand to my forehead, the weight of it all threatening to crush me.

For a moment, we stood in silence, the weight of the moment settling between us. Then, he moved to the table where the scattered records lay, their disorganized state reflecting the turmoil in my own mind.

"Let's start here," he said, his tone calm but purposeful. He reached for a stack of ledgers, his fingers brushing the edges of the worn pages with a careful precision. "There's always a pattern. We just need to find it."

I joined him, the initial awkwardness of working side by side gradually giving way to a shared rhythm. His sharp mind quickly identified patterns I had missed, his insights cutting through the chaos like a blade.

Together, we turned our attention to the records. His sharp mind quickly identified patterns I had missed, his insights cutting through the chaos like a blade. As he worked, explaining his findings in his steady, intelligent way, I felt the tension in my chest begin to ease.

"You see this?" he said, pointing to a series of transactions. "These payments—regular, but just small enough to slip under notice. They're siphoning funds out of the estate. It's deliberate."

"But how?" I asked, leaning closer. "I've reviewed these accounts a dozen times and never noticed."

"That's the point," he replied, his voice tinged with admiration. "It's subtle enough to avoid suspicion. But whoever is behind it didn't account for one thing."

"What's that?"

"That I'm stubborn enough to dig until I find the truth," he said with a faint smile, his confidence lighting a spark of hope within me.

"Please tell me, Jeremiah!"

"Wait!"

As he worked, he explained his findings in a steady, intelligent way, pointing out connections and discrepancies I hadn't noticed. "Look here," he said, sliding a page toward me. His finger tapped the column of figures, his voice tinged with excitement. "This expenditure is too high to be routine. Someone's funneling money where it doesn't belong."

"You're right," I murmured, the tension in my chest beginning to ease. Together, we pieced through the records, uncovering more signs of manipulation and deceit. The enormity of it all was daunting, but with him beside me, the task felt manageable—doable, even.

"There's a name here," he said suddenly, his voice drawing me from my thoughts. He held up a scrap of correspondence buried within the ledgers. The name scrawled at the bottom sent a chill down my spine.

"That..." I hesitated, the words catching in my throat. "That's Cedric's contact."

His expression darkened, but he only nodded, setting the paper aside with deliberate care. "Then we're on the right track."

Hours passed unnoticed as we worked, our quiet determination filling the room. At some point, the tension between us softened into something warmer, something that felt almost like hope. Despite the storm raging outside these walls, in this moment, I felt a glimmer of certainty.

Finally, he leaned back, rubbing a hand over his face. "This is enough for today," he said, his voice low but firm. "You need rest. Tomorrow, we'll keep going."

I nodded, exhaustion creeping into my limbs but my heart lighter than it had been in days. "Thank you," I said, the words inadequate for the gratitude I felt.

He smiled, a small, tired curve of his lips. "We're in this together now. Remember that."

As I watched him gather the scattered pages into a semblance of order, I felt the faintest flicker of something I hadn't allowed myself in so long: hope.

For the first time in weeks, I felt as though I could breathe. The pieces were beginning to fall into place, and with Jeremiah by my side, the impossible didn't feel quite so daunting. But a new fear took root. Cedric and Lady Henrietta were cunning and relentless. If they realized Jeremiah and I were working together again, their next move would undoubtedly be more ruthless.

"I'm afraid for you," I said softly, my voice breaking the comfortable silence.

Jeremiah looked up, his gaze steady and unwavering. "Don't be," he said firmly. "I'm exactly where I need to be—by your side."

His words wrapped around me like a shield, and for the first time in a long time, I felt safe. But even as hope blossomed, I knew the battle was far from over. Cedric and Lady Henrietta wouldn't go down without a fight, and the stakes had never been higher.

39

The Shadows of Doubt

The estate felt like a prison. Every corner seemed to hold a pair of scrutinizing eyes, every shadow a whisper of accusation. The Duke's relatives had always been vultures, circling with the patience of those who knew their time would come.

A carriage bearing one of the Duke's vassal, Sir Montague, arrived unannounced. His presence was a harbinger of trouble, his stiff demeanor and sharp gaze promising no pleasantries.

I had barely settled in the drawing room when Mary appeared, her face pale. "Your Grace, Sir Montague is here to see you. He... he insists it's urgent."

"Show him in," I said, my voice steady despite the knot forming in my stomach.

Moments later, Sir Montague entered, his steps measured but deliberate. He bowed with the barest hint of respect, his expression unreadable. "Your Grace," he began, his tone clipped. "I have come on behalf of the Duke's extended family. Certain... questions have arisen regarding the legitimacy of the child you carry."

The air seemed to vanish from the room, and my hand instinctively moved to my belly. "Questions?" I repeated, my voice firmer than I felt. "What exactly do they imply?"

Before Sir Montague could respond, Cedric entered the room, his presence commanding as ever. "Ah, Sir Montague," he said smoothly, his tone laced with polite disapproval. "I wasn't aware you intended to interrogate Her Grace today."

"This is not an interrogation," Sir Montague replied, though his tone suggested otherwise. "Merely an inquiry, Lord Harland. The Duke's family has a right to ensure the legitimacy of his heir."

Cedric's smile didn't waver, but a sharpness entered his gaze. "Her Grace carries the Duke's child. Any implication otherwise is both unfounded and offensive."

Sir Montague's lips pressed into a thin line. "Be that as it may, there are concerns. Does Her Grace possess letters from the Duke affirming the child's inheritance? Witnesses to confirm the date of conception?"

"Enough," Cedric said, his voice cold. "You overstep your bounds, Sir Montague. Her Grace has endured more than enough without having to defend herself against baseless accusations."

Though I was grateful for Cedric's defense, it did little to deter Sir Montague. He turned his piercing gaze to me, his expression unrelenting. "Forgive me, Your Grace, but these are matters of great importance. The Duke's legacy is at stake. Surely you understand the need for clarity."

I straightened in my seat, meeting his gaze head-on. "The Duke's legacy is well protected," I said, my voice steady. "I carry his child, and I will not allow his memory to be tarnished by insinuations."

"You've heard Her Grace," Cedric interjected smoothly. "Now, unless you have proof to substantiate these absurd claims, I suggest you take your leave."

Sir Montague hesitated, his jaw tightening, but finally, he inclined his head. "Very well. For now."

With that, he turned on his heel and left, his departure as abrupt as his arrival. The room fell into a tense silence, broken only by the faint sound of the carriage wheels retreating down the gravel drive.

"That man is insufferable," Cedric muttered, his polished demeanor slipping for a moment. "I'll see to it that he doesn't trouble you again."

"Thank you," I said softly, though the gratitude felt hollow. "But his questions won't stop with him. There will be others."

Cedric's expression softened, and he stepped closer, his voice low. "Then let them come. They will find no fault here, Your Grace. I won't allow it."

Despite his assurances, the weight of the encounter lingered. Cedric's defense had been timely and pointed, but it hadn't stopped the questions—and it wouldn't stop the whispers. The Duke's relatives wouldn't rest until they had what they wanted, and I wasn't sure how much longer I could fend them off.

As Cedric left the room, Mary appeared once more, her brow furrowed with worry. "Are you alright, Your Grace?" she asked, her voice trembling slightly.

I nodded, though the knot in my chest told another story. "I'm fine, Mary," I said, my hand instinctively moving to my belly. "But I fear this is only the beginning."

Mary seemed nervous, her hands trembling as she arranged my tea. "It's not right, Your Grace," she whispered, her voice trembling. "To treat you this way, after all you've endured."

I forced a smile, though my heart ached. "It's the way of things, Mary. The powerful will always find a way to press their advantage."

Her eyes filled with pity, a reflection of the helplessness I felt but couldn't afford to show. I sighed heavily, I'll have to discuss this matter with Jeremiah when he comes over later.

By mid-afternoon, I retreated to the library, seeking solace among the dusty tomes. But even here, the tension followed me. The door creaked open, and Jeremiah stepped inside, his presence steadying me in a way I couldn't quite explain.

"Your Grace," he said, his voice low and warm. "I thought you might need some company."

I looked up, offering him a faint smile. "Company or counsel, Lord Ravenscroft?"

He inclined his head, his lips twitching into the faintest hint of a smile. "Perhaps a bit of both."

I gestured to the chair opposite mine, and he settled into it with the ease of someone who had long since grown accustomed to the formalities of high society. Yet there was nothing calculating in his manner, no trace of the duplicity I had come to expect from others in my circle.

"The Duke's Vassal are relentless," I said after a moment, breaking the silence. "They question everything—my fidelity, my honesty, even my competence to manage the estate."

"And they will continue to do so," he replied, his tone matter-of-fact. "Because they fear what your child represents: the continuation of Rupert's legacy and their exclusion from it."

His words, though harsh, rang true. "I never wanted to fight them, Jeremiah," I admitted. "But it seems they won't rest until they've stripped me of everything."

"Then you must fight," he said simply.

I let out a bitter laugh. "And how do I do that, when even the servants look at me as if I'm a stranger in my own home?"

He leaned forward, his gaze unwavering. "By showing them that you are more than they believe you to be. The Duchess of Wakefield is not a title easily undermined. If you conduct yourself with composure and strength, they will see that you are worthy of it."

"And if they don't?" I asked, my voice barely above a whisper.

"Then you make them regret underestimating you," he said, his tone firm but not unkind.

"And how, exactly, am I to make them regret?" I asked, my voice sharper than I intended, though it wasn't directed at him. "The Duke's relatives are relentless. They twist every gesture, every word. Sir Montague didn't come here for clarity—he came to humiliate me."

Jeremiah studied me, his fingers steepled beneath his chin as he leaned back in his chair. "You're correct; Montague came to probe for weakness. And Cedric's defense, while timely, wasn't to protect you—it was to protect himself."

I stilled, my fingers tightening around the armrest. "You think Cedric put him up to it?"

Jeremiah's eyes narrowed thoughtfully. "Not directly. Cedric is too clever to risk being so overt. But it's possible he's nudging the Duke's relatives in this direction. He gains leverage if you're isolated—cornered with no one to rely on but him. Montague's arrival could have been a test, a way to gauge your reaction and solidify Cedric's position as your supposed ally."

The notion sent a shiver down my spine, but it made a disturbing kind of sense. Cedric had been quick to step into the void, offering reassurance and charm where others brought suspicion and scorn. Yet the timing of his intervention always seemed...too perfect.

"Cedric," I murmured, shaking my head. "He's playing a game I don't fully understand."

"But we can," Jeremiah said, leaning forward. "We can turn his own tactics against him."

My brow furrowed. "And how do we do that?"

Jeremiah's lips curved into a faint smile, his confidence unshakable. "We use Cedric's need for control to expose him. People like him thrive on being seen as indispensable—they manipulate from the shadows, but they crave acknowledgment. If we shift the narrative, subtly but deliberately, we can force him into the light."

I frowned, still uncertain. "How do you suggest we shift the narrative?"

Jeremiah gestured toward the folded letter I had tucked into a drawer earlier. "For one, we need to show that Cedric's actions aren't purely altruistic. Montague's visit was meant to rattle you, but it also proves the Duke's relatives are listening to someone. Cedric may not have summoned Montague directly, but he's likely behind the whispers fueling their doubts."

"And if we confront him?" I asked.

Jeremiah shook his head. "Not yet. A direct confrontation would give him the opportunity to deny and discredit. Instead, we start small. You need to reassert control over the estate—subtly, at first, by reinforcing your authority with the staff. You have allies among them, even if they're hesitant to show it."

A pang of frustration tightened my chest. "Even the staff seem to prefer Cedric. He's been meeting with them, making changes—"

"Changes that benefit him," Jeremiah interjected. "But loyalty among servants is rarely built on charm alone. Cedric's influence is surface-deep. If you take the time to engage with them—showing both strength and fairness—you'll find that loyalty is still within your reach."

I considered his words, my fingers drifting unconsciously to my belly. Jeremiah's confidence was infectious, and though doubt still lingered, a small ember of determination began to spark within me.

"And while you work on the staff," Jeremiah continued, his tone sharpening, "I'll handle the Duke's vassals."

I blinked, startled. "What do you mean?"

"Montague and his ilk need to understand that their actions will have consequences. I'll track their correspondence, intercept any additional letters, and uncover whatever scheme they're entertaining. If we can tie their actions back to Cedric—or even implicate him indirectly—we'll have the leverage needed to stop this inquiry in its tracks."

I hesitated, the enormity of his plan dawning on me. "You're willing to do all of this?"

Jeremiah's expression softened, a flicker of something unreadable crossing his face. "For you? Always."

The simplicity of his words sent a warmth coursing through me, though I quickly tamped it down. I couldn't afford distractions—not when my child's future was at stake.

"Very well," I said, my voice steadying. "What's the first step?"

"You'll need to resume small gatherings with the staff," he said. "Start by addressing those who seem hesitant—those who've remained neutral. Show them that you're still the Duchess of Wakefield, and that you value their loyalty."

I nodded, my fingers curling into my lap. "And the Duke's vassals?"

"Leave them to me," Jeremiah said, rising to his feet. His expression was resolute, his presence a steadying force. "By the time Cedric realizes what's happening, it'll be too late for him to counter."

As he turned to leave, I found myself calling out, "Jeremiah?"

He paused, glancing back.

"Thank you," I said quietly, my hand resting protectively over my belly. "For everything."

He inclined his head, his gaze lingering for a moment longer than necessary. "Always," he said again, his voice low.

40

The Shadow Watcher

The grandeur of the room felt like a mockery of the turmoil brewing beneath its surface. I sat at my desk in the small study, absently running my fingers over the edges of the estate ledger before me. Despite my best efforts, I couldn't focus on the columns of numbers. Jeremiah's warning echoed in my mind, his conviction as sharp as the intensity in his gaze.

"Please, don't trust anyone."

The words felt like a lock on my chest, heavy and suffocating. I'd always known the estate was filled with whispers and secrets, but the idea that someone might actively be watching me—that someone had followed us into the garden—left a deep unease that no amount of sunlight could chase away.

The sound of footsteps broke through my thoughts, and Mary entered the room, carrying a tray of tea and biscuits. Her presence, as always, was a small comfort, but even she seemed more subdued than usual.

"Mary," I said softly as she placed the tray on the table, "have you noticed anything... unusual lately? Any of the staff behaving oddly?"

She hesitated, her brow furrowing slightly as she set the teacups down with care. "Unusual, Your Grace? No, not outright. But..." She glanced toward the door, lowering her voice. "I did find it strange that Mrs. Clarke was asking about your morning routine the other day. She usually leaves that sort of thing to Mrs. Hawthorne."

I frowned. "Mrs. Clarke? What was she asking?"

Mary bit her lip, her hands twisting together nervously. "Just little things. When you take your tea, whether you prefer the drawing room or the study in the mornings. I thought it odd, but I assumed she was planning to surprise you with something."

It was a small thing, insignificant on the surface, but it added to the unease that had settled like a stone in my stomach. "Thank you, Mary. If you notice anything else, no matter how trivial, let me know."

"Yes, Your Grace," she said with quiet resolve, her loyalty evident in her tone.

Once Mary left, I stared down at the ledger, willing myself to focus. But my mind refused to settle. My thoughts kept returning to the garden—Jeremiah's warning, the shadowy figure, and the unshakable sense that unseen eyes were following my every move.

Later that morning, I left the study, seeking solace in the sunlit corridors. As I walked, my gaze caught on a small vase resting on a side table. It was tilted ever so slightly, its usual symmetry disrupted. Pausing, I ran my fingers along its rim, feeling a faint, sticky residue.

Wax.

Someone had likely used it to seal a letter, but why here, and why so carelessly? My unease deepened. Something wasn't right.

"Your Grace." A voice startled me, and I turned to see Mrs. Hawthorne approaching, her usual composed expression strained.

"Yes, Mrs. Hawthorne?"

"I wanted to bring this to your attention," she said, holding out a crumpled piece of paper. The edges were stained with ink, and her hand trembled slightly as she offered it to me. "I found it near the servants' quarters this morning."

I smoothed the paper carefully, my breath hitching as I read the hurried scrawl:

She's too close to uncovering it. Move the documents tonight.

The pit in my stomach deepened. "Did anyone see who dropped this?"

Mrs. Hawthorne shook her head, her lips pressed tightly together. "No, Your Grace. But I've kept it quiet for now. I thought you should see it first."

"Thank you," I said, my voice steady despite the storm building within me. "Please let me know if you find anything else."

Once she left, I stared at the note, my mind racing. What documents? And who was "she"? The message could refer to anyone in the estate—or perhaps it was meant for me. A cold resolve settled in my chest. I would not be blindsided.

That evening, Jeremiah arrived, his expression sharp as I handed him the note. He read it carefully, his brow furrowing as he tapped the paper lightly against his palm.

"Mrs. Clarke's sudden interest in your routine isn't coincidental," he said, his tone thoughtful. "And this letter... it suggests coordination. Someone's feeding instructions, likely through intermediaries. Mrs. Clarke could be one of them, or at least a useful pawn."

I nodded, my hands tightening in my lap. "And the fragment I found in the sitting room... there was ash in the fireplace and part of a letter. It mentioned 'illegitimate' and 'secure title.'"

Jeremiah's jaw tightened. "They're escalating," he said grimly. "This can't be ignored, Your Grace."

"I know," I replied, my resolve hardening. "But we can't act rashly. If Cedric or his allies think we're onto them, they'll cover their tracks before we can gather enough evidence to stop them."

"If they're destroying evidence, they must feel the pressure. That note"—he gestured to the paper—"tells me they're not ready to abandon whatever scheme they're plotting. If we can find the documents they're moving, we'll have leverage."

"Mrs. Hawthorne said she'd alert me if she finds anything more," I replied, glancing toward the window where the sky had begun to darken. "But we can't wait. If they're planning to move something tonight, we need to act."

Jeremiah stepped closer, his presence steadying me. "I'll watch the west wing," he said. "That's the least trafficked area at night—perfect for hiding or moving something without drawing attention."

I hesitated, worry gnawing at me. "Jeremiah... please be careful. Whoever's behind this isn't afraid of playing dirty."

His lips quirked into a faint, reassuring smile. "I've dealt with worse, Evelina. Trust me."

I watched as Jeremiah's expression shifted, his tone becoming more deliberate. "How is your progress with the correspondence, Jeremiah?" I asked, my voice betraying my worry and curiosity. I needed to know if there had been any breakthroughs—anything that could shed light on Cedric's schemes.

He exhaled, his brow furrowing as though weighed down by the enormity of the task. "I've been tracking it carefully, Your Grace," he began, his voice measured. "Sir Montague remains a suspicious link in all of this, but so far, I've found no concrete evidence of his involvement. I've set plans to intercept any additional letters that pass through his connections. If Cedric or the duke's vassals are coordinating, I'll uncover their correspondence and whatever scheme they're plotting."

His determination was evident, but his words left a knot of unease in my chest. "Do you think Sir Montague is the key?" I pressed, hoping for clarity.

"If he's not the key, then he's certainly a piece of the puzzle," Jeremiah replied, his eyes narrowing with resolve. "Someone's pulling strings, and I intend to find out who."

I hesitated for a moment, then asked, "And what's the plan now? How do we move forward?"

Jeremiah's gaze softened slightly as he considered my question. "I'll be watching the estate tonight," he said, his tone firm. "The west wing is the least trafficked area and perfect for moving something without being noticed. If they're planning to shift the documents, that's where I'll intercept them."

The weight of his words settled over me. "This is dangerous—whoever is behind this won't hesitate to do whatever it takes to protect their secrets."

"I know," he said, offering a reassuring nod. "But this is our chance to get closer to the truth. Trust me, Your Grace—I won't let them get away with this."

I held his gaze for a moment, the weight of our shared burden settling heavily between us. "But still, be careful, Jeremiah. I can't afford to lose you in this fight."

His lips quirked into a faint, fleeting smile. "You won't."

As he turned to leave, the note still in his hand, I felt a flicker of hope amidst the chaos. Together, we would uncover the truth. And together, we would protect what was mine.

41

The Stillness of the Night

The stillness of the night enveloped Wakefield Hall, a heavy, unnatural quiet that settled deep into my bones, making even the soft sound of my own breath feel intrusive. The moon hung low, its silver light spilling across the gravel paths and manicured hedges, casting shifting shadows that danced with an eerie grace. I stood near the stables, the scent of hay and damp earth grounding me as my eyes scanned the darkened windows of the estate.

Evelina's fragment of burned parchment weighed heavily in my pocket, a grim reminder of the stakes. It wasn't just about preserving Evelina's position or reputation—it was about safeguarding the life of her unborn child and the future of the Wakefield legacy. I couldn't allow Cedric or his allies to succeed in whatever scheme they were orchestrating.

Leaning against the shadowed stable wall, I let my eyes adjust to the dim light, every muscle in my body taut with vigilance. The estate was unnervingly quiet, the kind of silence that felt intentional. My instincts told me this was the moment to strike—late at night, when suspicion would be at its lowest. Yet the oppressive stillness made me wary. It was too quiet.

The servants' quarters were dark, save for a single faint light filtering through the shutters. Likely the night maid, finishing her duties. The west wing, where Evelina had discovered the ash and the damning fragment of parchment, was equally silent. Even the air seemed to hold its breath, as if the estate itself anticipated an imminent storm.

I prowled the grounds, my steps muffled against the soft earth. Each creak of the gravel or rustle of the hedges sent my senses surging into high alert. But there was nothing. No shadowy figures slipping between doors, no hurried whispers carried on the wind, no furtive movements betraying hidden agendas.

At the edge of the property, where the main house gave way to the sprawling gardens, I paused. The faint scent of wisteria lingered in the air, a fleeting reminder of the estate's beauty—a beauty that masked the rot beneath its surface. I pressed my back against the cold stone of the garden wall, scanning the dark expanse before me.

Had they realized we were watching? The possibility gnawed at me. Cedric wasn't careless, and if he suspected Evelina and I were onto him, he might have delayed his plans or moved the documents elsewhere. It was a frustrating possibility but one I had anticipated.

As the hours dragged on, the quiet persisted, stretching thinly over my nerves. I shifted my weight from foot to foot, the unease coiling tighter in my chest. Evelina had shown remarkable resilience, regaining control of the estate despite mounting opposition, but her position was far from secure. Cedric's influence lingered like a shadow, his manipulations subtle and insidious.

The memory of Evelina's strength—her quiet defiance in the face of overwhelming pressure—spurred my resolve. She shouldn't have to face this alone, no matter how fiercely she tried to protect me from the dangers swirling around her. Yet as the night wore on, the lack of activity began to erode my confidence. Were we looking in the wrong places? Had Cedric already acted, or was he simply waiting for the perfect moment to strike?

By the time the first light of dawn crept over the horizon, my patience was frayed. The estate remained as silent as it had been all night, its shadows unyielding. My shoulders sagged slightly as frustration and disappointment settled over me. Either Cedric's accomplices were more cunning than I'd given them credit for, or we'd misread their intentions entirely.

As I made my way back toward the stables, the faint chirping of birds signaled the start of a new day. The air felt heavier now, the unanswered questions looming over the estate like storm clouds waiting to break. Inside the stable, I leaned against a wooden post, running a hand through my hair. The quiet wasn't reassuring—it was foreboding. This wasn't over; it was merely delayed. The enemy wasn't retreating—they were regrouping. And that made them far more dangerous.

"Lord Ravenscroft."

The soft voice startled me, and I turned to see Mary standing in the doorway of the stables, her face pale in the dim morning light. She clutched a lantern, its weak glow casting flickering shadows along the wooden beams.

"What is it?" I asked, straightening immediately.

"I thought you'd want to know,My Lord" she began hesitantly, stepping closer. "There's been no movement tonight. Nothing unusual. But..."

"But?" I prompted, my unease tightening further.

"There's been talk among the staff," she admitted, her voice dropping to a whisper. "Whispers that Lady Henrietta and Lord Harland are planning something soon. They've been quiet—almost too quiet."

My jaw clenched. Cedric's strategy was clear. He thrived on calculated precision, waiting until the perfect moment to strike where it would hurt most.

"Thank you, Mary," I said, my tone firm. "Keep listening. Anything you hear, no matter how small, bring it to me."

She nodded, her worry evident even as she tried to mask it with loyalty. As she disappeared into the growing light, I allowed myself a moment to gather my thoughts.

The lack of movement wasn't a sign of retreat—it was the calm before the storm. Cedric wasn't backing down. He was waiting, planning, ensuring that his next move would strike with devastating precision.

With renewed determination, I left the stables and made my way toward the main house. If Cedric thought his silence would shake my resolve, he was mistaken. I had spent the night in quiet observation, but now it was time to act.

The storm was coming. And I intended to meet it head-on.

42

Mending Fences

The library had become our war room, its once-pristine shelves now shadowed by stacks of papers and ledgers. Evelina sat across from me, her fingers drumming softly against the desk as she skimmed another document. She looked weary but resolute, her earlier hostility melting away as necessity drew us together.

I leaned forward, my eyes scanning the letter I'd intercepted that morning. Cedric's signature loomed at the bottom like a mocking taunt. The contents were as damning as they were methodical. He had outlined a strategy to erode Evelina's credibility by spreading insidious rumors among the local gentry, planting doubts about her competence and moral character. Worse, he proposed leveraging forged documents to call into question the legitimacy of the child she carried, insinuating impropriety on her part. Every line dripped with calculated malice, revealing not just ambition but a deep-seated desire to ruin her entirely.

I handed the letter across the desk, watching Evelina's face as she read. Mary had found it first, tucked in Cedric's study beneath a stack of correspondence marked for destruction. She had rushed to show me, her face pale and her hands trembling as she recounted how she'd stumbled upon it while delivering fresh ink to his writing desk. The moment I saw the deliberate folds and Cedric's unmistakable seal, I knew it was critical. Evelina's expression shifted from confusion to shock, then settled into a cold, simmering fury.

"This," she said, her voice shaking, "this is the proof we needed." She set the letter down with a deliberate motion, her eyes lifting to meet mine. "He intends to destroy everything—my reputation, my child's claim, even the estate."

"Not if we move first," I said firmly, my gaze locking with hers. "He's underestimated you, Evelina. He thinks you're isolated and powerless. But you're not. Not anymore."

She hesitated, her fingers brushing over the letter. "You think this is enough to confront him?"

"On its own? No," I admitted. "But combined with the discrepancies in the estate accounts, the witnesses we've identified among the staff, and this..." I tapped the intercepted letter. "We have enough to force his hand. He's clever, but he's grown overconfident. That's his weakness."

Her lips pressed into a thin line, the tension in her shoulders betraying the vulnerability beneath her determination. "I've spent so much time wondering if I was imagining things," she confessed softly. "If I was seeing shadows where there were none. Cedric...he's always so charming, so careful. I thought maybe..."

"You thought maybe he was genuine," I finished, my voice gentler now. "That's what makes him dangerous, Evelina. He's a serpent who wears the mask of a savior. But you saw through him, even if it took time. That's what matters."

She smiled faintly, though the sadness lingered in her eyes. "Thank you, Jeremiah," she said, her voice quiet. "For not giving up on me. Even when I..." She trailed off, her gaze dropping to her hands.

"Even when you pushed me away?" I offered, a wry smile tugging at my lips.

She glanced up, her expression softening. "Yes. I thought I was protecting you. But I see now that I only made things harder—for both of us."

There was a pause, the weight of unspoken words hanging between us. Then she took a deep breath, straightening in her chair. "What's our next move?"

I appreciated her resolve, but I knew this had to be handled delicately. "We use this letter to bait Cedric into making a mistake," I said. "He needs to think he's still in control. The more confident he feels, the more likely he is to slip up."

"And how do we bait him?" she asked, her brow furrowing.

"By playing the part he expects," I said, leaning back in my chair. "You continue to rely on him publicly. Show no sign that you've seen through him. Meanwhile, I'll work behind the scenes to gather more evidence and ensure our allies are ready when the time comes."

Evelina nodded slowly, though I could see the unease flicker across her face. "I don't like pretending to trust him," she admitted. "It feels...wrong."

"I know," I said, my voice steady. "But Cedric thrives on the illusion of control. The more he believes you're in his pocket, the more he'll let his guard down."

She sighed, rubbing her temples. "I can't believe I ever let him get this close."

"You were doing what you thought was right," I said firmly. "You were protecting your child, your legacy. That doesn't make you weak, Evelina. It makes you human."

Her eyes met mine, and for the first time in days, I saw a glimmer of hope there. "You really believe we can stop him?"

"I know we can," I said without hesitation.

She took a deep breath, straightening in her chair. "So, what can we do first?"

"We weaken Cedric's influence," I said without hesitation. "We need to cut him off from his allies within the estate and undermine his credibility. If we can expose him publicly, the gentry will turn against him, and he'll lose his footing."

Her brow furrowed. "How do we do that without tipping our hand?"

"By leveraging the staff," I explained. "There are those who've already voiced concerns—quietly, of course. If we can encourage them to speak out, we'll create a ripple effect. Cedric thrives on fear and loyalty. Take those away, and he has nothing."

Evelina nodded slowly, her gaze sharpening with resolve. "And once his influence is gone?"

"We force him out," I said firmly. "With the evidence we've gathered, he won't have a leg to stand on. He'll be left with no choice but to leave the estate entirely."

Her lips pressed into a determined line. "It won't be easy. He's cunning, Jeremiah."

"So are we," I replied. "And we have the truth on our side."

The tension between us softened as we refined the plan, our shared resolve strengthening with every word. Evelina began to open up, sharing her frustrations and fears with a candor that surprised me.

"I've spent so much time feeling like I was failing," she admitted, her voice quieter now. "As a duchess, as a mother-to-be...even as a woman. Cedric fed into those doubts. He made me feel like I needed him to survive."

"You don't," I said simply. "You never did."

Her gaze lingered on mine, a small, grateful smile touching her lips. "You've always believed in me, haven't you?"

"Yes," I said, the word carrying more weight than I'd intended. "Even when you didn't believe in yourself."

She reached across the desk, her fingers brushing mine in a gesture so brief yet so profound that it left me momentarily breathless. "Thank you, Jeremiah," she said softly. "For standing by me. For coming back, even after I tried to push you away."

I covered her hand with mine, my grip firm but gentle. "I told you once, Evelina—I'm here for you. No matter what."

As the candlelight flickered around us, casting long shadows across the room, I felt the beginnings of something stronger than just trust. It was a partnership forged in fire, a shared determination to protect what mattered most.

And though the road ahead was fraught with danger, I knew one thing for certain: together, we could weather whatever storm Cedric had in store.

43

The Gathering Storm

The library was quiet, save for the steady scratch of my pen on parchment and the occasional low murmur from Jeremiah as he flipped through ledgers. Outside, the sky was a patchwork of gray, the looming clouds mirroring the tension coiled within me. Each passing moment brought us closer to the confrontation I both dreaded and anticipated.

For days now, Jeremiah and I had worked tirelessly to uncover every thread of Cedric's deceit, piecing together a web of evidence that could not be ignored. Intercepted letters, physicianed estate records, unexplained financial transactions—it was all there, each piece damning in its own right. Together, they painted a picture of calculated betrayal that could topple Cedric's carefully curated façade.

"Here," Jeremiah said, sliding a sheet across the desk toward me. His voice cut through the quiet like a blade, sharp and focused. "This letter. Cedric directed the solicitor to expedite the sale of the estate lands. He didn't even bother to hide it under your name this time."

I picked up the letter, my fingers brushing against his as I did. The parchment felt heavier than it should have, as though the weight of Cedric's treachery was pressed into its fibers. My eyes scanned the bold handwriting, the curves and slants of Cedric's script almost mocking in their arrogance. He had instructed the solicitor to conduct a "review and reassessment" of the recent additions to Wakefield's holdings, aiming to expedite their sale. The phrasing was cold and transactional, with no regard for the people who worked those lands or the legacy they represented. He hadn't forged my signature—he had simply assumed no one would dare question him.

"It's so brazen," I murmured, setting the paper down with trembling hands. "He truly believes he's untouchable."

"Desperation breeds arrogance," Jeremiah replied, leaning back in his chair. His gaze was unrelenting, his calm a steady counterpoint to my rising anger. "Cedric knows his window to gain control is closing. The closer you get to delivering the heir, the harder it becomes for him to undermine you."

I met his gaze, the firelight casting shadows across his face. His expression was resolute, a stark contrast to the storm of doubt churning inside me. "Do we have enough to confront him?" I asked, my voice steady despite the tightness in my chest.

"More than enough," he said. "Between the forged documents and his attempts to undermine estate management, no one could argue his innocence."

My eyes drifted to the stack of evidence on the desk, a fortress of proof built piece by painstaking piece. It was solid, undeniable. And yet, the thought of standing before the council, laying bare Cedric's schemes, filled me with trepidation.

"You'll need allies on the council," Jeremiah said, his tone shifting to one of quiet intensity. "They're not just a formality—they're the key to cornering Cedric and Lady Henrietta. If you can sway them, Cedric's entire strategy falls apart. But you must approach them carefully. Present the evidence without hesitation, and appeal to their sense of loyalty to the Wakefield legacy."

I nodded, his advice grounding me. "I'll need to address more than the evidence," I said quietly, tracing the edge of the ledger with my fingers. "They'll expect me to falter, to crumble under their scrutiny. I have to show them I'm capable of leading, of protecting this estate and my child."

"You don't need to show them anything you aren't already," Jeremiah said firmly. "You're the Duchess, Evelina. You've already proven your strength. All you have to do is let them see it."

His confidence steadied me, and for a moment, I allowed myself to believe it. "Then we focus on the strategy," I said, sitting up straighter. "I need to be prepared for anything Cedric or Lady Henrietta might throw at me."

Jeremiah's expression sharpened, his focus shifting into the precise, calculated demeanor I had come to rely on. "They'll likely challenge the legitimacy of your evidence," he said. "You need to be ready to counter their accusations without letting them rattle you. Stick to the facts. Don't let them twist your words."

"And the council?" I asked, scribbling notes in the margins of my papers.

"Half of them are loyal to you, or at least to the Wakefield legacy," he said. "They'll side with whoever they believe can maintain stability. Your role is to show them that stability lies with you—not Cedric."

I looked up, meeting his intense gaze. "And if they waver?"

"Then we give them a reason not to," he said, his tone steely. "That's why this evidence is so important. Cedric's arrogance is his weakness. Use it against him. Show them the chaos he's already sown, and they'll see he's not the leader they want."

His words steadied me, grounding me in the certainty of our evidence. For the first time, I felt a flicker of confidence, a glimmer of hope that I could face this battle and emerge victorious.

As the clock struck midnight, I leaned back in my chair, exhaustion tugging at my resolve. "We've done everything we can," I said softly.

Jeremiah nodded, his expression gentler than before. "You've done more than enough, Evelina. The rest is just execution."

I met his gaze, the warmth in his eyes chasing away the last remnants of doubt. "Thank you, Jeremiah," I said quietly. "For standing by me, even when I tried to push you away."

He inclined his head, his smile faint but sincere. "I made a promise—to Rupert and to you. But keeping it isn't just about duty." His voice softened, and though he didn't say more, the unspoken words lingered between us. It was more than loyalty to Rupert that bound him to my side. It was something deeper, something he couldn't yet name aloud.

The words hung between us, a silent vow that carried more weight than I could express.

44

The Duchess's Resolve

The missive lay on the desk, its ink stark and accusing against the creamy paper. It had arrived without ceremony, delivered by one of the kitchen maids who claimed to have found it tucked into the folds of a tea towel. The message was brief, each word laced with malice:

Beware of Cedric Harland. He plans to ensure your child never sees its inheritance.

I read the note twice more, the words hammering in my chest like an ominous drum. My fingers trembled as I set it aside, forcing myself to breathe. This was the third warning I'd received, each more urgent and chilling than the last. Whoever was sending them had no reason to lie, and the pattern was becoming impossible to ignore.

"What does it say?" Jeremiah's voice broke the silence. He stood by the window, arms crossed, his steady gaze fixed on me. The sunlight framed him, lending his presence an almost otherworldly solidity.

I hesitated, my fingers hovering over the note. Then, with a resigned sigh, I handed it to him. "Read for yourself."

His expression darkened as he scanned the words, his jaw tightening with barely suppressed anger. "It seems our suspicions were well-founded," he said, his voice low and dangerous. "Cedric isn't just maneuvering for power—he's planning something far worse."

"And yet, I've let him stay," I murmured, guilt threading through my voice.

"I've allowed him access to the estate, to the staff. To me."

"You did what you had to do," Jeremiah said firmly, setting the note aside. "Playing along gave us time to gather proof, to understand his game. But now it's time to stop playing."

I met his gaze, drawn to the quiet strength in his eyes. "What do you suggest?"

"A formal meeting," he replied without hesitation. "With Cedric, Lady Henrietta, and the key members of the estate. Confront him openly, but carefully. He's clever, Evelina, but he thrives on shadows and whispers. Drag him into the light, and his schemes will start to crumble."

"And what if he retaliates?" I asked, my voice trembling slightly. My hand moved instinctively to rest over my belly. "What if this provokes him to act faster? The baby..."

Jeremiah's jaw tightened, his resolve hardening. "That's why we have to act now," he said, his tone sharpened with urgency. "Every moment Cedric remains in control of this estate is another moment of danger for you and the child. The warnings are clear, Evelina. He won't stop until he gets what he wants. We must remove him before he can act on his threats. His influence, his schemes—they must end now. Delay could cost far more than we can afford."

My pulse quickened, fear and urgency intertwining in my chest. "Then we need to be sure," I said, my voice steadier now. "If we're going to confront him, we need every piece of evidence, every ally ready to stand by us. He can't be allowed to twist this in his favor."

"We have enough to force his hand," Jeremiah said, his tone softening slightly. "The intercepted letters, the discrepancies in the accounts, and the witnesses among the staff. Cedric's power lies in his secrecy. Expose that, and he has nothing."

I nodded, the weight of his words settling heavily over me. "And if he tries to strike back?"

"We'll be ready," Jeremiah said simply. He stepped closer, his presence a steadying force. "But you can't hesitate, Evelina. The safety of your child depends on this. Cedric has made his intentions clear, and he won't stop unless we stop him first."

I turned toward the far wall, where my late husband's portrait hung in solemn grandeur. Rupert's eyes, forever captured in a mix of sternness and warmth, seemed to meet mine. For so long, I had carried the weight of his legacy like a shroud, fearful of failing him, of being unworthy of the trust he had placed in me. But now, staring at his image, I felt something shift.

"I'll defend our child," I whispered, my voice steadying with each word. "And I'll defend Wakefield. Cedric won't win. Lady Henrietta won't win. This is my family, my legacy, and I will not let them destroy it."

Jeremiah stepped beside me, his presence a quiet but unyielding support. "You're stronger than they know, Evelina," he said, his voice low and certain. "And you're not alone in this fight."

I glanced at him, his words wrapping around the fear in my chest like a protective shield. "You've always been there for me," I said, my voice trembling slightly. "Even when I didn't deserve it. Jeremiah... I don't know how to thank you for everything you've done. For everything you've risked."

His hand lingered near mine, a fleeting connection that seemed to carry the weight of unspoken emotions. "You don't have to thank me, Evelina," he murmured, his gaze steady. "You and the child... you're my reason to stay. My reason to fight."

The depth of his words struck something raw within me, and for a moment, the room seemed to quiet around us. "I care about you, Jeremiah," I admitted, the words falling softly but firmly between us. "More than I should, perhaps. But I... I can't let anything happen to you. You mean too much to me."

"Nothing will happen to me," he promised, his voice a steady reassurance. "Not while I'm here to protect you. And I'll do whatever it takes, Evelina. Whatever it takes to see you and the child safe."

As the first rays of dawn spilled through the library windows, I stood tall before Rupert's portrait, the note clenched in my hand like a weapon. My other hand instinctively moved to rest over my belly, a protective gesture that steadied my resolve. The battle was far from over, but for the first time in weeks, I felt ready to face it.

Whatever they had planned, I would meet it head-on. For my child. For

Wakefield. And I would win.

45

The Council

The council chamber was imposing, its high ceilings and towering windows casting long shadows across the room as I entered. Each member of the Duke's council was seated around the grand oak table, their expressions ranging from curiosity to skepticism. The weight of their gazes pressed against me, but I held my head high, letting the authority of my position bolster my resolve.

Jeremiah had been clear: "They are the key to cornering Cedric and Lady Henrietta. If you appeal to their loyalty to the Wakefield legacy and present the evidence decisively, they will have no choice but to align with you."

I stepped forward, the sound of my heels echoing in the cavernous space. "Gentlemen," I began, my voice steady, "I have called you here today because the integrity of this estate is under threat. What I will present may shock you, but it is the truth—a truth I cannot allow to remain hidden."

There were murmurs of surprise, a few glances exchanged among the council members. I reached for the stack of documents Jeremiah and I had painstakingly compiled, laying them on the table with deliberate care.

"This," I said, gesturing to the forged contracts, intercepted letters, and financial discrepancies, "is evidence of Cedric Harland's betrayal. Unauthorized sales of estate lands, financial discrepancies meant to enrich himself while destabilizing Wakefield. He has acted in direct violation of my authority as Duchess and the wishes of the late Duke."

I produced the most damning piece, holding it up for all to see. "This letter, signed by Lord Harland himself, directed a solicitor to expedite a review and reassessment of the recent additions to Wakefield's holdings. He presumed to act without my knowledge or consent. This is not only presumptuous but reveals his intention to divide the estate to consolidate his own power."

One of the elder council members, Lord Whitby, adjusted his spectacles and leaned forward. "These are grave accusations, Your Grace. Do you have proof that links these actions directly to Lord Harland?"

"I do," I replied, my voice unwavering. "The letter bears his signature and specific instructions to the solicitor to bypass my authority. He has not only ignored his station but sought to dismantle the stability of this estate for his own gain." I passed the damning document to Whitby, who examined it with a furrowed brow before nodding grimly.

"And what of Lady Henrietta?" another councilman asked. "What role does she play in this?"

"Lady Henrietta has conspired alongside Lord Harland," I said, producing further evidence of their correspondence. "Their communications reveal a coordinated effort to undermine my authority and ensure my child never inherits Wakefield."

The murmurs grew louder, anger and disbelief rippling through the room. I let the moment hang, then raised a hand to silence them. "I understand your outrage, but this is not the time for mere indignation. I need your support to take decisive action. Together, we can ensure the safety of Wakefield and its rightful heir."

Lord Whitby nodded, his expression firm. "You have my support, Your Grace. The evidence is irrefutable."

A pause hung heavy, then another councilman, Lord Andrews, leaned forward. His voice was careful, but sharp. "Your Grace, we will lend you the full weight of our authority to act decisively. But it comes with a condition. The presence of Lord Ravenscroft, a man unrelated to this house, is... unorthodox. If you are to lead with our backing, you must sever your reliance on him."

The room fell into a stunned silence. My instinct was immediate refusal—

Jeremiah was my most trusted ally, the anchor that kept me grounded amidst the chaos. But as my gaze flickered toward him, I saw the slightest motion of his hand—a subtle signal to agree.

My throat tightened, but I forced my voice steady. "Very well," I said. "If that is what it takes to secure the future of this estate and my child, I will honor your request."

A murmur of approval rippled through the room, and Jeremiah's expression remained neutral, though his eyes carried a message I understood too well: There was no other way. This sacrifice, however painful, was necessary.

As the meeting concluded and the council members dispersed, Jeremiah approached me, his expression unreadable. "You made the right choice," he said quietly.

"Did I?" I asked, my voice barely above a whisper.

He nodded, his voice filled with quiet conviction. "You did. Trust me, Evelina. This is the only way forward."

I managed a faint smile, though my chest ached with the weight of what I had agreed to. "Then we move forward. Together, as far as we can."

His hand brushed mine briefly, a fleeting gesture of reassurance. "Always," he murmured.

The following morning, I dressed with care, choosing a gown of deep green velvet that exuded both elegance and authority. Mary fussed over my hair, pinning it into a style that was simple yet dignified.

"You look like a true Duchess, Your Grace," she said, her voice thick with pride.

I managed a faint smile, my nerves coiling tightly in my stomach. "Let's hope the council thinks so too."

As I descended the grand staircase, Jeremiah waited at the bottom, his posture steady and his expression unreadable. He offered his arm, and I took it without hesitation, drawing strength from his quiet presence.

"They'll expect you to falter," he murmured as we approached the drawing room. "But you won't. Remember the plan. Stick to the evidence. Let them see the leader you are."

I nodded, my grip tightening on his arm. The weight of the moment pressed down on me, but I refused to let it break me.

Together, we entered the drawing room, the air thick with tension as every gaze turned toward us. Lady Henrietta and Cedric sat to the left, their expressions sharp with calculation. The estate council members were seated to the right, their faces carefully neutral.

I stepped forward, my posture straight and unyielding. The room fell into a hushed silence, and for the first time, I felt the full power of my title.

I was the Duchess of Wakefield. And I was ready to defend what was mine.

46

The Duchess's Stand

The grand drawing room was a battlefield, though it bore no weapons or blood. Instead, the stakes were etched into every tense expression, every sharp glance exchanged across the polished mahogany table. The sunlight streaming through the tall windows did little to warm the atmosphere. It illuminated the gathered faces, each etched with anticipation, skepticism, or, in Cedric's case, barely concealed frustration.

I stood near the head of the table, my hands resting lightly on the edge, drawing strength from the solidity of the wood beneath my fingertips. Behind me loomed my late husband's portrait, his stern yet kind gaze a silent reminder of the Wakefield legacy I was sworn to protect. To my left sat Jeremiah, his quiet presence a steadying force, his focus unwavering as he observed the room. He said nothing for now, waiting for the right moment to strike.

Cedric lounged opposite me, his posture feigned ease, but I caught the flicker of annoyance in his eyes. Lady Henrietta sat nearby, her hands clasped in her lap, her expression the picture of practiced civility. Yet her sharp gaze betrayed her readiness to strike at the first opportunity. Around us, the estate council members shifted in their seats, their murmured conversations fading as I straightened, commanding their attention.

"Thank you for convening today," I began, my voice steady despite the tight knot of tension coiled in my chest. "There are serious matters concerning the management of the Wakefield estate that must be addressed. I believe it's time for clarity—for all of us."

Cedric's smirk curled at the edges. "Clarity, Your Grace? That sounds ominous. Surely this isn't necessary. We all have the estate's best interests at heart."

I met his gaze, unflinching. "Do we, Lord Harland? Because what I've uncovered suggests otherwise."

Jeremiah slid the intercepted letter across the table, the faint scrape of paper against wood reverberating in the otherwise silent room. The council members leaned in to examine it, their eyes scanning the damning words that detailed Cedric's unauthorized plans to sell estate properties.

"This letter," I said, my voice calm but firm, "was addressed to a solicitor and outlines intentions to sell portions of the estate without my consent or knowledge. It bears Cedric's name."

Cedric's expression darkened as murmurs rippled through the room. "Your Grace," he said, his tone smooth but taut, "surely you must understand. The estate requires swift decisions—decisions you've been too... preoccupied to make." His gaze flickered briefly to my abdomen, a deliberate move that ignited a spark of anger in my chest.

"Preoccupied?" I repeated, my tone sharp enough to cut through the murmurs. "Is that what you call carrying out my late husband's wishes? Maintaining the estate he entrusted to me?"

Lady Henrietta leaned forward, her tone laced with sweetness that felt like venom. "Your Grace, no one is questioning your dedication. But managing an estate of this magnitude requires... practicality. Cedric has only acted to preserve the Wakefield legacy during this delicate time."

"Delicate," I echoed, my voice cool. "Interesting choice of words, Lady Henrietta. If Lord Harland's intentions were so noble, why act in secret? Why not bring these plans to me or the council?"

Her practiced mask slipped for a fraction of a second before she recovered, her smile tightening. "I'm sure Cedric only sought to relieve you of unnecessary burdens."

Cedric seized the opportunity, his voice rising with feigned indignation.

"The truth, Your Grace, is that your position is complicated. Your pregnancy, while... hopeful, leaves the estate in a precarious situation. Decisions must be made swiftly, and I acted in the estate's best interests."

I tightened my grip on the edge of the table, forcing my tone to remain even. "And you believe selling portions of Wakefield without the Duchess's consent serves the estate's best interests?"

The council's murmurs grew louder, their unease palpable. I reached into the stack of papers Jeremiah had prepared and pulled out the letter bearing Rupert's signature and seal. I held it aloft, letting its presence command the room.

"This," I said, my voice ringing with authority, "is a document signed by the late Duke of Wakefield, explicitly affirming my role as the estate's manager until my child comes of age. Rupert's wishes were clear, and I will not allow them to be undermined."

The council members exchanged glances, the weight of the evidence shifting the room's dynamic. Cedric's composure cracked, his smirk replaced by a scowl.

"With all due respect, Your Grace," he snapped, "your judgment is clouded. The rumors, the scandals—do you truly believe your presence strengthens this estate?"

Before I could respond, Jeremiah's voice cut through the tension like a blade. "Lord Harland, you overreach."

All eyes turned to him as he rose from his seat, his posture commanding. His calm, measured tone carried a sharp edge, each word deliberate. "The Duchess's judgment is not what's under scrutiny here. What is under scrutiny is your disregard for the Duke's clear instructions and your blatant attempts to undermine the rightful authority of this estate."

Cedric's face flushed with anger. "And you, Lord Ravenscroft? What authority do you claim here? Shall we discuss your involvement—your questionable proximity to the Duchess?"

Jeremiah didn't flinch, his gaze steady as he replied. "You're welcome to discuss it, but I doubt the council will find your deflection convincing. The evidence speaks for itself. The Duchess has upheld her duty, despite your interference. If anything has threatened this estate, it's your reckless ambitions."

The council's murmurs grew louder, their support for Jeremiah evident in their nods. Cedric's fists clenched, his composure unraveling as Jeremiah's words dismantled his arguments.

"Enough," Lady Henrietta interjected, her voice sharp. Her gaze sharpened further, and her next words dripped with venom. "But there is another matter, Your Grace, one that lingers in whispers throughout the estate. How can we be certain this child you carry is even the Duke's? The timing, after all, raises questions."

The room froze. The air turned icy, and my hands gripped the edge of the table to keep steady. I refused to let the slander unsettle me. I met her gaze head-on, my voice cutting through the silence like steel. "Lady Henrietta, those are grave accusations you make. If you intend to question the legitimacy of my child, I demand you present proof. Baseless insinuations have no place in this room—or in this estate."

A murmur rippled through the council, the weight of my demand silencing even Cedric for a moment. Lady Henrietta's expression faltered briefly before she masked it with a thin smile. "Proof? Perhaps time will reveal the truth, Your Grace."

I straightened, drawing strength from the outrage coursing through me. "Until such time, Lady Henrietta, I suggest you tread carefully. Spreading such malicious claims not only insults me but the late Duke's memory. And I assure you, the consequences for slander will be severe."

Jeremiah's voice broke the tension. "This meeting is not for baseless allegations but to address clear, documented violations of the Duke's wishes. Let us return to the matter at hand."

The council stirred uneasily, their expressions a mix of shock and disapproval as they exchanged glances. Some nodded in agreement with Jeremiah's calm assertion, while others leaned closer to each other, whispering in low tones. The weight of Lady Henrietta's accusation had clearly unsettled them, but my firm unwavering response and her demand for proof had shifted the dynamic. Murmurs of support began to ripple through the room, voices rising as council members voiced their disdain for such unfounded claims.

"Lady Henrietta's suggestion is beyond the pale," one elder councilman said, his voice carrying a note of reproach. "The Duchess has always acted with dignity and in line with the Duke's wishes. Casting aspersions on her honor is both reckless and unbecoming."

Another councilwoman, her brow furrowed in thought, added, "The evidence provided against Lord Harland is far more substantial than any whispered rumor about the Duchess. We must focus on what is tangible and proven."

Cedric shifted uncomfortably in his seat, his composed facade slipping further as the council's mood turned against him. Lady Henrietta's sharp gaze flickered around the room, catching the waves of dissent but doing little to conceal her growing frustration.

Sensing her chance to regain the upper hand, Lady Henrietta leaned forward, her voice honeyed but laced with sharpness. "Your Grace, while you may command respect in this room for now, sentimentality does not run an estate. The Wakefield name requires practicality and bold leadership, not mere defiance. Your child—legitimate or otherwise—does not guarantee stability."

The murmurs in the room swelled, a mixture of shock and disapproval. My fingers gripped the edge of the table tightly, fighting to contain the fire rising within me. How dare she question my child's legitimacy in such a public forum? Straightening my posture, I let the anger in my chest sharpen my words.

"Lady Henrietta, I will not permit such baseless slander to linger in this room," I said, my voice cutting through the tension like steel. "You have no proof, only whispers, and that is a dangerous line to walk."

I turned my gaze toward the council, meeting each member's eyes as I swept the room. "I have shown you the evidence of Lord Harland's misdeeds—facts, not gossip. If any member of this council finds value in Lady Henrietta's baseless claims, speak now. Otherwise, let us remember our purpose today: the preservation of this estate."

The council members exchanged uneasy glances. Some whispered among themselves, while others sat back with contemplative frowns. Finally, an elder councilman cleared his throat, his voice carrying weight. "The Duchess is correct. We cannot dwell on rumors. The evidence against Lord Harland is substantive, and that is where our focus must remain."

A councilwoman leaned forward, her brow furrowed in thought. "Lady Henrietta's accusations are unbecoming and detract from the gravity of today's discussions. This estate deserves better than petty insinuations."

"Before we proceed further, there is something that must be addressed." I turned my focus directly on Cedric, who sat with a forced composure that barely concealed his unease. "Lord Harland," I began, "I accuse you of more than mismanagement. You have made deliberate attempts on my life and the life of the child I carry."

Gasps rippled through the room, but I pressed on. "There was the falling pot in the gardens, the horse that inexplicably broke loose, the carriage with its broken wheels, and the improperly installed ladder that could have caused a fatal fall. Each of these incidents occurred after you entered this estate and replaced many of the trusted servants. Can you explain this?"

Cedric's face tightened, and he shook his head, his voice steady but tinged with indignation. "These accusations are baseless, Your Grace. You have no proof, only conjecture. Accidents happen on large estates; to claim otherwise is paranoid at best."

I smiled, though it did not reach my eyes. "Perhaps I am paranoid, Lord Harland. But all of these 'accidents' began after you arrived and made sweeping changes to the staff. Are you saying that replacing loyal servants had nothing to do with this string of misfortunes?"

Lady Henrietta rose from her seat, her voice sharp and defensive. "This is preposterous! You have no evidence to link my son to any of these supposed incidents. He has done nothing but work tirelessly to support this estate in your time of weakness."

"Weakness?" I repeated, my voice cold. "You speak of weakness, Lady Henrietta, yet you conveniently forget the poisoned tea that nearly cost me my child. And who was it who suggested bringing Lord Harland into the estate afterward? It was you."

Lady Henrietta's face flushed with anger. "That incident affected me as well! If I were behind it, why would I endanger myself?"

I leaned forward, my voice lowering to a dangerous edge. "What if the poison used was an herbal concoction that only affects pregnant women? That would certainly explain why you suffered no lasting harm."

The room erupted into murmurs, council members shifting uncomfortably in their seats. Cedric's composure cracked further, his fists clenching as he glared at me. "This is nothing but a calculated attack to discredit me," he said, his voice rising. "Your Grace, if you have evidence, present it. Otherwise, these allegations are slander."

One of the elder councilmen cleared his throat, his tone measured but firm. "The Duchess raises valid concerns. While circumstantial, these incidents cannot be ignored, especially given their timing."

Another councilwoman spoke up, her brow furrowed. "It does seem too convenient to dismiss. If there is even a possibility of deliberate harm, we must act to protect the Duchess and the estate."

Lady Henrietta's voice cut through the murmurs. "You are all letting paranoia cloud your judgment! Cedric has only ever acted in the best interests of Wakefield."

"And yet," I said, standing tall, "the best interests of Wakefield do not align with deceit and manipulation. Cedric has brought instability, not strength. For the sake of my child and this estate, he must be removed from Wakefield immediately."

The weight of my words settled over the room, the council exchanging uneasy glances. Finally, an elder councilman spoke, his voice solemn. "The safety of the Duchess and the heir must take precedence. Until these matters are resolved, Lord Harland's presence at Wakefield poses too great a risk."

Cedric surged to his feet, his composure shattered. "This is an outrage! You have no right to cast me out without evidence!"

Jeremiah stepped forward, his voice steady and commanding. "The council has spoken, Lord Harland. Your actions have undermined the trust necessary to govern this estate. For the good of Wakefield, you will leave."

"No one can force my son to leave just because of false accusations without proof. So, prove your accusations, Your Grace!" Lady Henrietta's jaw hardened and her voice sounded like she was holding back anger.

I straightened, my voice sharp as I added, "And who said I have no evidence?"

Cedric's face reddened, his composure breaking further. "This is absurd! You have no concrete proof, just circumstantial claims. These are nothing but wild accusations to tarnish my name."

Lady Henrietta rose abruptly, her tone dripping with indignation. "This is beyond reason! My son has devoted himself to the welfare of this estate. To accuse him of such heinous acts without undeniable proof is malicious slander."

I stood up and looked at everyone. "The proof you are asking for is in this bottle," I said as I removing a small bottle from the folds of my gown, "was found in Lord Harland's quarters. It contains Veratrum."

Gasps rippled through the room. Cedric's eyes widened, his face draining of color before he spoke, his voice laced with indignation. "This is absurd! I am being slandered! Your Grace, you cannot seriously believe—"

I raised a hand, silencing him. "I have witnesses. Mrs. Hawthorne, a senior servant of this estate, saw you handing a vial to a dismissed servant shortly before the poisoning incident. Furthermore, Mr. Benson, the butler, has testified to the discovery of this bottle in your chambers."

The council turned to Cedric, their expressions a mix of shock and anger. Lady Henrietta rose from her seat, her face a mask of cold fury. "This makes no sense! Cedric has no reason—"

"No reason?" I interrupted, my voice rising. "He seeks control of Wakefield, and what better way than to destabilize it? To cast doubt on my capabilities as Duchess? Poisoning was not just an attack on me but on the very foundation of this estate."

The room erupted in heated whispers. Cedric's protests grew louder, his voice cutting through the noise with desperation. "This is an outrageous lie!" he shouted, his composure slipping. "I demand this farce ends now! These accusations are baseless, and I will not stand here and be defamed in such a manner!"

Jeremiah's voice rose above the din, calm but edged with authority. "Enough. The evidence is undeniable, Lord Harland. The testimonies and the poison bottle found in your chambers leave no room for your denials. You have betrayed the trust of this estate and its rightful Duchess."

Lady Henrietta's mask cracked further, but she said nothing as the council's murmurs reached a crescendo. The room buzzed with whispers, council members exchanging sharp glances and hurried conversations. Cedric's voice cut through the clamor, rising in desperation. "This is preposterous!" he shouted, his face flushed. "These accusations are built on lies and falsehoods! I demand to see these so-called witnesses and examine their credibility!"

"You will have your opportunity, Lord Harland," one councilwoman interjected coldly, her voice firm above the noise. "But the evidence is substantial, and your protests do little to erase the weight of it."

"Substantial?" Cedric snapped, his composure fully unraveling. "This is a witch hunt, orchestrated by those who wish to see me disgraced! Mother, surely you can see this is a calculated move to undermine us both!"

Lady Henrietta's gaze darted around the room, her lips pressed into a thin line as the murmurs swelled again. She opened her mouth to respond, but the elder councilman's voice boomed above the chaos. "Enough!" His stern expression quelled the noise, and he turned his attention to Cedric. "This is a grave matter. The council must deliberate at once."

As they withdrew to confer, Cedric glared at me, his veneer of charm shattered. "You've made a powerful enemy, Your Grace."

I met his gaze, unflinching. "No, Lord Harland. You made that choice the moment you betrayed this estate. Now you will face the consequences."

The power had shifted back to me, but I knew the fight was far from over.

"Your Grace, you may have won this round, but this estate is not sustained by sentiment or idealism. Mark my words—you will face challenges greater than these."

I met her gaze, unyielding. "And I will face them, Lady Henrietta. But know this—any further interference will be met with legal consequences. This estate belongs to my child, and I will protect it with everything I have."

Her expression hardened, but she rose gracefully, signaling the end of the confrontation. Cedric followed suit, his parting glance filled with venom.

"This isn't over," he murmured as he passed me.

"No," I replied, my voice firm. "But when it is, you'll find yourself on the losing side."

As the council dispersed, offering quiet words of support, I allowed myself to exhale, the weight of the confrontation pressing heavily on my shoulders.

Jeremiah approached, his expression softening as he crouched beside my chair. "You were brilliant," he said quietly. "You stood your ground, Evelina. That's more than a victory—it's a declaration."

I managed a faint smile, the tension easing slightly. "I couldn't have done it without you."

His smile deepened, his gaze steady. "You could have. But I'm glad you didn't have to."

For the first time in weeks, I felt a flicker of hope. The battle wasn't over, but with Jeremiah by my side, I knew I wouldn't face it alone.

47

The Calm Within the Storm

The nursery was a quiet haven amidst the chaos. The soft hues of cream and lavender, chosen by Rupert long before we ever dreamed of children, seemed to breathe calm into the room. The gentle light from a single lamp cast a warm glow over the delicate furnishings, illuminating the carved edges of the bassinet and the embroidered curtains swaying slightly in the draft. Here, in this untouched sanctuary, the weight of the outside world seemed to dissipate, replaced by a fragile sense of peace.

I traced my fingers along the bassinet's intricate woodwork, imagining the day when a tiny form would rest there, safe and loved. The faint scent of lavender lingered in the air, a soothing balm to my frayed nerves. For the first time in months, I allowed myself to hope—not just for survival, but for a future worth fighting for.

I lowered myself into the rocking chair by the window, my hands instinctively cradling my belly. The storm clouds outside churned, dark and unruly against the fading daylight, a mirror to the turmoil that had become my life. The confrontation with Cedric and Lady Henrietta replayed in my mind, their venomous words mingling with my own quiet victories. I had stood my ground, exposed their schemes, and, for now, the estate was secure.

And yet, the victory felt fragile, like a fine piece of porcelain perched on the edge of a shelf. One push, one careless move, and everything could shatter. I rocked gently, letting the rhythmic motion ease my thoughts, the creak of the chair blending with the soft patter of rain against the window.

The echoes of the council meeting lingered—Lord Whitby's stern nod of approval, the murmured agreement of the others, and the condition they had placed upon their support: distancing myself from Jeremiah. It had been the most bitter pill to swallow, and though I understood its necessity, the thought of severing ties with him tightened something unbearable in my chest. He had said little after, his quiet acceptance more painful than any argument would have been.

A soft knock at the door startled me from my reverie. "Come in," I called, my voice steadier than I felt.

Jeremiah entered, his presence filling the room with an unexpected warmth. His coat was damp from the rain, his hair tousled by the wind. He hesitated at the threshold, his gaze sweeping over the nursery before settling on me. The tension in his shoulders eased as he stepped closer, though his expression was lined with weariness. "I thought I might find you here," he said, his voice low.

I offered a faint smile, gesturing to the chair beside me. "It's the only place that feels untouched by all of this," I admitted. "As if the nursery exists in its own little world, waiting for something pure and good."

He took the seat, his posture relaxed but his gaze intent. "It will," he said, conviction threading his words. "And it will be worth everything you've fought for."

The weight of his words settled over me, grounding me in a way I hadn't realized I needed. "I wasn't sure I could do it today," I confessed, my voice barely above a whisper. "Standing before them, knowing how much they hate me, how far they're willing to go..."

Jeremiah leaned forward, his elbows resting on his knees. "You didn't just stand before them, Evelina. You faced them head-on and won. That's no small thing."

I looked down at my hands, my fingers tightening over the curve of my belly. "Sometimes, I wonder if I'm strong enough. If I can truly protect my child from all of this—the scheming, the lies, the danger."

He reached out, his hand covering mine with a gentle but firm reassurance.

"You are strong enough," he said, his voice low and certain. "I've seen it. You've faced every challenge they've thrown at you, and you've come out standing. You're not just protecting your child, Evelina—you're securing their future."

His words stirred something deep within me, a flicker of courage that had been smothered by doubt. "It doesn't always feel like it," I admitted. "But hearing you say that... maybe I can start to believe it."

Jeremiah's lips quirked into a small smile. "You don't have to believe it all at once. Just hold onto the moments when you do."

The storm outside cast flickering shadows across the walls, the sound of rain growing heavier. I turned my gaze back to the bassinet, imagining the tiny life that would one day fill it with laughter and cries. "Thank you," I said softly, turning back to him. "For everything. For standing by me when it would have been easier to walk away."

His hand lingered on mine for a moment longer before he leaned back, his expression thoughtful. "I made a promise to Rupert," he said. "But staying—it's not just about that promise anymore. I'm here because I believe in you, Evelina. And I'll be here as long as you need me."

The sincerity in his voice brought a warmth to my chest, easing the chill that had lingered there for so long. For the first time in what felt like forever, I didn't feel alone in this fight.

I rose from the chair and crossed to the small cabinet near the window. From a hidden compartment within, I withdrew a vial. Turning it in the lamplight, I revealed it to Jeremiah with a faint smile. His expression shifted from calm to sharp curiosity.

"The Veratrum poison," he murmured. "The one found in Cedric's quarters?"

I nodded, watching his reaction carefully. "The very same."

Jeremiah frowned, his brows furrowing. "But the traces of the original poison were never found. How did you...?" He trailed off, realization dawning in his eyes.

I held his gaze, unflinching. "I made it. The evidence, the testimonies—they were necessary to remove Cedric and secure the estate. Cedric may have been guilty of many things, but this particular crime? It needed to be ensured."

His silence stretched, the storm outside a faint echo to the turmoil I saw in his expression. Finally, he spoke, his voice low. "You risked everything to orchestrate this."

"I did what I had to," I replied firmly. "Cedric was a threat to my child and to Wakefield. If I hadn't acted, he would have found another way to destroy us."

Jeremiah leaned back, exhaling slowly as he regarded the vial in my hand. "You've always been stronger than I gave you credit for," he admitted. "But this... Evelina, this path isn't without its dangers."

"I know," I said quietly, placing the vial back in its hiding spot. "But it's done. And now, we can finally move forward."

Jeremiah's reflection in the window remained steady as the storm raged on. "Let's hope Cedric doesn't find a way to return from this," he said softly.

"They'll come again," I said quietly. "Lady Henrietta, Cedric—they won't stop. They'll find another way."

"Let them come," he said, his voice a quiet challenge. "If he does, we'll be ready."

I nodded, my gaze fixed on the storm. The fear was still there, the uncertainty—but so was the resolve. I would not falter. For my child, for Wakefield, for the future I now dared to dream of, I would stand.

The storm might rage, but I would weather it.

* * *

Stay tuned for the continuation of Evelina and Jeremiah's story in "The Duke's Heir" (Provisional Title)

About the Author

Leontine Blythewood is a Regency romance writer who revels in scandal, intrigue, and the thrill of conflict. She likes to create tales of stolen glances, whispered secrets, and the razor's edge of propriety. She also wants her stories to leave readers wondering who will emerge unscathed-or delightfully ruined.

Beyond the drama of her novels, Leontine lives a quieter life. An avowed feline devotee, she finds inspiration in her feline companions' unpredictable natures and unmistakable disdain for society's rules.

Printed in Dunstable, United Kingdom

70775295R00127